One wife gone missing,
and one body found
add up ... to murder ...

My father is an eloquent man with few words.

Rather than spoil the moment by reminding him I wouldn't be staying in Dacus, I filled the silence by asking, "Tell me about Melvin Bertram." That name had danced around the edges of my brain all day.

"Whatever made you think of him?"

"I ran into Mr. Earnest this morning. He commented how interesting that we'd come home at the same time, me and Melvin Bertram."

"He's back?"

My dad's not as plugged into the town gossip as my mother. Which might not bode well for his newspaper venture.

"That's what Mr. Earnest said."

"If anybody'd know, it'd be him, I reckon. 'Course, Bertram's got family in town—a brother. Might be visiting for Thanksgiving."

"Why do I know the name?"

"Don't you remember? Several years ago? His wife disappeared. Everybody figured he'd killed her."

Southern Fried

Cathy Pickens

St. Martin's Paperbacks

30314 9379

Library of Congress Catalog Card Number: 2003058548

ISBN: 0-312-99553-9
EAN: 80312-99553-9

Printed in the United States of America

St. Martin's Press hardcover edition / April 2004
St. Martin's Paperbacks edition / March 2005

St. Martin's Paperbacks are published by St. Martin's Press, 175 Fifth Avenue, New York, NY 10010.

10 9 8 7 6 5 4 3 2 1

To my parents, Paul and Kitty, who laid before my sisters and me a wealth of choices and challenged us: "What are you doing for the good of the world?" And to my husband, Robert, whose love, support, and humor are beyond words. This book is dedicated to them, with all my love.

Acknowledgments

Thanks to the original Mystery Mavens—Paula Connolly, Dawn Cotter, Terry Hoover, Susan Luck, Nancy Northcott, and Ann Wicker—and to the DSSG (you know who you are): You took me in and made me better. Thanks to P. J. Coldren, die-hard Malice contest reader who sent Avery on her way. And thanks to Susan Dunlap, mystery writer and mentor extraordinaire.

One

A couple of county cop cars and several pickups, one loaded with an air compressor, crowded around the boat landing at Luna Lake. Pudd Pardee, head of the county rescue squad, leaned against the front fender of a rust-red truck that sported a bumper winch. As I parked my dad's pickup alongside, Pudd jabbed his elbow into the ribs of a tall kid propped next to him. Judging from their gaudy laughter, they were sharing some guy humor.

Pudd heaved himself upright as I strolled over.

"Well, if it idn't Miz Avery Andrews, attorney-at-law."

"Thought you boys were out here dragging the lake for a body," I said, tilting my head to stare up at Pudd's unimpressive five-foot-eight height. "You're making it look like open-mike night at a comedy club."

"You know how this bidness can be sometimes, A'vry. If we didn't keep our sense of humor, pretty soon these dead bodies'd git to us." Pudd punched his companion in the ribs and cocked him a sly look, then hitched up his jeans and arced a stream of tobacco juice past the bumper of his truck, barely missing his young buddy's work boot.

"Pudd. Get serious a minute. The sheriff sent word. She's holding Donlee Griggs for murder? He's confessed to drowning Pee Vee Probert?"

"So you're defending Donlee? Figured you would. Him bein' so sweet on you and everything. He's always been partial to that red hair of yours."

I've always thought it more a burnished gold, but whatever. And Donlee developed crushes on any female unwary enough to smile at him.

"Yep." Pudd sighed expansively. "He'uz sittin' around the table at Maylene's just last week, goin' on and on about how the overhead lights in the courtroom lit up your hair like golden sunshine."

My eyes narrowed to slits, a look I practice to cross-examine particularly loathsome witnesses. Didn't faze Pudd, though.

Up until two weeks ago, I hadn't seen Donlee since high school. Then I'd been appointed to represent him in a bail hearing on a drunk-and-disorderly charge. An unusual occasion for a class reunion, for sure.

"Think you'll be able to get him off?" Pudd asked. "Or will you two be carrying on your star-crossed love affair through a wire mesh window?"

That didn't deserve a response. I shoved my hands into my jacket pockets and mimicked his good ol' boy slouch, staring toward the lake and ignoring Pudd.

Something about this rescue scene didn't register

as real, though the usual contingent of Ghouly Boys were present—the rescue squad guys and police scanner junkies. One old boy dangled his legs off the tailgate of his truck while he finished off a Bud. Another little clump included a couple of county deputies. Neither of them had missed many blue plate specials at Maylene's.

In all, maybe fifteen guys stood around in various poses. And all pretended they weren't sneaking glances in my direction. Something odd about their collective casual air. Or maybe I just expected more intensity at a murder scene.

Donlee had been stuffed into the backseat of a sheriff's cruiser parked at the far edge of the picnic area. His full-moon face brightened when he caught my eye. He lifted his cuffed hands and actually waggled his fingers at me, flashing a gap-toothed grin.

Donlee had been a six-foot-seven goofball even in high school. I'd received my share of do-you-love-me-check-yes-or-no notes shoved through the vents in my locker. I couldn't quite believe he'd killed somebody. But isn't that what folks always say? "He never seemed like the type."

I kept staring toward Donlee but didn't waggle my fingers back at him.

"You know why he committed this heinous act, don't you?" Pudd asked, feigning seriousness and trying to pretend he didn't see Donlee making nose prints inside the cruiser window. "Tragic, itn't it? It 'uz his true love for you that drove him to it."

Pudd's companion—a dark, lanky kid barely out of high school—snorted. When I turned my back on

Donlee to glare at him, he shifted his attention to a puddle of Pudd's tobacco spit. At least my slit-eyed stare worked on somebody.

But it didn't stop Pudd. He just kept smiling. He'd always liked a good joke, but I hadn't figured out the punch line on this one. Joking about this just seemed mean-spirited. So I ignored him.

The Donna Karan suit I'd put on for my official lawyer visit with Donlee wasn't heavy enough for an early-morning visit to a boat landing. The November breeze off Luna Lake—which was really more of a pond—nipped through my silk blouse.

"Any idea where the body is? Or how long it might take to locate it?" I tried to get Pudd to focus on the fact that somebody had died. Anything to avoid having to consult with my client. It was just too sad.

Pudd kept staring and grinning and working his tobacco wad. The guys scattered in clusters around the lake's edge alternated between studying the water and sneaking looks over at us. They seemed to be eyeing us more than the activity on the lake.

"Nope," Pudd said.

The breeze wasn't strong enough to push up waves. Bubbles appeared at regular intervals on the lake's dark surface.

"How long can those guys stay under there?" Even the thought of it felt cold.

"Aw, they can swim all day with those suits. The ones freezing their arses off are those two numb-skulls bobbing around in that boat out there."

In a two-seater flat-bottom johnboat, two men huddled in camouflage-green jumpsuits and jackets. Every now and then, one would crane over the side as if he could see something in the greenish-brown water. Then, turtlelike, he'd poke his neck back into his coat collar.

"Those guys love it," Pudd said. "Gives 'em a chance to practice."

"Practice?" He wasn't taking any of this seriously enough. My next question was cut off by the arrival of another pickup. It slid to a stop behind my truck.

The newcomer's door popped loudly as it opened, then squawked shut. As soon as he slammed the door shut, I found myself face-to-face with the reportedly dead Pee Vee Probert.

"Pee Vee!" Pudd threw up his hands in mock surprise. He had shifted from comedian to dramatic actor in the time it took Pee Vee to slam his door. "You're alive!"

"'Course I am, nidjit. Heard you all 'uz dragging the lake. Come on the scanner. Found anythin' yet?"

"Actually," I observed wryly, "you're not supposed to be here."

He jammed his hands on his skinny hips. "Sez who? Hit come over the scanner." Like that was all the permission he needed.

"No, I meant you're not supposed to be here." I pointed at the ground where we stood. "You're supposed to be *there*."

With his lips pursed in his sun-dried face, Pee

Vee's gaze followed my pointing finger to the lake. He stared for a few seconds at the small rivulets the breeze made on the lake and at the two guys sitting, like a couple of sillies, in the boat. Then he looked at me as though he might need to put some distance between himself and a crazy person.

"What the—"

Pudd couldn't hold it a second longer. Tobacco-stained spit spewed from his rubbery lips, and he doubled over as far as his protruding belly would allow, sounding like a Macy's parade balloon with the air hissing out of it.

Pudd guffawed. "You ain't got sense enough to know you drowned, Pee Vee."

Pee Vee looked bewildered. But I was a few hundred yards ahead of Pee Vee on this one. Not that that was hard to do.

"Donlee Griggs apparently told these guys he drowned you in the lake," I explained.

"He never!" Pee Vee's voice shrilled.

"No, he didn't. But he—"

"—called the dispatcher." Pudd pinched his thumb and forefinger across his eyes to wipe away tears of laughter. "Told 'em he'd held a gun on you, off the dock over there. Kept you swimming till you drowned. He said—" Pudd's voice cracked like that of a twelve-year-old in the church choir. "He said it 'uz over a woman."

Pudd poked at his companion. The kid kept eyeing me nervously.

"*That* woman," Pudd blurted, pointing at me.

"I never!" As Pee Vee whirled on me, his indignation carried his voice up another octave.

We'd drawn a crowd by this time. The rest of the crack law enforcement team who'd gathered around the boat ramp joined us for a close-up.

"Donlee said seeing A'vry had rekindled the old high school romance"—Pudd's eyes were streaming from the effort of his tale—"said he needed to do something extry-ordinary to get her attention. Said a murder trial would let the two of 'em spend plenty of time together. Preparing his defense and all." Pudd pulled a handkerchief with a fraying hem from his hip pocket and wiped his eyes.

"I never!" Pee Vee announced, but less shrilly.

"Thank you, Pee Vee," I said as graciously as I could. My cheeks were burning. I hoped it looked like windburn rather than humiliation.

I'd skipped breakfast for a stupid prank. I couldn't be angry with Donlee. He really was stupid. But Pudd and some of the rest of this crew would pay. I didn't know how or when, but they'd pay. I felt like the village idiot—or, worse yet, like little Avery Andrews playing mommy-dress-up. A gangly hometown kid, the brunt of a goofy, embarrassing joke. I might as well be making nose prints on the window myself.

At least the rescue guys had gotten in some practice dives. Fuming, I turned toward my truck, careful not to skin my shoe heels on the gravel. Donlee could stay locked in the back of the cruiser awhile longer, for all I cared.

Sudden movement on the lake caught my attention. Two divers broke the water's surface about fifty feet out, and swam furiously toward the boat ramp.

Something about the urgency of their movements affected everyone. Several men migrated toward the point where the two swimmers would come ashore. One of the fellows out in the boat fumbled with the tiny motor, trying to catch up with the divers.

They arrived practically together, and both flopped down onto the rough ramp with a recklessness that surprised me, considering they wore neoprene suits. That roughed-up concrete ramp could cut like broken glass.

Carrying his fins, the first swimmer jerked his mask off, gasping.

"A car," he croaked. His mouthpiece swung against his chest as he duck-walked in his booties up the ramp. "A car down there."

The second diver had not joined the crowd on the ramp. Instead, he'd veered straight for the trash barrel chained to a pole at the lake's edge, flapping across the grass in his fins. He leaned over and vomited up his toenails, with expressive, ungentlemanly sounds.

The older diver, the one telling the story, turned a peculiar pea-soup color around his lips and spoke louder, trying to drown out the sounds from the trash barrel. "An old one, from the looks of it. At least a seventies model." He swallowed hard and glanced at his flippers.

His timing was flawless. His companion with the

weak stomach ceased his retching at the same moment he announced, "There's a body inside."

A body. The crowd shifted, glancing at one another, moving a half step closer in—and closer to each other.

"Been there awhile, I'd say. But it was—" He paused and swallowed. Pudd, who stood directly in front of him, took a step back. Just in case the guy got queasy.

The diver, his face pinched into a tight circle by his rubber hood, shook his head. "It was—I've never seen anything—it's like a skeleton. But it's covered in this yellowy-white stuff. Looks like soap. It's—"

The retching sounds at the barrel started up again, though weaker than before. My own stomach gave a slight heave.

Some of the guys stared over their shoulders at the lake, their interest obvious. Others watched the older diver, now in the center of a loosely drawn circle. Everyone tried to ignore the guy at the barrel.

"We need to get that thing lifted," Pudd announced. "See what we got. Let me pull the truck down there, see if that winch can do the trick."

The onlookers stared alternately at the lake or the ground, talking with a quiet animation, not-so-secretly glad the show had taken a macabre turn.

I counted quickly. The crowd had grown to about thirty Ghouly Boys—a couple of trucks with volunteer fire stickers on them, some county cops, some passersby, and a handful from the rescue squad. Not a lot of entertainment options on the Tuesday before Thanksgiving, I guess.

"I doubt that winch'll do it," the diver commented to nobody in particular as Pudd maneuvered his truck, front end forward, onto the ramp.

The younger diver, who'd been studying the inside of the trash barrel, now stood at limp attention beside the ramp. No one stood with him, whether to avoid his shame or the smell, it was hard to say.

When Pudd stopped his truck and started to unwind the winch, the younger diver stepped forward to unhook the cable. Nobody interfered; everyone was anxious to let the guy redeem himself.

The older diver waddled to the front of Pudd's truck. "Somebody ought to radio for a wrecker, just in case."

"Aw, this'll pull a dump truck, Carl," Pudd huffed, bent over his task.

"That thing's mired up right bad in the mud there. I'm not too sure—"

Pudd cut him off. "We'll giv'er a try."

The younger diver had already headed out into the water as the electric motor on the winch hummed, feeding out the cable.

His partner shrugged, pulled his mask into place, took a couple of puffs on his mouthpiece, and flopped down the grass bank like a B-movie swamp creature returning to his own.

Pudd might have every confidence in the superiority of his equipment, but obviously not everyone shared his optimism. From a county car to my right,

I heard background radio squawks interrupted by a deputy calling to town for a wrecker.

"We-ell."

A drawling voice at my shoulder startled me. I'd been so focused on the figures disappearing under the murky water, trailing the wire cable, that I hadn't heard Dale Earnest come up behind me.

"Mr. Earnest."

He missed a beat when I offered my hand. In Dacus, women don't offer to shake hands with their father's barber. It would take me a while to relearn the social norms.

"Good to see you, Avery," he said, clasping my hand in both of his. "Your dad told me, when he came in for a haircut last week, that you'd be coming home."

How very diplomatic. Dale Earnest had certainly heard about my coming home from sources other than my dad—sources less inclined to be charitable about the circumstances of my return.

The quizzical look Mr. Earnest fixed on me, and the gentle, saccharine politeness of his tone, told me he knew more than my dad would've told him. The circumstances of my firing were too complicated to be adequately absorbed by the grapevine. So I wondered which tendrils had reached the cracked-leather pump chairs in Mr. Earnest's barbershop.

"Came up to drain the water lines at the cabin," he said. "Wasn't expecting this much excitement."

I smiled. I knew we'd both pretend that he knew nothing at all scandalous or questionable about me.

A couple dozen cabins sat tucked back among the pines on needle-strewn winter-weedy banks around a small, still lake. Luna Lake, only twenty minutes north of Dacus, serves as a busy weekend getaway in summer but sits largely abandoned in cold weather.

"Whoa!"

A shout from the ramp stopped conversations in the clustered groups. Pudd swung around and into the truck cab, as fast as his bulk would allow, to reach the brake. Pudd's young buddy cut off the winch's motor and scuttled out of the way before the truck, on a slow slide toward the water, could run him down.

"Shoulda tied that thing off on a tree," Mr. Earnest observed. "Winch'll pull the truck underwater 'fore it pulls that car out."

Pudd got the truck stopped and several of the Ghouly Boys gathered around to hatch another plan.

Mr. Earnest nodded. "Don't use the cabin much anymore," he said. "Might not keep it. With so many Yankees coming in, I can probably get a good price for it."

I nodded. Mr. Earnest, his hands jammed into the pockets of his L.L. Bean jacket and his bald head shining in the weak sunlight, could've been mistaken for one of those retired Yankees. Until he opened his mouth.

"I hear tell you've moved into your granddad's cabin up here." He squinted at me. "That a good idea?"

"Well, it'll do until I decide on something more permanent. Mom and Dad tried to get me to stay with them. But the cabin needed some work. It's a nice change, after living in Columbia."

"You sure it's safe?" Mr. Earnest asked bluntly. "Not too many folks up here this time of year."

"I'll be fine." I didn't elaborate. Years ago, my grandfather had not only taught me to shoot, he'd bought me a nice little S&W .38 and educated me on the advantages of hollow points.

Mr. Earnest leaned against the hood of a county cop car, settling in to watch the lake. "You setting up practice in Dacus?"

"No. I'm just working out of Carlton Barner's office temporarily." To keep busy, I picked up court appointments and guardian ad litem cases that the county's other attorneys avoided like plague-ridden rats. I'd left Columbia a few weeks ago without a clear plan in mind, but with no reason to start a real job search until after the holidays.

He nodded, staring at the lake. The winch whined weakly, straining to dislodge the car from its mud bed. Mr. Earnest didn't seem in any hurry to get about his business.

"Funny, you and Melvin Bertram coming home at the same time."

"Who?" I settled back against the car hood next to him.

"Melvin Bertram. You too young to remember him?" He sighed, his round belly shifting beneath his crossed arms. "He's been gone, law, I guess ten or fifteen years now. Time sure has a way of getting away from you."

I nodded. The pace of conversation and most else in Dacus now struck me as odd. I'd been away almost ten years, to attend law school and then to practice law. In that time, I'd forgotten the circadian rhythms of my growing up, the paced conversations with deep currents. The pauses, in some cases, spoke more than words. He was saying something important. I waited, hoping I could hear it in the pauses.

He continued. "Yep, probably closer to fifteen years. Were you gone by then?"

"In high school," I said. But Melvin Bertram's name rang only a faint bell with me.

I studied the trees that rimmed the small lake—scarcely more than a shirttail full of water, in my Aunt Letha's words. The leafless hardwoods sketched stark patterns against the watered blue sky. A half dozen docks jutted around the lake's rim, though the only boat visible was the rescue boat.

"Peculiar he'd come to mind," Mr. Earnest said, then sloughed off the topic like a too-warm overcoat. "How's your momma and daddy doing? Can't believe he decided to buy that old newspaper."

I smiled, mostly to myself. "Yep. He's been getting a lot of ribbing about that." My father had surprised the Rotary Club one day by announcing that he'd bought the *Clarion*, after a working life as a mechanical engineer. "He says the paper's only assets are a bunch of old machinery, and he can keep that running as well as anybody."

Mr. Earnest chuckled, his belly heaving. "That's 'bout true."

The rumbling arrival from Todd's Wrecker Service interrupted our slow conversation. Whoever had radioed into Dacus for a wrecker without giving Pudd's winch a chance to prove itself had been wise. But, before the wrecker could maneuver into place, Pudd petulantly had to rewind his cable and back his truck out of the way, the tires spitting gravel.

The spectators perched around staring, like we didn't have anything better to do with our midmorning.

Which I didn't. I could've walked over to get Donlee Griggs sprung from county detention. Donlee's alleged victim stood a scant twenty yards from me, jeans riding low on his skinny hips and brown locks stringing over the neck of his grubby flannel shirt. So avoiding a murder charge would likely be a formality.

But I wasn't in any hurry. Especially since that goofball had planned all this just so I would rush to his aid.

Pudd's laughter still burned my ears. I really should make a phone call to assure that the wheels of justice began to grind. But I needed a little while to nurse my pique—and my embarrassment. You really can't go home again.

The wrecker kept feeding cable to the divers.

I couldn't help being surprised at myself. True, the tense boredom and promise of drama here reminded me of a courtroom. But two weeks ago, I couldn't have imagined propping my rump against the hood of a car, staring across the lake and shooting the breeze with the guy who cuts my father's hair. I'd been too busy calculating billable hours and buzzing around Charleston or Columbia in my black BMW from lunch meetings to hearings to late-night preps for morning depositions. Killing an hour or two in the company of a bunch of county employees and police scanner addicts wouldn't have been on my agenda.

Now I had nowhere to run. And not much to run around in since I had no leased BMW. My closetful of business suits hung in the only closet I could claim—in my old room at my parents' house; the lake cabin boasted only wall pegs. And my most important client sat periodically stamping nose prints onto the window of a county cop car.

The wrecker cable drew taut as the motor ground loudly. A few of the cops gathered at the bottom of the ramp, right where the wrecker would flatten them if its brakes failed.

Out on the lake, the johnboaters positioned themselves closer to shore. They wisely stayed a safe distance away from the taut cable as it disappeared into the water. The onlookers stared, most not speaking now. Several minutes went by, filled only by the sound of the winch and the intermittent squawk of two-way radios. Then the water at the base of the boat ramp churned.

In a bubble of muddy water, the car's rear end appeared. Even with most of it still underwater, the car dwarfed the bobbing two-seater boat. The juxtaposition of the two objects jarred my senses. Cars aren't routinely resurrected from watery graves.

Slowly, as the truck's winch continued to whine, more of the car lifted into view. The sheet metal had rusted to a mottled red-brown shade. The mud-caked tires hit the submerged end of the ramp.

Johnnie Black stopped the winch, leaving only the car's trunk and rooftop visible.

The divers, belly-floating beside the car, seemed to be checking the underside of the car.

"Good thing it 'uz right side up," one of the amateur rescue experts standing near me commented. "Otherwise they'd've had to flip that sucker in the water."

Several watchers drew in closer, forming a tighter ring around the drama. Not close enough to get in the way, but eager not to miss any of the good stuff.

One of the divers flipped a hand signal to the wrecker operator, who started pulling up cable again. Slowly.

The car inched up the ramp. Water streamed down the sides in muddy rivulets. Reddish-brown stains coated the window glass, leaving a color like someone had tried to wash away dried blood. Distinguishing between the rusty parts and the red mud was impossible.

I'm no good at identifying makes and models, but the sedan sported a boxy broad trunk and a mass of sheet metal that current gas mileage restrictions won't allow. A Ford decal decorated the trunk.

The car's rear end crept up the ramp. The onlookers craned, necks extended like vultures' for a better look. The front seat wasn't yet visible.

As the car emerged from the water, the front end canted sharply downward. But I didn't have to move for a better look. The car's passenger obliged me by floating into view against the rear window.

I'll never look at a kid's Magic 8 Ball in the same way again.

Murky water filled the car. Inside a shape floated into view, undefined at first. Then the face—or what remained of it—drew close to the window and took form through the murk. A human head. Not exactly a head. But not quite a skull either. A waxy yellow padding outlined the cheeks, jaw, and neck. The eye holes gaped, hollow and black.

Floating limply, the head tilted. The grinning teeth tapped once against the glass. Then the apparition floated back into a shapeless form in the murk.

The guy who'd been glad they hadn't had to flip the car clamped his hand over his mouth and stifled a gagging sound.

Two

The unexpected resurrection at the lake must have unnerved me more than I realized, for I immediately made two mistakes: stopping by my parents' house and calling Sheriff L. J. Peters.

L.J.'s guffaw as soon as she heard my voice told me she'd already learned about Donlee and the invented drowning of Pee Vee Probert. Pee Vee himself had shown up at the detention center to ask Donlee why he'd tried to drown him when he, Pee Vee, hadn't even been at the lake. Then the two of them had headed off in Pee Vee's pickup.

"Practically arm in arm," L.J. said. "Probably headed to Tap's to celebrate Pee Vee's near-death experience."

Tap's Pool Room, the bar where Donlee worked and where Pee Vee regularly drank. And where Donlee drank and alternately lost and remorsefully reclaimed his religion.

"They'll most likely both be back down here in detention by sometime tomorrow morning," L.J. finished in a wry tone.

I hoped Pee Vee was the only one drinking to celebrate that he hadn't drowned. I didn't want a late-night call from Donlee.

As soon as I hung up the phone on L.J.'s barking laughter, my mom corralled me.

"You finished, Avery? Then you can come with me to the Frank Dobbins circle meeting."

"I don't—"

"Those ladies would love to see you, now that you're back in town. Some of them probably haven't seen you in years."

"I really need—"

"And you're already dressed up. Though you need to spot-clean the hem of your jacket. Looks like you backed into something."

She stuck the corner of a kitchen towel under the faucet, then proceeded to damp-mop the back of my blazer.

"Mom, I really need to stop by the hardware store—"

She picked a couple of stray red-gold hairs from my jacket. "Stayin' up at that cabin isn't one of your better ideas, Avery. Lord only knows, though, you're as pigheaded as your grandfather ever had time to be. Anything could happen up there. Take that drowning this morning—"

"Mom, nobody drowned this morning. A guy made the whole thing up. It was a joke."

"Still, that car with the body in it. That's not the kind of place you need to be staying by yourself. Who'd they think it was?"

"I don't know." I didn't want to think about it

right now. I suppressed a shudder. The picture was too fresh in my mind—and too gruesome.

The drowning, I could believe she'd heard about. How she knew about the submerged car already was beyond me, though not much happens in Dacus that Mom doesn't know about, mostly through her various projects.

Come to think of it, Donlee Griggs had been one of her little projects. She and I would have to have a talk about that one of these days.

But not right now. Right now, we were on our way out the door to the Frank Dobbins circle meeting.

I couldn't very well insist on driving, since I didn't have a car. Nothing made me question what would become of me more than reminders that I had no wheels. I'd have to attend to my lack of transportation, probably sometime after I attend to my lack of gainful employment.

Mom scooted through a yellow light in front of the Lutheran church and banked in a sweeping circle, with several bags of cans collected for recycling rattling across the back of the minivan. She parked in a diagonal space beside the church, her front wheels perched on the sidewalk.

I've never been certain what function the Frank Dobbins circle meetings serve—or even who Frank had been. Mostly, it seemed, a group of ladies got together at one another's houses or in church social halls and chatted about books, ate cucumber sandwiches, and then, I assumed, spent the rest of the afternoon burping up cucumber.

My mom, being a sensible woman, didn't seem

to fit. But she went anyway. I suspected it enabled her to enlist the aid of these ladies, their Sunday School classes, and their husbands' checkbooks in her projects. You can't save the world without adequate resources.

The cooing and chirping that greeted me fell in sharp contrast to the hands-in-the-pockets stares that had met me at Luna Lake that morning. But the arm-patting and polite comments masked some of the same kinds of questioning looks.

The tallest woman in the room neither smiled nor genteelly patted arms. From her vantage point near the cut-glass punch bowl, she spotted us as soon as we came through the door. She set her collision course accordingly. The lesser ships floating in her path did little to impede her progress, but her salutation reached us before she did.

"Avery. Glad you brought her, Emma."

Seeing my great-aunt Letha in contexts other than family gatherings always brings the enormity of her into stark relief. Aunt Letha is a large person by any measure, but against lesser mortals, those less able to withstand her onslaught than her own family, she is formidable indeed.

Letha is my mother's aunt. My great-grandmother died in childbirth while producing my grandfather, Avery Hampton Howe. Two decades later, my great-grandfather remarried and sired three daughters, Aletha, Hattie, and Vinnia. When my great-grandfather later buried his second wife, Aletha assumed what all considered her birthright: the role of matriarch. She'd held the unelected office ever since.

"Aunt Letha, it's good to see you." We don't waste a lot of time hugging in my family, but a handshake seemed particularly awkward. So I simply smiled.

"Good thing you're here. Getting out's the best thing. Best thing to still wagging tongues." Letha shot a look at a pillowy lady standing nearby in a tight print dress. "Afraid a mule's gonna kick you, stand close to it. It'll still kick. But it won't hurt nearly as bad," Letha said, not quietly.

The pillowy lady's expression froze under her wiry gray curls. Like a possum caught in headlights, she couldn't even bring herself to scurry away. I had no idea what they'd been saying about me before I got there, but Aunt Letha's unveiled remarks left little doubt that this pinch-faced woman had been in on it.

Aunt Letha turned her attention to me, and I tried not to wince. Her directness can be rough, even on those she might intend to protect. "Good thing you're pulling your hair back like that," she said. "Makes that long hair look more professional. You need to meet Sylvie Garnet. She may have a wonderful opportunity for you. If you'd bothered to stop by this week, I'd have told you about it sooner."

My mother comes by her penchant for hard-luck cases honestly, though Aunt Letha is more formidable in her aid to the downtrodden. The downtrodden better be moving pretty quick or Letha can steam right over them.

"Drat. Don't see her right now. But I'll introduce you. Whatever were you doing hanging around up at the lake this morning? Hattie, Vinnia. Avery's here. Avery, you come by tomorrow. We need to go walking."

My other two great-aunts joined us, rescuing me from further cross-examination. I really didn't want Aunt Letha asking me about the lake.

We exchanged pleasantries, and I promised to get my mom and dad over for lunch after church. My great-aunts didn't mention the submerged car or Donlee's stunt—which boded badly for my reputation. Either they didn't know—which was unlikely— or the story circulating was so embarrassing they dared not mention it. Maybe they were still so embarrassed for me over the loss of my job, they hadn't had time yet to fret over how I'd managed to attract the attentions of Donlee Griggs.

Had anybody asked, I couldn't really explain the loss of my job. I still wasn't sure why I had snapped that day in court, listening to my own expert witness shamelessly perjuring himself to win my medical malpractice case. I play to win, but not at all costs. Not with an expert willing to stretch the truth beyond all recognition. I snapped. By the time I got through angrily goading Hilliard and he got through exploding, the judge declared a mistrial, the insurance company I represented settled with the injured baby's family, and I was out of a job. True, I should've controlled myself in court. But my reasons were too complicated to explain in casual conversation. So I'd just keep smiling and pretending along with everybody else in Dacus that nothing had happened.

As I looked around for Mom, Letha returned to grab my elbow and steer me at an alarming pace past clusters of dainty little ladies. I feared we'd topple someone over, bobbing as they must in Aunt Letha's wake.

"Avery, you remember Sylvie Garnet."

We both nodded politely. Of course I knew her, in that way you know your parents' contemporaries. She looked a bit grayer and a tad shorter than I remembered her—a phenomenon I'd noticed since coming home. The whole town seemed older and smaller.

Of course, Sylvie Garnet still stood taller than I, slender in a willowy way, like my sister. She wore a rich red-orange Pendleton wool skirt; the matching sweater sported patchwork suede leaves. Her hair, brushed back from a well-defined widow's peak, lay in Queen Elizabeth steel-gray waves, and she carried herself with the rigid decorum I remembered.

"Avery. I've been meaning to call you. We're so thrilled you've come back here to Dacus." The words rolled off in a honeyed drawl that, this close to the mountains, had to be an affectation. "I understand they had some excitement up at Luna Lake this morning." She smiled expectantly. I just smiled back. News did travel fast.

When I didn't volunteer anything, she continued, without looking too disappointed: "My husband has been anxious to talk to you. In a professional capacity." She leaned forward and tapped my forearm lightly. "Something at the plant he has questions about. He's certain you'll know more about it than these local boys, you being with the Calhoun Firm and all."

"I'll certainly be happy to talk to him." I patted my blazer pocket as if searching for something. "I didn't bring any business cards with me." Actually, I didn't have any cards. "He can reach me at Carlton Barner's office."

"Oh." Her eyebrows raised. "Are you going into practice with Carlton?"

"No. But he's been kind enough to give me the use of an office and his staff for a while."

Whether Harrison Garnet would be able to reach me by calling Carlton's office remained to be seen. For some unspoken reason, Lou Wray, Carlton's receptionist, had developed a palpable dislike for me. Whenever we were out of his earshot, she all but growled and hissed. What she would do to a phone inquiry from Harrison Garnet unsettled me a bit, but right now I had no alternative.

"Actually," Sylvie said, "the matter seems rather urgent. Something about an environmental inspection. I'm not really sure." The shake of her head and the wave of her hand gave an unconvincing imitation of the uninvolved housewife. "Why don't you just stop by this afternoon? After the meeting here, of course. I'll call him and let him know you're coming. Looks like they want us to take our seats. You go by the plant this afternoon."

She patted my arm again to punctuate those last

words, then dismissed me by seeking out a seat with two women I didn't recognize.

Aunt Letha had set sail for another part of the room, so I swerved by the refreshment buffet to snag something before I took a seat on the back row. With finger food, you have to choose carefully to get something substantial while not appearing gluttonous—although some of the ladies, their midsections uncomfortably harnessed by girdles and their swollen feet spilling over their DeLiso Deb pumps, really packed away the cheese straws, petit fours, and mixed nuts without appearing self-conscious.

When I joined her, Mom smiled reassuringly, artfully ignoring my chicken puff–stuffed cheeks. I had skipped breakfast.

I also missed most of the program—something about a new book on the diaries of a Confederate war heroine. Tuning out the speaker—and squelching any thought of the body at the lake—I focused on the immediacy of what might be my first serious client. Picking up an appointment from the guy's wife would have been an odd way to go about things at the Calhoun firm. But not in Dacus.

The only thing I knew about environmental law involved recognizing it as a tricky, regulation-laden area. I'd spent my practice life as a malpractice defense litigator. But as of a few weeks ago, I'd started from scratch. Environmental law might be as good a place to start as any—and more interesting than wills, divorces, fender benders, and real estate closings, the meat and bread of small-practice law.

The thought of general practice terrified me. I'd been used to an elaborate support network of specialist lawyers, paralegals, a law library, computer research capabilities, and a billing office. I knew how to defend a medical malpractice case, but little else. Armed only with Carlton's receptionist, who'd obviously like to see me stuffed and mounted, I felt daunted. But that was only if I was candid with myself.

I squirmed, not paying much attention to the speaker, a gray man with a light lisp. He garnered a pleasant titter from the audience at some anecdote of Civil War sexual politics.

Not for the first time, I mused about exploring other career options. After all, I'd been given a fresh start, a clean slate. In my darker moments, I'd mentally practiced auditioning for some of those other options. "Would you like fries with that?" made my stomach clench, but "Hi, welcome to Wal-Mart" wouldn't be too bad.

I kept returning to the same conclusion. Law school had left me completely unprepared for practically everything. My sister stays home, raising my niece and nephew, gardening, canning vegetables, cooking standing rib roasts, and sewing her own clothes. I'm domestically challenged by brown-and-serve rolls. And seventh-grade home ec had been the last time anyone had let me near a sewing machine. While attempting to create a pair of hot pants, I'd stitched the cuff of my shirt to the left front and back of the shorts, then broken the needle and jammed the machine. In trying to free me, while maintaining control of twenty home ec students armed with scissors and pins, my teacher almost burst into tears.

Thinking back on it, she'd probably reconsidered her career options that day. She'd suggested I join the marching band, then she'd married the next May and quit teaching. I mentally skimmed past the marriage option. Law school had broken me of the dating habit. Few people have any idea of the kind of people who go to law school. And practicing law broke me of the habit of a social life.

So here I sat, in the Lutheran church social hall, accepting the fact that at the ripe age of thirtyish, I didn't have many directions in which to head.

But at least I had an appointment with Harrison Garnet. Sort of.

I grabbed Mom and scooted out of the meeting as quickly as we could.

"Sure you can borrow the van," she said. "Just drop me by the house. Oh, and can you take those aluminum cans by the fire station? For their burned children project."

Bags of empty Coke and beer cans collected from Tap's filled the back of the van, rattling every time we stopped, started, or turned a corner.

"I probably should put those things in your dad's truck. They do get a little pungent, don't they?"

"You can't very well have Dad riding around with his truck full of beer cans. What would First Baptist's board of deacons say?"

Mom laughed as she parked the van in front of the house. "It'd be almost worth it to find out. Good luck. See you for supper?"

"Sure. Thanks." I crawled over behind the wheel, then wrestled my skirt back where it belonged. The matter-of-fact way my parents handle the most dramatic upheavals amazes me. Then again, they tend toward a flair for the dramatic in the most ordinary circumstances.

Garnet Mills sat a couple of blocks off north Main Street, nestled into a neighborhood of small mill houses, a scattering of house trailers, and a few large old white clapboards, two that offered rooms for rent.

The grounds looked unkempt and unprosperous. Rust pocked the chain-link fence surrounding the parking lot. Grass sprouted through the cracked asphalt. Paint peeled from the metal doors of the loading dock.

Inside, two green vinyl chairs sat on either side of a dusty plastic fern in the makeshift waiting area, and ancient gray-green metal desks furnished the business office. But the receptionist, who probably doubled as office manager, didn't park me there. She immediately ushered me past a half dozen desks; three women of assorted ages talked on phones, typed on an old Selectric, or pushed papers around.

Mr. Garnet's office walls were painted a rosy taupe, and the cherry furniture hadn't come from the same army surplus sale as the desks outside. The subdued good taste evidenced Sylvie Garnet's hand at work here. Not flashy, not new, but it clearly drew a line between out there and in here.

While Sylvie Garnet and her decorating taste had remained the same, Mr. Garnet had changed. I remembered him as a small man, slightly shorter than his wife, with a fringe of bright white hair circling his shiny head. I'd never seen him in anything but a dark gray suit, exuding an air of authority, a masterliness. None of that had changed. What had changed was the wheelchair he swung around his desk to greet me.

"Mr. Garnet. It's so nice to see you again."

"Avery. My, haven't you grown up. Your dad keeps us posted on you and your sister, at the Rotary meetings. Despite all his bragging, he didn't tell us how pretty you were."

Feeling awkward, I fought the urge to bend over to address him and gratefully sank into the chair he motioned me toward.

"Thanks for stopping by. Sylvie told me you were in town. You may be just our answer for this little matter we're facing."

"I certainly hope I can be of help." I pulled out my leather notepad and Waterman pen, for some reason needing the comfort of the familiar tools of my trade. "Perhaps if you could give me some background."

Mr. Garnet rolled behind his desk. Seated behind the protective barrier of his walnut fortress, with the

wheelchair out of sight, he looked more like the suc-
cessful businessman I'd known all my life. Garnet
Mills produced cheap upholstered furniture, a low-
end operation with the kind of jobs that now often
move to Mexico.

"In a nutshell, Avery, I've got some environmental boys coming tomorrow to audit my records. And
they want to know, while they're here, if they can
look around the plant site." With thumb and forefinger, he lined up his desk blotter precisely with the
edge of his desk. Other than a brass lamp and a ma-
hogany in-box—which sat empty—the desk lay
clear of clutter. Either he was extremely organized
or he didn't have much to keep him busy.

"We're just a small-town operation and don't often deal with the environmental boys. I want to be
protected. To tell you the truth, I feel a bit like a
sheep waiting to be shorn." He smiled disarmingly.
"I understand those boys can play hardball. I just
want to make sure we're covered."

"I understand." I tried to sound reassuring, but I
scarcely knew where to begin. "Have they served
you with any papers? Do you know of any complaints? Or is this a routine visit?"

He shrugged. "The guy called, wanted to know if
he could come tomorrow afternoon. I assumed this
was routine, but I wanted to make sure. You know,
protect myself. You hear about these regulators running a police state."

I nodded. He probably spent his afternoons listening to conservative talk radio shows. "Best to be

prepared. What sorts of records are you required to keep?"

He looked puzzled, so I quickly added, "Do you use or store any hazardous materials on the premises?"

He snorted politely. "You mean other than the liquid correction ink the girls out front use? I understand that's toxic or hazardous or some such. We're supposed to keep paperwork on that. Can you believe it?"

"A Material Safety Data Sheet." I nodded and hoped I'd gotten the name right. "The paperwork can be quite onerous."

"You can say that again. Not sure how we're protecting the environment if we're killing all those trees for the paper to keep records on."

I nodded and pretended to jot myself a note.

He continued. "Of course, we use glues and stains in our operation. Heck, even empty paint cans have to get special treatment these days. We contract with a waste hauler. As far as I know, we're okay."

"What exactly would you like me to do?"

He shrugged, with both palms up in an eloquent question. "You tell me. Anything we need to do? To protect ourselves?"

"Do you have anyone designated with special responsibilities for compliance?"

He pursed his lips, digesting my question, then shrugged. "The plant manager, I suppose. He keeps up with that stuff. To be honest, I pay as little attention to it as I can. Haven't ever found out what all that record-keeping and environmental nonsense has to do with running a business."

"Perhaps I could meet with him. As long as the records are in order—"

"He's off this week. Took some vacation. Slow time of the year, Thanksgiving to Christmas. Orders really slack off until after the first of the year."

I tapped the end of my pen against my bottom lip. "Maybe we should try to have this visit postponed." It would buy me some time to figure out what I was doing. "If your compliance guy's not here to answer any questions they may have—"

"How about a tour of the plant?" He abruptly moved to another topic without responding. "If you're gonna be representing us, you might as well get a feel for our operation here."

With one hand on his desk, he steered himself around the corner. "Would you hand me those crutches, there behind the door?"

Propped against the wall beside my chair stood short metal crutches with circles that he slid over his forearms. He wiggled out of the chair. "This'll be easier going, if you don't mind walking with a slowpoke."

I opened the office door and followed him out. I wondered what had happened that he now needed crutches or a chair. He maneuvered with remarkable agility for a man who'd come to the use of crutches late in life. I'd remembered Mr. Garnet as a member of the hunting and fishing club, the fellows who used their Luna Lake cabins as headquarters for the manly pursuits of deer hunting and escaping their wives.

On our stroll around the plant, I began to question any optimism I might have felt at becoming the new corporate counsel for Garnet Mills. The mandatory postings about wage and hour laws were displayed near the time clock, but ear protectors were as likely to be dangling around a worker's neck as sticking in his ears.

The plant seemed busy, with lots of people and all the machines operating. Most of the time, the noise level kept conversation to a minimum, with Mr. Garnet yelling occasional comments into my ear. I caught snatches of what he said.

Despite the bustle and the noise, the plant didn't appear particularly prosperous. The aged machinery, bolted to the worn, blackened oak floors, stood caked with years of greasy gray dust.

We stepped through a small side door onto the loading dock. Even here, the noise didn't subside much. A diesel truck's engine idled, its gaping back door accepting forklift loads of boxes. The other loading bays sat empty.

"It's not fancy," he said, as if he'd read my expression too clearly, "but it gives three shifts a paycheck every other week."

We walked to the end of the dock. I clenched my teeth against the late-afternoon chill. The contrast from the warmth in the plant didn't seem to affect Mr. Garnet, but I was glad when we moved into a patch of sunlight.

The employee parking lot stretched behind and beside the loading dock area. I glanced at my watch.

"We run three full shifts here right now. And glad we can do it. Had to lay off a shift a few years ago. During the recession. That's hard on folks."

We stood at the sunny end of the dock, surveying the parking lot for no particular reason that I could see. Near the gate, where employees would enter and leave the lot, a fellow tinkered over a motorcycle. Wearing a battered leather jacket and his hair pulled back from his shiny forehead into a curly gray ponytail, he looked the quintessential burly seventies biker turned middle-aged. Except for him, we were the only people outside the plant.

I nodded toward the figure at the gate. "Who's that?"

Mr. Garnet shrugged. "Seen him around. Don't really know. He waits around for somebody at shift change."

Which wasn't for another hour. Mr. Garnet and I should have a chat about his potential liability for third-party criminal conduct on his premises. If this were my plant, I wouldn't want folks hanging around. In too many instances, estranged husbands shoot their wives dead in parking lots after work.

As we surveyed the loading area, a slight-built man came around the edge of the building and crossed the lot. Seeing his rolling gait and crooked arm—clear marks of cerebral palsy—I wondered what doctor had messed up at his birth. Then I shook my head, trying to lose the image. Too much time spent as a malpractice attorney had colored my vision.

Before the lank-gaited fellow's path could intersect with the biker, we turned back toward the offices. I followed Mr. Garnet's lead through the plant. I wasn't sure about the next step. I felt stupid as it dawned on me that I'd never had to ask a client to pay me. The Calhoun Firm had standard rates. And standard contracts. And a billing department. And a collections process in case things didn't go well.

I had none of those things. I didn't even know the going rate for lawyers in Dacus, though it was surely considerably less than my billable rate at the Calhoun Firm. But probably better than the hourly fee the county paid for representing indigent criminal defendants.

Once we were back in his office, Mr. Garnet remained propped on his crutches. "Avery, can you be here tomorrow afternoon when that inspector shows up?"

"Certainly." I jotted a note, as if I might need a reminder. That would give me this evening and tomorrow morning to give myself a crash course in environmental audits. "And thank you for the tour."

"Like I said, you need to know what we're about here if you're going to represent us." He smoothly slid the right crutch off his arm and extended his hand to shake mine. "I suppose you'll want me to sign something. That's how you lawyers usually work, isn't it?" He snorted a laugh.

I smiled, hoping I looked more like a lawyer than

I felt. "We can draw that up later. We'll take care of first things first—that inspector."

"Fine. Tomorrow after lunch, then?"

I walked back through the short gauntlet of green desks and busy women. They stopped their chattering or slowed their work as I walked by. Not sure of the protocol, I nodded a generic good-bye to the group.

As I drove slowly across town toward my parents' house—which didn't take all that long in a town the size of Dacus—my brain raced. I needed a sample contract of representation. And, more important, I needed to prepare for the inspection visit tomorrow.

Carlton Barner's office boasted only copies of the *South Carolina Code* and *South Carolina Reports*—the state's statutes and appellate court decisions—which would be of no help. Camden County had no official law library, although the resident judge's office had the regional court cases and federal statutes.

Which also wouldn't help much. Digging through statutes and case law on something like this would be time-consuming and almost useless, even assuming I had a starting point for a case law search, which I didn't. I had no computer research hookup—the legal services are expensive, even if I had the hardware—and I didn't know anybody in Dacus who'd bothered to subscribe.

What I needed was a quick how-to on environmental inspections and audits, something that would tell me what to expect, what they could get away with, and what I could help Garnet manage. Plenty of lawyers must have found themselves in my shoes, so somebody would have written some kind of short cut. I'd just drive to Columbia to the law library.

The digital dash clock blinked 2:25. A three-hour drive. Well, actually, a little less than that. I'd burned up that road enough weekends trying to escape the sandy pine barrens around Columbia in search of red clay and roads that didn't go in straight lines. So I knew exactly how long it took.

"Of course you can use one of the cars," my mom said. "Better yet, get your father to ride with you. He just pulled up outside."

I had changed into jeans and a Clemson sweatshirt and we hit the road, with my dad driving, by three-thirty. Though I hated to drag him along on my harebrained mission, I had to admit I appreciated the company. And it gave us the first real chance we'd had to talk since I'd come back home.

By the time we got to Greenville, we'd chatted about the newspaper—mostly about the working order of the equipment, including the delivery truck. Then, once on I-385 South, we settled into a discussion of how to drain the cabin's water heater to check the heating coil and how best to insulate the water pipes.

"Nobody's ever really used that place during the winter. Your grandfather would go up every now and then. But nobody's used it hardly at all since he died. And that's been, what? Seven or eight years?"

I nodded. After my first year in law school. Avery Hampton Howe, himself a lawyer, had been unabashedly pleased with my decision to go to law school, even though some in the family considered my choice more than a little disreputable—common and off-color, even.

I'd been named for my grandfather. And I'd adored him. He'd died unexpectedly the week after my first-year finals, if death at the age of ninety can truly be unexpected. I missed him sorely—his counsel and his wisdom. But I'd often had the uncanny sense that he sometimes stood nearby, nodding silently, rooting me on. If only he could whisper in my ear how to handle an environmental audit.

"Your granddad would've been pleased that you've come home," my dad said, as if reading my thoughts. "Of course, we all are."

I snuck a quick glance at him out of the corner of my eye. His eyes were fixed on the road ahead. I could have hugged him. Something in his tone, and in those few words, resounded as a vote of confidence. Confidence I sorely needed. Somehow, in those two short sentences, he'd managed to tell me I was okay. That coming home hadn't been a failure, but an inevitability.

My·father is an eloquent man with few words.

Rather than spoil the moment by reminding him I wouldn't be staying in Dacus, I filled the silence by asking, "Tell me about Melvin Bertram." That name had danced around the edges of my brain all day.

"Whatever made you think of him?"

"I ran into Mr. Earnest this morning. He commented how interesting that we'd come home at the same time, me and Melvin Bertram."

"He's back?"

My dad's not as plugged into the town gossip as my mother. Which might not bode well for his newspaper venture.

"That's what Mr. Earnest said."

"If anybody'd know, it'd be him, I reckon. 'Course, Bertram's got family in town—a brother. Might be visiting for Thanksgiving."

"Why do I know that name?"

"Don't you remember? Several years ago? His wife disappeared. Everybody figured he'd killed her."

Three

"Killed his wife?"

"That was the rumor," Dad said. "One day, she upped and disappeared. Likely just ran off. But you know how stories pick up wind."

"Mr. Earnest said it was a while ago. Ten or fifteen years?"

Dad pulled around a loaded semi on a hill. "Fifteen, I think. Don't you remember Melvin? His dad and Harrison Garnet were partners for a time in a couple of businesses."

"No. But I do remember somebody a few years older than me who went missing. She'd been a cheerleader when she was in high school." Funny, the things you remember.

Dad signaled, pulled back into the cruising lane, then said, "Melvin—he was the youngest of two or three kids—he'd come back from college and hung out his CPA shingle. Then he married Lea Hopkins, a secretary at Garnet Mills. A bit younger than him. Her folks were from up on the mountain, so I didn't know them. I remember the mill offered a reward when she went missing. Folks posted her picture around after she disappeared."

Garnet Mills. I kept getting reminders of how small my world had become.

Dad continued. "She just disappeared one day. More comes back to me as I think on it. She'd packed up some paints and a canvas or some such one Saturday morning. Took her car, left the house, and never came home. Didn't take anything else with her. No clothes, no money out of the checking account. Just never came home."

"What did they think happened to her?"

He shrugged. "Some folks just figured she'd run off. Even folks who knew her, that didn't seem to surprise them."

"What about her husband?"

He shrugged. "Don't know, really. Doesn't take much to get folks talking. Gossip said she had a boyfriend, that she'd taken off with him. But it struck everyone as odd that she never came back and nobody ever heard from her."

"Her husband—Melvin—left town?"

"Um-hmm. A year or so later. Upped and moved. To Atlanta? Somewhere. Guess having people look at you and wonder what you did to run your wife off finally got to him."

"Worse yet, having people wonder if he'd helped her disappear. That'd be creepy." If he'd killed her, it'd be bad enough. But if he hadn't, imagine enduring the suspicious stares and whispers.

"Honey, you've been hanging around the courthouse on criminal docket day way too much lately," he said with a chuckle.

I snorted in reply and propped both my feet on the dashboard. "So nobody's heard from her since."

"Not's far as I know. Not that anybody'd have any reason to tell me."

"They might have a reason now. You own the newspaper, don't you?"

Dad just shrugged, then he pulled into a fast food place off the interstate and we grabbed some burgers. I would've preferred a Confederate Fried Steak at Yesterday's in Five Points. I'd only been gone from Columbia a couple of weeks, but I already knew how much I'd miss those batter-fried steaks.

The law library caters to students and not the average attorney, so I could get in four or five hours' work before they closed—enough to turn my brain to mush, but also enough to help me earn my fee tomorrow.

While I worked, Dad visited a suburban handyman superstore, perused the local newsstand, and then came back and snoozed on a sofa tucked in a corner of the library. I finished my library research shortly before midnight and didn't run into a soul I knew.

The trip to Columbia prompted a rare moment of silent confession. I had to admit to myself that I wrestled with the—what? humiliation? embarrassment?—of losing my job. Somewhere inside, I still wondered if it branded me a failure. Mostly, I felt angry, angry that refusing to cover up for somebody's lies cost me so much. But shouldn't I be feeling something else? Missing something? Aside from a few colleagues at work, I really had no friends in Columbia. I'd grown chummy with none of my clients—corporate medicine and insurance aren't particularly warm and fuzzy, not the kind of clients Perry Mason kept in touch with after the credits rolled.

I'd been too busy to get to know anyone in my condo complex. My law school buddies had moved to other cities, so we kept in touch irregularly. And I'd sporadically attended a large church, specifically for the advantage of sitting in an anonymous pew, to be entertained by the music, moved by the message, and out the door in time for lunch.

After I finished work, we didn't take time to cruise through my old neighborhood. I felt oddly relieved as Dad steered us toward I-26 North. The ease with which I could flee this city surprised me; I had no reason—other than those chicken-fried steaks, the law library, and The Happy Bookseller— to even look back.

We got in so late that I stayed at my parents' house, then I slept later than I'd intended. A mauve silk blouse in the closet went with my black suit, so I could dress for my afternoon meeting at Garnet Mills without having to drive back up the mountain.

Mom had left a note on the kitchen counter:

Working at First Fruits Food Bank this a.m.
Plenty for breakfast. Help yourself.

Armed with a toasted blueberry bagel and some kind of fruity hot tea Mom had mixed in with the Earl Gray, I sprawled on the sofa with my photocopied law articles and a highlighter pen.

When the phone rang, I caught it on the third ring, thinking it might be Mom.

"Miz Andrews?"

"This is Avery."

"The attorney?"

"Yes." I tried to sound businesslike, instead of like a kid answering her parents' phone. The voice—one I didn't recognize—sounded deep and rich, with only a trace of an up-country drawl.

"Miz Andrews, we haven't met. I apologize for calling you at home, but I wasn't sure how else to get in touch with you. My name is Melvin Bertram."

"Uh. Yes?" Surely he'd gotten used to awkward silences over the years. "Mr. Bertram."

I hoped my voice didn't hint that I'd spent part of last evening rehashing gossip about him.

"Miz Andrews, I wondered if we might meet. I'd only take a few minutes of your time. And of course I'd pay your regular rate. I have a couple of—questions."

Oh, whoa. What in the heck? "Certainly, Mr. Bertram. When would be convenient for you?"

"Whatever would suit you, Miz Andrews. I'm the one imposing on your time."

And offering to pay for it. I liked this guy already. But why was he calling me? "Would you prefer this afternoon? Or sometime next week?"

"This afternoon would suit me nicely. Shall we

meet at—" He chuckled. "That's a tough one, since neither of us has an office in town."

"I'm sharing office space with Carlton Barner." I glanced at my watch. "I have an early-afternoon appointment, Mr. Bertram. I should be finished by four." I couldn't judge how long I'd be at Garnet Mills, but that should leave me a safety margin.

"Near the courthouse?"

"Yessir. In the next block, toward town." I'd have to get there well ahead of him, to keep Lou Wray, the receptionist, from sharpening her claws on him.

"Four o'clock, then. I look forward to it."

His deep voice flowed smoothly over the phone line. What had I thought a man suspected of killing his wife would sound like? Somehow not that intriguing. Or that courtly.

The glance at my watch had startled me into action. I scurried around dressing for my return to Garnet Mills. I pictured an environmental inspector as punctilious, on time, in a rumpled but respectable suit, with graying hair and steely, suspicious eyes. So I dressed in a tailored suit and rushed to be on time.

Both the inspector and Harrison Garnet kept me cooling my heels in Garnet's dingy plastic outer office for twenty minutes. Finally, a kid in an olive double-breasted Italian suit and slick hair announced himself to Rita Wilkes, the keeper of Harrison Garnet's gate.

"Jason Smith. I have an appointment with Mr."— he peeked inside his uncreased, unstained leather folio—"Harrison Garnet."

Rita stood on the other side of the waist-high

swinging gate that corralled me and Jason Smith outside the shabby domain over which she ruled. Her only reply came as an upraised eyebrow.

"Jason Smith." He repeated it carefully, as if everyone must have heard of the young hotshot sporting a suit that would be out of style before his misplaced self-confidence could be shattered on the rocks of reality.

"From Environmental—"

"Ah, yes," Rita Wilkes interrupted. She'd wanted him to dangle an appropriate amount of time. Or maybe Jason Smith wasn't what she'd expected in a government functionary. The way he clipped his words reminded me of some of the Calhoun Firm's Ivy League hires—the ones who never lasted.

"Would you both step this way, please?" She held open the gate. Jason Smith went through first, and I followed. A glance over his shoulder indicated his slight surprise at my presence, but he didn't say anything.

We moved in a line through the office, with Rita leading. He swaggered in front of me, the draped fabric of his jacket and pants adding to the sashaying motion of his walk. He smoothed a hand over his mafioso hairstyle as Rita held open the door to Harrison Garnet's office.

Meeting with his lawyer for a few minutes before the government inspector showed up would've been wise, to my way of thinking. Showing us both into his office as he finished up a phone call left Jason Smith and me eyeing each other warily.

"I'll see you this evening," Harrison said, then carefully replaced the receiver and smiled benignly up at both of us.

"I'm Harrison Garnet." He offered his hand to Jason Smith. "Forgive me for not standing."

"Jason Smith." Jason held his notebook carefully to keep his jacket from sweeping the desktop and leaned across to grip Garnet's hand enthusiastically.

"You've met Avery Andrews? Our counsel?"

Jason turned, his eyebrows raised. "Avery." He squeezed my hand with too much force, really seeing me for the first time.

"Mr. Smith," Garnet said, "we haven't had an inspector from your agency visit us before. Your time is valuable and I don't want to waste it, so you'll have to let us know what you need."

"I'm just here to look around. Perhaps to take a few samples, a few pictures." He stood, feet apart, notebook held with both hands against his thighs.

"Fine. Where do you need to start?"

A flicker across his face was hard to read. Surprised at Garnet's openness? Or did he not know where he wanted to start?

I took advantage of the lull. "Mr. Smith, may I first ask the purpose of your visit?"

He cut his eyes from Harrison Garnet, seated behind his desk, to me.

"To inspect the premises for compliance with the environmental protection regulations of the federal government and the state of South Carolina."

An answer that wasn't an answer. "Certainly. A

part of your regular inspection process? Or," I paused, "in response to a complaint?"

The tip of his tongue wet his lips. "We've had a complaint."

I nodded, as if I'd suspected as much. In fact, I thought, *Oh, shit.* A routine inspection might be one thing. But a red flag sent up by a complaint—even a complaint by the proverbial disgruntled former employee—meant a different scope of investigation, a different road map for Jason Smith to follow.

"And what was the nature of the complaint?"

"A-ver-ee." He drawled my name with condescension. "You must know that environmental complaints may be kept strictly confidential."

I smiled my tiny smile again. "Complainants, Jason, not complaints," I drawled back. "I didn't ask who made the complaint. I asked the nature of the complaint."

He hesitated. We both had sense enough to know that revealing too much about the complaint might reveal too much about who made the complaint.

"Surely, Jason, you must realize that our only desire is to help provide answers to your questions and to get to the bottom of this. Garnet Mills certainly doesn't intend to violate—knowingly or otherwise—the environmental protection laws. But, without some idea of what you're looking for, our ability to assist you will be limited." My voice positively purred.

Jason Smith revealed his discomfiture only by a slight shifting of his spraddle-legged stance. But he replied without hesitation, "Perhaps we could start with a brief visual inspection of the plant site. Then we could discuss further the information that I'll need."

Before I could reply, Garnet, who'd watched our exchange as if it were a tennis match, pushed his wheelchair back from his desk. The movement drew Jason's attention. He stared at Garnet's wheelchair. Probably much as I had. Had Garnet become blind to those unthinking stares, the impolite shock? Or did he just politely ignore the reactions he got?

"Suppose we take you around the plant, answer your questions. I'm sure we can get this cleared up quickly." Garnet used the edge of the desk to pull himself upright, then fitted his crutches around his forearms.

"Avery, would you get the door?"

His tone of voice said he wasn't asking my opinion, so I didn't give it. I didn't want to indicate to Jason any disagreement between client and counsel, so we proceeded along the same path my tour the day before had taken.

I trailed behind Garnet and Jason, watching the two men, paying particular attention to what drew Jason's attention. He bounced through most of the plant tour, playing social, get-to-know-you games with Harrison Garnet and politely attending to the tour monologue.

Garnet's tour didn't take us from the beginning of the operation to the end. The direction seemed governed by the shortest distance between points rather than production flow, so we saw the areas closest to his office first, then moved to the more remote parts of the plant.

Jason didn't make any notes or linger over anything or ask any questions whose answers interested him—not until we arrived in the part of the building where a handful of workers fitted and glued wooden furniture frames together.

Jason Smith started paying attention when we got there.

"What sort of glues do you use, Mr. Garnet?"

Harrison Garnet paused in his recitation. "Whatever we can get at a decent price. Everything's gotten so expensive lately."

I wanted to kick him—or one of his crutches—and tell him to answer the question. Nothing more. Don't volunteer. Don't embellish. Don't give economic or political commentary. But he still wasn't asking for my advice.

Jason Smith nodded appreciatively. "I'd like to have a look around outside now." He glanced at Garnet's crutches, probably without realizing that he'd done it.

As if he had something to prove, Garnet heaved himself around. "Right this way." With his shoulders churning, he plowed toward an exit and the rear loading dock.

Jason, for all his fresh-faced shallowness, knew what he was looking for. And Harrison Garnet hobbled right along without even asking what it was. Or how much trouble he would be in if Jason found it.

Was Garnet really that naive? Conceivable. As a lawyer, even I knew precious little about the

environmental field. Except I did know that guys
who wear suits could end up doing jail time alongside bruisers named Bubba. Either Garnet didn't
have anything to hide or he didn't know it needed to
be hidden.

On the dock, Jason assumed his cocky stance,
surveying the back parking lot as if he owned it.

"How long has this plant been here, Mr. Garnet?"

"This original building's been here since the for-
ties. Initially it housed a garment manufacturing
plant. We took it over in the midfifties. Expanded
quite a bit in the early years."

Again, Jason murmured politely, studying the
parking lot. "I'm trying to picture your layout here. I
believe a creek runs along that back part of your
property?"

"If you can call it a creek. Barely enough water in
there to wet the rocks. We use city water and sewer
here."

Jason nodded, staring past the sunlight glinting
off the parked cars toward the tree line half a football field away. Then he turned back toward the door
we'd exited from, not bothering to finish his tour of
the loading area. "I'd like to take a look at some of
your paperwork now, if you don't mind."

Garnet registered only a tinge of surprise—or
maybe disappointment—then turned toward the
door. "Sure—"

"Excuse me, Mr. Smith." I'd played the strong,
silent type long enough. "Before you go on a fishing
expedition through the company records, I'm going
to have to ask you again the purpose of your search.

I'm sure you understand." The syrupy drip of my voice did little to soften my insistence.

Harrison Garnet looked over his shoulder at me but didn't struggle to turn around.

Jason Smith, sensing a break in the ranks, waited. When Garnet didn't speak, Jason focused on me. "As I've indicated, I'm not required to reveal my source—"

"And as I've indicated, I believe you are required to state the subject of the complaint." I had no idea if that was true. But if he weren't required to tell, he should be.

I half expected him to put his hands on his hips and taunt me: *Well, I'm not telling. Nyeh, nyeh, make me.*

How many guys like Jason had I known? Over-confident, ego-inflated white boys heading into a world where they couldn't get by on a paucity of brains and plenty of family connections the way their frat brothers had in the past. Headed into a world where women and guys who weren't white or well connected would flail the tar out of the likes of them. And they'd conveniently be able to blame affirmative action, reverse discrimination—anything but their own cockiness and lack of experience. And lack of humility.

"Your attitude certainly isn't in the spirit of cooperation as, together, we try to resolve this matter," he said.

Bullshit. "Maybe we could be more help in resolving this matter if we knew what this matter is."

We'd squared off, with Harrison Garnet closed

out of our little tête-à-tête. Garnet maneuvered awk-wardly around so he could watch us. Jason Smith appealed to him. "Mr. Garnet, if I could simply see your records for—"

"Mr. Smith, I don't know how to make this any clearer. Without more information about what you need to see, I can't let you pillage about in my client's files. Those files contain confidential customer information, trade secret process information—any number of things that are proprietary and valuable."

I had no idea if any of that was true, either. But I was on a roll. And I resented his continuing end-runs around me to Garnet.

"I'm afraid I'll have to ask you to supply a search warrant before you go any further."

Muscles on either side of Jason's jaw shot out in tight knots. "If you want to play hardball, Miz An-drews—"

"Now, wait a minute." Harrison Garnet wobbled a bit, trying to enter the fray.

"You can simply tell the judge what you're look-ing for and he'll spell it out in the warrant. Then there won't be any misunderstandings."

"Mr. Garnet has already given consent to an in-spection. It's too late—"

"No, it's not." *Nice try, Junior.* "He consented to show you the plant. On advice of counsel, he'll need to see an administrative search warrant before you can see the company's records."

Jason's jaw muscles worked overtime. "Very

well, Miz Andrews. But plan on seeing me—and my supervisor—here first thing tomorrow morning. Accompanied by a search warrant allowing us access to the records. If you want to do this the hard way, I assure you that can be arranged."

Harrison Garnet's gaze trailed from Jason Smith's reddened face and locked on me. Without a word, he told me I'd better know what I was getting him into.

Four

Holding off Jason Smith, Boy Regulator, lacked the finality of a victory, but at least I'd won the skirmish—and gained a twinge of that *ha, beat you* that I hadn't felt in a while. Where that set the battle lines, I wasn't sure.

If I took time to admit it, I also felt a twinge of *oh, shit*. Angering the little twit in the olive Italian suit likely hadn't been the smartest thing I'd ever done. But every instinct I had said he knew exactly what he was looking for. And Garnet and I still wouldn't know when or if he found it—until it was too late to explain or rectify.

I'd bought enough time to evaluate the records myself. I just hoped I would understand what I saw. The complaint apparently hadn't alleged anything life-threatening, urgent, or irreversible, which meant Jason the wonder kid would have to wait until after Thanksgiving. No judge would give him an administrative warrant—valid for only twenty-four hours—for Thanksgiving Day.

Harrison Garnet hadn't seemed too concerned.

At least not concerned enough to review the records with me after Jason left, despite my insistence. I tried to set a meeting for first thing Friday morning, though I doubted that would give us enough time to adequately prepare for the junior G-man's return. But he said he'd call.

Did Harrison Garnet know what Jason wanted? Did that explain why he wasn't worried? Or did he not have enough experience to worry? He was a difficult man to read.

I had an hour before my appointment with Melvin Bertram, so I drove to my great-aunts' house on North Main and parked out front. I studied the house. This lengthy holiday visit to Dacus felt odd. Everything in Dacus, everything that had been normal and accustomed in my life before, now shone in stark relief. Against what? The backdrop of my life as a lawyer? As I studied my past, the light seemed to have shifted or to have grown brighter. Not the blinding light that floods in the side door of a movie theater at the end of a matinee. More like the stark quality of light on a fall afternoon, when the crisp air holds little humidity and the edges of everything seem sharper.

From behind the privet hedge that crowded the sidewalk, the rusty, spicy smell of boxwood enveloped me. The hoop-skirted branches of a magnolia tree, that staunch representative of the indestructible South, sheltered the entire right front yard.

Anyone who associates magnolias with their waxy, iridescent white flowers has missed the essential nature of magnolias. Every time I see a magnolia, I remember my first visit to Charleston days after Hurricane Hugo hit. Stalwart oaks, downed or damaged, trashed the streets. Even the palmettos once used to build fortresses stood ragged. But the magnolias, despite wind and flood, hadn't lost a single waxy leaf, as though their skirts had scarcely been ruffled. Daintiness is disconcertingly deceptive in magnolias.

The stiff, shoe-size dead leaves scratched harshly as I kicked them down the front walk. The white clapboard house, always in need of painting no matter how recently it had been done, had stood on this spot for a hundred years.

I twisted the turn bell in the center of the front door. The mechanical jangle carried easily to the back part of the house. Usually I went in and out the back door, but for some reason, today I felt like a more formal call.

"Avery." Aunt Letha flung open the door without first parting the lace curtains. "You should have phoned first. You're just in time." The odor of mothballs and Aunt Letha's gardenia perfume wafted over me.

She backed me onto the porch and slammed the door, rattling the windowpanes. Aunt Letha's rottweiler, a black mass of spoiled dog flesh named Bud, strutted at the end of his leash like one of Hannibal's elephants. The family suspected he'd been named for an old boyfriend. Aunt Letha wouldn't say.

"Where—"

"Come on." She left me blowing in her wake like dried leaves in a wind. When she hit the sidewalk, I noticed her Rockports.

"Aunt Letha, I've got on pumps. I can't walk in—"

"Sure you can. If you can't keep up with an old lady like me, you're in a sad state."

Bud's thick nails rasped along the magnolia-leaf carpet. I've never had sense enough to know when to back down from a challenge. I trotted down the sidewalk after them.

Aunt Letha towers over me. Despite her bulk and her age, an impression of energy and activity encircle her like an aura. She steamed down Main Street while I clopped down the root-broken sidewalk behind her. She cut right on the first side street, marched through the gates at Memorial Park, and plopped down on a bench near the praying hands statue. A block and a half. Bud looked around, sighed deeply, then stretched out on the grass, his legs out behind him like a frog awaiting dissection.

"You walk every day, Aunt Letha?"

"Every day." She sat spraddled on the weak-legged bench, her turquoise pull-on slacks strained at the knees. "Almost."

We settled into a companionable silence. The graveyard—the only one in Dacus, if you didn't count the country church cemeteries scattered outside town—covered the two blocks behind the Lutheran church. Weathered granite and marble monuments, some with lettering scrubbed away by wind and water, were sprinkled thickly all around us. Most stones bore the family names of original German settlers.

Flowers brightened the graves—some clamped onto the tops of headstones, some in metal canisters stuck into holders, others on spindly legged wire stands. In odd contrast to the solemn, fall-colored plastic and fabric flowers, I noticed several Mylar balloons, shining and dancing in the sun. Balloons on graves? I didn't comment on them. Aunt Letha surely had a well-rehearsed diatribe on Mylar and Lutherans that I didn't need to hear.

"Got any clients yet? Besides that white trash you've been picking up at the courthouse."

"Yes'm, I do, as a matter of fact. Two new ones this week, it looks like."

"Harrumph," she answered. "It's a wonder. Avery, you're gonna have to mind what kind of folks you find yourself attracting. What kind of clients you gonna have, you keep associating yourself with weirdos like that Donlee Griggs? That boy acted like he'd been struck stupid by lightning when he was in my eleventh-grade history class. And time has not improved his lot. What few synapses the unfortunate circumstances of his breeding left him, he ruined with drink."

I nodded. No argument from me on that.

"You realize folks are going to have enough trouble taking you seriously."

I half turned to get a better look at her.

"Can anything good come out of Nazareth, Avery? If folks've known you any stretch of time, they have trouble believing you have a lick of sense. That's just the way it is with folks."

Her biblical turn implied a generic reference, not one directed solely at me, except as illustration.

"You have to give people a reason to take you seriously, Avery. People in this town still remember you wearin' those shiny red satin shorts and those white leather boots off down Main Street."

"I never—"

"Don't tell me. I stood right there and watched." Bud stirred at the sharpness in her tone, ready to leap to her defense, should the need arise. Of course, he'd never actually had to defend Aunt Letha. How could the need ever arise?

"Marched right down Main Street in it."

The occasion she referred to leapt from a distant memory. "Aunt Letha," I said, exasperated. "I was three years old. In the Christmas parade, for Pete's sake."

"People remember, Avery."

"You were three years old once, in this same town." Though, even as I said it, I had trouble imagining it. "People don't have any trouble taking you seriously."

"Never pranced down Main Street in red satin and white leather boots with my bare legs a-shinin'."

"And a baton, Aunt Letha. I twirled a baton."

"Dropped it a time or two, best I remember."

Hard to argue with fact.

We sat, studying the gravestones and the bobbing balloons and listening to the distant traffic sounds.

Casually, as though searching for nothing more

than companionable gossip, I asked, "What do you remember about Melvin Bertram?"

"He's back in town, I hear."

"Um-hmm."

"I remember his younger brother in high school. His parents aren't from here. Moved in after Melvin would've been in my class, best I remember."

Which meant they'd been in Dacus some decades—still newcomers, by Dacus measure.

"His father was with one of the new plants that moved in about that time. From somewhere over in Georgia. Sordid doings, that about his wife."

"Whose wife?"

"Melvin's, of course. She upped and disappeared. Must have been"—she calculated in her head—"fifteen years ago. That was the high school's centennial celebration. I remember Melvin's mother on the covered dish committee with Vinnia. Tiny, chirpy like a bird. Always wore shoes with a strap across the instep."

Tiny, next to Aunt Letha, could mean almost anything.

"I don't remember Melvin," she continued. "His brother was a smart kid. Better in math than in the verbal arts. You could tell he had to be an engineer—or whatever else that type might turn to. Couldn't do much else."

Like my dad, the engineer turned renaissance newspaper publisher.

"But, my, the talk that steamed around town about that wife of his. Lea Hopkins, she was in high school. And quite a little piece of work, even then.

Not that old-lady schoolteachers were supposed to know about such, but the football team apparently passed her around with more completions than they did the football."

I snuck a glance at Aunt Letha, my eyes wide. To be a lady of a certain age, her practical earthiness could jolt me sometimes.

"She headed off to college, but within a year or two, the engagement announcement, photo and all, appeared in the newspaper. Melvin was a bit older than she, but only four or five years. Not enough to be unseemly, you know. Settled in, him working as a CPA. She typed or something in the office at Garnet Mills. I remember because, of course, when she didn't show up for work and all the talk started, they interviewed everybody who knew her."

As we sat, side by side, staring across the gray-brown autumn lawn and the cold stones, a figure limped through the gate from the south side of the graveyard.

"Who's that?" I asked, recognizing the man I'd seen in the Garnet Mills parking lot, the one who'd approached the biker at the gate.

"Nebo Earling. Visiting his momma's grave, I guess. She died years ago, bad to drink. His daddy took off long before that—nobody ever had any idea who he was, though they suspicioned about one or two."

He limped away from where we sat, toward the far side of the park. As we watched, he stooped at a grave, picked up an arrangement of yellow and or-ange flowers, studied them, then chunked them haphazardly back into the vase. He moved a couple of graves down, chose a bunch of bright red silk flowers, limped across to another grave, and placed the flowers in the empty vase.

"Look at him. I know that boy hasn't got good sense, but even a jaybird knows when it's stealing." Letha shrugged. "Reckon if anybody cares, they'll spot their flowers and reclaim them." She sighed expansively and crossed her arms. "Yep. One Thursday Lea took the afternoon off. To go up the mountain to paint, she'd said. 'Least, that's what she told Rita Wilkes."

Rita Wilkes. The woman who presided over the Garnet Mills office. No wonder she acted as if she owned the place. She'd been there forever.

"But Lea didn't show up for work the next morning. They called her husband. And later the cops. Fact that Melvin hadn't raised a hue and cry when his wife didn't come home all night struck folks as odd. That, more than anything, fueled the suspicions. Don't they always say look around the house when somebody gets murdered, likely a loved one did it?" She nodded sagely.

"They think he murdered her?"

She shrugged. "He sure didn't give folks much reason to think otherwise. Didn't appear concerned when nobody heard from her, first for days, then weeks. And practically the whole town knew they hadn't been getting along. Lea blabbed everything she knew to those hens at work. And they, of course, blabbed to everybody else in town. Once Lea went missing, it all became especially interesting. And the way she behaved left plenty for folks to be interested in."

I had faint glimmers of memory about the case, one of those peripheral intrigues that had mostly affected adults. Fifteen years ago, I'd been in high school and too busy trying to outgrow Dacus to worry about small-town tales, so the details had passed me by.

"He left town himself, which didn't help anybody's opinion of him. The whole thing was sordid and trashy. But folks usually get no better than they deserve."

I glanced at my watch. I'd need to be leaving before long. Now probably wouldn't be a good time to mention the name of my afternoon appointment.

Four rows of headstones over from where we sat, a faded blue Buick—one of those gas guzzlers nobody could afford to drive very far—stopped on the two-rutted gravel drive that cut through the graveyard. A lean man, grayed and stooped, folded himself out of the driver's door and walked around to unlock the trunk, then ambled loosely the few steps to a nearby grave. I watched, amazed, as he used a whisk broom to brush leaves and imaginary dust off the bronze plate on the ground.

He carefully picked a couple of stray fall leaves from the silk flowers that exploded from the bronze vase. Another trip to the trunk brought clippers to trim some grass straggling from the edges of the marker. Another brushing with the whisk broom and he straightened stiffly, one hand on his hip. He stood only a moment, studying his handiwork, retraced his steps, cranked the yacht-sized Buick, and crunched down the gravel drive.

Aunt Letha didn't comment on the performance. She found the oddest things perfectly ordinary.

"I've got to run, Aunt Letha. I've got to meet somebody in a few minutes. Mind if I leave my car at your house? It's about as quick to walk to the office from here."

"Sure, hon."

She looked me up and down as I stood and smoothed my skirt. She didn't say anything. Her look said she wanted to, but she restrained herself with some effort. I never know which is worse—the comments she makes or the ones she refrains from making.

"Bye, Bud. See you later, Aunt Letha."

I walked through the grass alongside the gravel drive. I'd taken enough risks with skinning the heels of my pumps. Of course, after mincing through the grass, I'd have to remember to check my heels for clods of mud.

I entered Carlton Barner's office through the front door of the asbestos-sided old house. Our arrangement was so temporary, he hadn't seen fit to give me a key to the back door. I'd fallen into this layover office after my mom had a chat with Carlton's cousin about me "coming home." I hadn't wanted to argue. I certainly hadn't expected to be so thankful for a haven in which to hide from my own unemployment.

Back in my clerking days in law school, I'd
worked for a small personal injury firm. One client
had been so banged up in a car accident that he
hadn't been able to return to his traveling sales
job for almost two years. He introduced himself to
everyone as a consultant—even though he never
could show me any income from clients. I'd thought
his reaction pathetic and odd, but now I realized how
much of myself had been defined by my job—my
condo, my car, my wardrobe, my acquaintances, my
time, my life. All gone. So now I told people I was
in town for a while, sharing space with Carlton
Barner, to keep from having to say "I have no job."

Today, clients filled Carlton's waiting room. On
second glance, maybe two clients and accompany-
ing family members.

Of course, that meant two more clients than I had
waiting. As I stood on the worn hallway carpeting
and looked through the receptionist's window, I had
qualms about Melvin Bertram meeting me here.

I glanced at my watch. I was plenty early for our
appointment, but too late to make other arrangements. If everybody in town knew the stories Aunt
Letha knew, news of this meeting would make the
rounds by suppertime.

Was I overreacting? Nobody remembered old
gossip or grudges like Aunt Letha.

Unless it was Lou Wray, the gorgon receptionist.
Why all Carlton Barner's clients weren't arranged in
the entry hall as frozen stone statues, I'd never
know. After Melvin Bertram showed up, her sharp

tongue would be slicing open old gossip before the dinner bell at the textile mill sounded.

"Miz Wray." I leaned through the receptionist's window, trying fruitlessly to get her attention. "Miz Wray."

She waited a count of three before turning slowly. Not that she seemed to be doing anything important, sitting at the farthest of the three desks. Nothing more important than ignoring me, that is.

"Miz Wray, I'm expecting a client at four. When he arrives, could you tell him to come on back?"

Her only reply came as a marked tightening around the corners of her mouth. But it spoke eloquently. I'd keep my ear out for Melvin Bertram.

Carlton had loaned me the office he'd set up for his summer clerks. Spartanly furnished, it sat at the end of the hall past the kitchen and directly across from the bathroom door.

The most attractive feature of the nondescript house was that it stood only a block from the courthouse. The small rooms were brightened—and made cooler—by the ten-foot windows. Its high ceilings dated from the 1920s, designed for hot, un-air-conditioned Southern summers. In late autumn—even on mild November afternoons after I'd walked a few blocks in the sun—the rooms settled into a damp chill difficult to shake.

I paced between my office door and the kitchen, trying to keep an eye on the front door without drawing too much attention.

Fortunately, Melvin arrived five minutes early. At

least I hoped it was him as I whisked down the hall to greet him before the barracuda could swim out from her hidey-hole.

"Mr. Bertram?" When he cocked his head expectantly, I added, "I'm Avery Andrews."

He gave me a cool, firm handshake, his grasp gentle and strong. I half expected him to cup my hand in both of his, one of those courtly, Sunday-morning handshakes.

"Thank you for seeing me, Miz Andrews."

"Avery. Please."

I tried not to stare. He looked perfectly average—average height and weight, his sandy hair held only highlights of gray. Midforties, judging from what I knew of his history, though he didn't look it. Dressed in navy corduroy slacks and a patterned pullover sweater, he looked like a business executive on vacation. Not like a man who, by his mere presence, fanned the gossip fires sizzling around town.

I led him into my office and took a seat beside him in the chairs in front of the desk.

"So, Mr. Bertram. What—"

"Melvin. Please."

I nodded.

"This is a bit awkward," he said, turning to face me. "If what I'm about to ask you is inappropriate in any way, please tell me. But I'd like to ask your opinion about—a couple of things."

Clients often launch into long explanations to avoid telling me what they've come for, trying to avoid the unpleasant but true. I nodded and leaned forward slightly, hoping to encourage him to get on with it.

"I understand you were at Luna Lake yesterday when they discovered a submerged car."

Whatever I'd expected, that wasn't it. I nodded.

He paused, studying my face, no doubt seeing my surprise. "I understand it was a 1978 Ford Thunderbird."

I shrugged. "I don't know much about makes and models of cars. It was old. And rusted. And had a Ford emblem on the trunk. That's about all I know."

"Red? With a white top?"

"Hard to say. It was almost solid rust."

"And—there was a—skeleton inside?"

"That I can tell you." I shuddered, remembering that Magic 8 Ball skull.

"Could you—could—well, tell anything about—" Words failed him, but the desperation in his eyes spoke what he couldn't say.

"No. To tell you the truth, the car wasn't far enough up the ramp to allow the water to drain out. About all I can tell you is it was a skeleton. And, to my untrained eye, that of an adult."

I didn't mention the peculiar deposits on the face bones. For one, it had looked too weird and I didn't know how to describe it. For another, Melvin Bertram didn't look like he could deal with that picture in his mind any better than I could. Whatever pictures did parade across his brain, they were apparently gruesome enough that he didn't press for any more details.

"May I ask, why are you asking me about this?" I suspected, but I needed to hear it from him.

He sat back in his chair, his sigh deflating his desperation. Not completely, though.

"The sheriff came to see me today. At my brother's house. I'm visiting for the holiday." He paused. "The car has been identified as my wife's. The license tag and description match hers. Pending an autopsy—which will be delayed because of the holiday—Sheriff Peters expects the body inside will be hers."

His voice died out, as if he'd saved just enough air to say that last sentence, but had no more in him. He stared at the top of my desk, not seeing the legal pad or my Waterman pen or the absence of billable cases. Then he continued. "Of course, she's been gone for fifteen years. I don't suppose a delay for the medical examiner's Thanksgiving meal is really going to make much difference."

What could I say to that? "I'm so sorry, Mr. Bertram. Melvin." To keep from staring at him, I glanced down. A clod of mud clung to the heel of my pump.

He shifted in his chair. "I just needed to confirm some things. I heard you'd been there. And I wanted to know what parts of Sheriff Peters's innuendo I could believe. Trust me," he said, eyeing me with an even gaze. "I learned fifteen years ago that cops can shade the truth any color they want it to be. Different sheriff, I know. But same mentality, I figure."

Different sheriff, all right. Fifteen years ago, L. J. Peters had been with me in the—what? ninth or tenth grade at Dacus High. L.J. was Lucinda Jane to her mother but L.J. to those of us who had lived in fear of her. By high school, L.J. had abandoned her daily ritual of slamming me against the bathroom wall, a sort of exercise regimen for her through most of elementary school. She'd given that up for more mature pursuits, like sneaking cigarettes behind the gym and sneaking glass-pack mufflers past the Highway Patrol. Lucinda Jane had grown up— and I mean up, to about six feet—and become sheriff of Camden County. That thought frequently frightens me.

"Guess L.J. hasn't changed a lot since I last saw her," I mused.

"You know Peters?"

I nodded.

"I forget what it's like to live in a town where you expect everybody to know everybody else. And everything."

That last comment was loaded. He fixed me with his steady blue-flecked gaze, as if trying to read how much I knew. And trying to decide how much he wanted me to know.

He decided quickly. "Avery, thank you so much for your time." He pulled a slip of paper from his pants pocket. "My brother's address. You may bill me there."

"I really didn't do anything," I said, as I accepted the proffered slip of paper. "But if I can be of assistance, please give me a call."

We did the handshake thing, and he left without causing any discernible ripples among the group waiting to see Carlton. Lou Wray stayed out of sight.

I needed to consider more permanent arrangements for my life, make some calls. Network, as they say. This arrangement with Carlton and the Dragon Lady would serve temporarily—but, thanks to the Dragon Lady, only temporarily.

What that meeting with Melvin Bertram had been about, I couldn't tell. He obviously hadn't learned anything he hadn't already known. I shrugged mentally. Might as well call it a day. And a busy one it had been, meeting with both my clients in one day.

I went to retrieve Mom's van from Aunt Letha's house. As I covered the handful of blocks up Main Street, Dacus's version of rush hour—which lasted all of five minutes—moved past on both sides of the crape myrtle–filled median. Daylight faded fast and no one else walked the sidewalks.

Past the central business district, which filled only three or four blocks, Main Street became a hodgepodge of houses. The newest one probably dated to 1950. A few were stately and multistoried, a couple boasted wide verandas. Most were nondescript clapboard or brick.

Dacus claimed no special architectural heritage. No grand, glorious past. No landed gentry with elegant town homes. Downstate South Carolina claimed that pride, where the plantation owners—or the modern version, the sharecropper leaseholders—kept their families in town and away from the grubbiness of actual work.

Dacus, nestled into the foothills of the Blue

Ridge, had first been settled by Germans searching for some place that looked like home. And it had attracted an independent, almost asocial cast of characters over the decades. But they all knew work. And didn't much revel in hollow neighborliness. I hadn't understood the difference until my exile downstate. For such a small state, South Carolina maintained a rare diversity, in accents, work ethic, social proprieties. And temperatures.

The crispness in the air invigorated me. The weather statistics always show a five- or ten-degree difference over the 150-mile distance to Columbia. But the cheek-chilling bite of fall never shows up accurately in those numbers. I loved the way the air felt here.

I bent to unlock the van door just as Aunt Hattie nosed the 1980 LeSabre onto the sidewalk, peeking around the driveway shrubs before she pulled into the street. I waved and walked to the passenger window, on Vinnia's side.

"Avery," she called over the top of the window as she cranked it down. "Come go with us."

"Where you off to?" I leaned against the car door.

Hattie, the older of the two by eighteen months, grasped the steering wheel in both hands. Tall and angular, she had no trouble seeing over the car hood's acreage, and she commanded it with the same authority she'd exercised over generations of biology students. Or pupils, as she referred to them. Disparagingly, I'd always thought.

Grandmotherly-looking Vinnia, shorter by close to a foot and softer and rounder, nestled back in the passenger seat. "To church. The Sunshine Girls are going to the community Thanksgiving service out at South End Baptist. Hattie, you remembered the keys to the church bus?"

"Of course." Hattie, used to bossing high-schoolers around, tolerated Vinnia's remindings. Vinnia had mothered five children and couldn't get out of the habit.

"Church bus?"

Vinnia nodded. "The Sunshine Girls—of course, we just call them that, but we'd take any men who lived long enough to qualify—"

Hattie snorted at that. "—and could keep up with us."

A frightening prospect for some man of certain years to find himself mixed up with a bunch that included my great-aunts.

"Anyway, we're all going together. Hattie and I take the bus around to pick up the girls who can't drive after dark."

"You drive the church bus, Aunt Hattie?" I was picturing the repainted Blue Bird school bus that usually sat parked behind the church.

"Certainly." She leaned over enough so she could get a clear view of me. "Have for years."

I hesitated, about to tread on dangerous territory. "Aunt Hattie, do you have a commercial driver's license?" Hattie had retired from teaching five years ago—and that had been more than a decade after most of her contemporaries had retired.

"Whatever for?"

"Well, it's required now. To operate a commercial

vehicle. It's like the old chauffeur's license." Only the requirements are much more stringent.

Hattie propped her left arm on the steering wheel so she could lean farther across the front seat. I knew, in a momentary flash, what it must have been like to accidentally knick an earthworm's intestine in her biology class.

"I've been driving that bus to pick up those girls since before I taught you to rollerskate, Avery." She didn't have to say anything else.

Vinnia scrunched back against her seat so I could have the full force and effect of her older sister. But Vinnia, too, fixed me with her soft blue eyes. In a pitying tone, she said, "Avery, honey, sometimes you know just enough to spoil everyone else's fun. It's not a becoming trait, sweetie."

I tapped the car door lightly, surrendering gracefully. "You all have fun."

I hoped my smile smoothed things over. What cop in his right mind would stop the Sunshine Girls? All the cops had probably had Aunt Hattie's biology class. They likely wouldn't go out of their way to encounter that stern stare again.

I waved as Aunt Hattie bumped the Buick's back tire over the curb.

The sun had dropped below the trees. Suddenly, the drive up the mountain to the lake cabin seemed a cold, lonely trek.

Something about this time of day, hanging between daylight and dark, always distresses me. I try to stay busy until good dark. Somehow, then it's okay. But the death throes of daylight and the loneness of an empty house and the inevitability of the evening news and a microwave dinner were things I wanted to avoid. Or to share with someone.

I turned toward my parents' house.

Five

The chaos at my parents' house built to a crescendo on Thanksgiving morning. Aunts Letha, Hattie, and Vinnia joined my parents, my sister Lydia and her husband, my niece and nephew, two Japanese exchange students from the college, and some drug rehab kid my mother had taken in. I hoped the newcomers were all sufficiently rehabbed and ready to deal with my family in full force and volume.

The aunts had henpecked each other and the dinner to pieces before the time came to set it on the table. During the morning, I'd snatched glimpses of the Thanksgiving Day parades on TV, roughhoused with my niece and nephew (until our mothers yelled at us to knock it off), and—as my contribution to the traditional holiday feast—burned the bottoms on the brown-and-serve rolls. Fortunately, Aunt Hattie had also made biscuits.

The first lull in the noise came when we bowed our heads for the blessing. Then the only sounds came from the television in the den and mouselike crunching sounds from my niece, Emma. Her

mother—my sister—and I caught each other sneaking one-eyed glances in Emma's direction. I
grinned. My sister glared. Everybody else waited
for Emma to bless the food, while Emma tried to
swallow the pecan she'd snuck off the top of the
sweet potato casserole.

As usual, the food tasted like home and the conversation was stereophonically loud and familially
funny.

"What time's the bowl game?" Emma asked. At
seven, she'd suddenly become a big football fan. I
suspected my dad had worked on her secretly; he'd
spent years as the family's only true believer.

"Who's playing?" Vinnia asked. She probably
didn't know a football had a point on both ends.

"Clemson, Vinnia." Hattie nodded sagely. Probably mentally planning on being on her way home by
kickoff time.

The conversation ebbed and flowed; sometimes
two conversations overrunning each other. I sat back
and listened. Was this what it felt like to awaken
from a coma? The food was better, the kids' knock-
knock jokes were funnier, the parade floats more
elaborate, my family more special to me than ever
before. Everything had an intensity I couldn't describe, as if I'd been banished somewhere far away
and had come home when I never thought I'd see it
again.

I bent over another mouthful of dressing and
blinked back a tear that stung my eye. Silly, but it
felt good to be back here. I'd never missed a
Thanksgiving at home, at this same table, with the

same menu and these same people. Well, except for the two exchange students and the drug addict.

But it felt like the first time in very long memory: the first time I hadn't had the pressures and vagaries of school or a law practice; didn't have Winn Davis, my former managing partner, leaving sexually explicit voice-mail messages; didn't have the pressure of maintaining impossible levels of billable hours.

Of course, considering the number of billable hours I'd worked this week, I should've returned Jake Baker's call offering me a job in Charleston. But rather than rehearse "Welcome to Wal-Mart" or contemplate working with the state's most audacious ambulance chaser, I sat back and counted my blessings.

The mention of Melvin Bertram's name roused me from my maudlin reverie.

"You don't say," Hattie said. "Didn't know he was back. For good?"

"Or bad," Aletha countered.

We'd collectively begun cleaning and stacking plates and moving serving dishes from the dining room table to the kitchen counters. Mom had shooed the teenagers and little kids out of the kitchen toward the television or other diversions. My dad disappeared out the back door. On any other day, he would clear the kitchen by himself, but he doesn't dare interfere with the great-aunts.

"I heard at the beauty parlor yesterday something that, if I'd known it, I'd forgotten it," Vinnia said.

"As if that made sense." Letha vigorously shook crumbs from the place mats into the sink.

Vinnia paid no heed. "I heard that Melvin Bertram's wife—do you remember her? Lea Hopkins, she was. She and Sylvie Garnet's son had been keeping time together, at one time. And now, here little Harry is, running for governor."

"He's what?" Aletha demanded.

"Running for governor. That's what Sylvie announced at the Ladies Auxiliary Wednesday morning. Of course, this is very preliminary. But Sylvie said the party higher-ups had sought him out."

"Seems awfully young to be a governor."

"Not really. He's forty-something. He'll always look young, until he just suddenly runs to pot. He's that type."

Perennially youthful, but doomed. Good description of Harry.

"The shocking thing about the conversation—" Vinnia stopped loading plates into the dishwasher and leaned toward her audience with a conspiratorial air. "Maeve said this affair continued even after Lea married Melvin Bertram. I was positively shocked."

Hattie shook her head. "That girl was never any better than she ought to be. Might explain why she popped home from college so quick and took that clerking job at Garnet Mills. Could see Junior practically every day, that way."

"How can somebody do something like that?" my mom asked. "I'm sorry if I sound naive. But just how do you go about carrying on an affair with your husband or wife around? Especially in a town this size. Law, I can just see me carrying on with somebody. Even assuming I knew how somebody could do such a thing. I mean, how do you—well, the whole idea is embarrassing."

"Explains why people in town remember the rumors fifteen years later," Letha said. She rinsed the okra-and-beans pot and handed it to Hattie to put in the dishwasher. "And explains why nobody ever thought she and Bertram would stick it out."

"That's all for this load," Hattie said. "Just stack the rest over there."

I gave the stove top a final wipe with glass cleaner and a towel about the time Dad stuck his head in the back door and beckoned me.

"Avery, you got a sec?"

Outside, the faint but warm November sun glinted off the cars in the drive.

"I got a surprise for you. If you like it, that is."

He led the way toward the garage, a wooden stand-alone that leaned slightly akilter. The wooden doors stood open to either side, and backed into the space was my grandfather's 1965 Mustang convertible. Red.

The car and I were roughly the same vintage. My grandfather had been in his late sixties when he'd bought it, brand-new. As a kid, I'd thought being squired around in that car defined *special*.

I approached it with reverence, as I always had. "I can't drive this."

Dad shrugged, his hands jammed in his jeans pockets. "I know it's not as fancy as that car your firm provided for you. But I thought, until you could get something else—"

"No, Dad. It's not that. It's—well, a classic now. I'd be scared to death to drive it."

"I've been tinkering with it. The carburetor needed cleaning and rebuilding. Carbs are tricky things. But she'll do until you get something else. I mean, you're welcome to borrow my truck whenever you want to. Especially if you think this old thing'll break down on you somewhere. But—"

"No, Dad. It's great. I'll take good care of it. You've got it looking great."

I hugged him quickly, taking him by surprise. Then I turned to inspect the passenger side, so he wouldn't see the tears in my eyes.

"Thanks, Dad. This is—really special." I swallowed hard. "Granddad loved this car, didn't he?"

Dad puffed a laugh out. "He sure did. Even though everybody in town thought him a damned fool. Just made him that much more determined." He patted the car's hood affectionately. "He'd be glad to know you're using it."

"Avery!" My mom called from the back stoop. "Avery! Telephone!"

Just inside the door, the phone receiver lay on the kitchen counter. I pulled the cord tight so I could stand in the laundry room, in hopes of hearing over the sounds of the dishwasher and the television.

"Avery?" The voice sounded familiar, but I couldn't place it immediately. "I apologize for bothering you at home on a holiday. This is Melvin Bertram. I really need your help."

His voice sounded different on the phone—richer, more honeyed. In person, his voice sounded deep, but somehow sharper.

"Yes?"

"Sheriff Peters has come to escort me to her office. She has some questions, she says."

"On Thanksgiving?" Even for L.J., that crossed the bounds of propriety.

"She did let me finish my pumpkin pie."

I could hear sounds at his house not unlike those emanating down my own hallway. "Where are you now?"

"Still at my brother's house. He lives on Lake's Edge, so we're close to town."

Lake's Edge consisted of larger, established homes huddled around the edge of a pond. Distinctly middle-class prosperous, the thing that made the neighborhood truly exclusive was the size of the pond.

"Sheriff Peters thought we might be more comfortable at her office rather than here, with my brother's kids and cousins." His voice drew away from the phone. I figured he had turned to acknowledge L.J. in the conversation.

"Let me speak to L.J. Is she there?"

Melvin didn't say anything to me, but I heard some indistinct muttering, then L.J.'s voice boomed in my ear.

"A'vry. Shoulda known you'd land back in town and git yourself mixed up in some nonsense that's none'a your business."

"Happy Thanksgiving, L.J. Since Clemson made

it to a bowl game this year and Carolina didn't, this is how you decide to spend your holiday?"

She sounded as though she was working a toothpick through a compacted wad of turkey as we spoke.

"Can't put a criminal investigation on hold, A'vry."

"But it could wait until tomorrow."

L.J. made a smacking sound—probably shifting her toothpick. "'Bout the time some shyster starts tellin' me I need to hold off questioning her client, I gotta wonder what she's hiding. Or what she wants time to cover up."

"For Pete's sake, L.J.—"

"Gotta go. Since Mr. Bertram has graciously consented to help us with our investigation—"

"L.J. Tell Mr. Bertram I'll—"

I bellowed into a dead receiver, as if my voice could actually carry over the severed connection to Melvin, to tell him to watch what he said until I got there.

I turned down the hall to ask Mom if I could borrow her van. I didn't have the nerve to presume I could actually take the Mustang. It was too special. But Dad silently appeared, the keys dangling from his fingers.

Without a word of protest, I solemnly took the keys and left out the back door.

I didn't take time to exult over the car. The vinyl smelled of ArmourAll, the gas gauge sat on full, and the clutch required a surprisingly long reach—quite a stretch for my short legs. But I moved easily from driving my smooth, German-engineered BMW to this loose, loud, punchy little redneck car. An original Mustang without power steering is nobody's definition of an easy car to drive. But I could see how mastering one bred its own arrogance. I quickly knew why my grandfather had loved this powerful, pouty car.

I had to hurry. Too many really good confessions take place in the car on the way to the police station. I couldn't do anything about that. But I could make it to the station almost as quickly as they could.

This wasn't a fresh crime—one that had just happened, with a perpetrator dying to unburden himself to a casual and caring cop. And I reminded myself that Melvin Bertram had accumulated more experience in criminal interrogation than I had. After all, he'd started fifteen years ago.

I pulled into the Law Enforcement Center parking lot, a block down from the courthouse. County cop cars scattered the lot, along with a few civilian cars. Cops' off-duty cars? Or those of some Thanksgiving Day visitors? Did families come eat turkey dinners with their locked-up loved ones? No telling which was L.J.'s car.

I hadn't seen L.J., except in passing, since the night we'd graduated from high school. But I recognized her immediately, right up to her bowl-cut black hair. As they walked side by side down the hallway toward me, she eclipsed Melvin, who wasn't a small man. L.J. wore a dark blue uniform, her shoe box–size brogans clapping the tile floor with a military slap. I'd come in the lot door, so she must have her own parking space somewhere else.

"L.J. Long time." I offered my hand.

She scanned me up and down before she took my hand, her narrow eyes dark under her dark bangs. "A'vry." Her expression said she disapproved of something. Maybe my wool slacks and burgundy cashmere cardigan were too fussy for her taste.

"Melvin, I assumed from our aborted conversation that you were requesting counsel during your questioning."

L.J.'s eyes narrowed. Her right hand lightly touched the butt of her holstered pistol. That's what she'd been missing when we were in high school: that heavy belt slung with nasty-looking items—shiny handcuffs, a stick in a leather case, a radio of some sort, and that businesslike gun. She lovingly fingered her belt and motioned us toward an open door to her left.

Not unlike a movie-set designer's concept of an interrogation room, this one had a small battered metal-topped table and four mismatched chairs. I chose a wooden one with scarred rungs to prop my feet on.

The room, stuffy, crowded, and not quite clean, didn't boast a two-way mirror. But a shoe-box cassette recorder, the cord running from the table to a wall outlet, sat on the distant edge of the table.

L.J. straddled a chair on the opposite side of the table from Melvin and me and commandeered the tape recorder.

While she fumbled with the cassette, I caught Melvin's attention and raised my eyebrows in an unspoken question. He shrugged slightly. If that meant he didn't know what had prompted this, then maybe nothing damaging had happened in the car.

Sitting in that cramped room as L.J. set things up, it struck me how easily Melvin managed silence. Even knowing its value as a technique for eliciting information, I found myself struggling to leave the silence alone. But Melvin just sat.

He wore a pinstriped oxford shirt and khaki pants, with his gray-flecked sandy hair cut short. His metal-framed glasses were not round enough to look owlish, but lent his face a knowing air. Casually dressy for a holiday at home. He looked like somebody used to business attire and not quite willing to revert to the faded jeans and nappy sweatshirts of a comfortable homecoming.

"Today is Thursday, November twenty-third," L.J. spoke into the small microphone. "Present are L.J. Peters, sheriff of Camden County, Melvin Bertram, and Avery Andrews, present as his attorney. The time is now two-fifteen P.M.

"Mr. Bertram, as you are aware, a car matching the description of your wife's car was discovered submerged in Luna Lake earlier this week."

Melvin nodded.

"Please answer into the microphone."

I didn't point out that she hadn't actually asked a question.

"Yes."

"Were you aware that the tag number was the one registered to your wife?"

"Yes. A deputy informed me of that . . ." He paused. "Yesterday?"

L.J. stared at him a bit longer than comfort would allow. Her skin looked pocked and waxy under the overhead lights. And her eyes were squintier than I remembered—narrow, black slits.

"Dr. Edwin supplied us with your wife's dental records. We were fortunate that he's in town and still practicing." Dr. Edwin, wildly white-haired and wizened, had been leaning between the dental chair and spit sink so long he had trouble standing up straight.

"The forensic odontologist in Charleston has agreed to review the case for us tomorrow."

Boy, they'd worked quick if they'd already gotten the records to Charleston together with the body and had a specialist lined up.

"Mr. Bertram." She paused for dramatic effect. "Can you tell us whether the body in the 1978 Ford Thunderbird pulled from Luna Lake Tuesday of this week is that of your wife, Mrs. Lea Hopkins Bertram?"

Melvin kept his gaze steady, fixed on L.J. But he said nothing.

L.J. just stared, waiting.

If the truth be told, Perry Mason reruns were as close as I'd ever gotten to a real police interrogation. So I treated this like a civil deposition with a lot of money on the table. I sat and waited.

Melvin didn't rush to confess anything. Or deny anything, either.

Melvin studied the scarred tabletop. Perhaps coming to grips with something he'd known for fifteen years?

"Sheriff." He finally broke the silence. "I don't know any more about that than you do."

L.J. didn't respond immediately. She just stared. Finally, brushing the tabletop with her palm, she said, "That's your tale. I'm sittin' on mine."

I sat, letting the tape hiss through the recorder. L.J. was trying to provoke a reaction—a tactic I'd used myself in depositions when I wasn't scoring any points.

Melvin met her stare, his lips pressed together in an obvious effort to keep control. If this was L.J.'s normal demeanor with bereaved widowers, she'd have trouble come reelection time. Nope, this was her "you're a suspect" demeanor. But what did she have to lose? Melvin wasn't registered to vote in this county.

Finally, L.J. reached for the microphone. "Thank you, Mr. Bertram." She pronounced the interview concluded and read the time from a wristwatch the size of a pie plate.

Then she escorted us into the hallway. "We'll be in touch, Mr. Bertram." That ended it. No reminiscences with me about our high school days or questions about our families. She swung off down the hall, her right hand lightly checking the butt of her automatic.

Melvin turned to me, his face weary, the skin slack. He suddenly seemed older than he had yesterday.

"Could I trouble you for a ride home?" One corner of his mouth grinned wryly. "I'd rather not ask the sheriff, if you don't mind."

"I'm parked back this way."

Outside, he stopped at the top of the short set of concrete steps. "Why, even when you know the only possible answer, does that answer still have the power to—hurt so?"

"I'm sorry." I touched his shoulder, not sure what he wanted. But clearly he needed some acknowledgment of the import of what he'd just learned. "I know this must be difficult."

He grabbed the metal handrail and began a shambling descent. "But why? Why should it be difficult? Haven't I known—probably for all of the fifteen years—that she had to be dead? Well, not all. Not at first. At first, I hoped—"

He stopped again at the bottom of the steps. "I thought at first she'd just left for a while, that she'd be back. But sometime—I can't really remember when—I began to know that she had to be dead. It never came as a revelation. Just grew as a certainty. No word. No financial record. No—nothing."

He sighed. The sunlight showed more of the gray in his sandy hair. "Pretty soon, I forgot what she looked like. I studied her pictures—I memorized her pictures. I knew I would always recognize the pictures. But I wondered, would I recognize her? The not knowing was maddening. What had I done? Or not done? Had she run off with someone? Had she gotten sick or been hurt? What—"

His rush of words stopped as suddenly as it had started. He shook his head, as if clearing cobwebs and bad memories.

"Thank you for coming down, Avery. I'm sorry to

have interrupted your holiday. I wasn't sure what—
well, what the sheriff had in mind."

"You did the right thing. Be careful with L.J. She's
smarter than you might think. And persistent. I don't
know what today was all about. But she'll be back."

He nodded. "They always are."

He climbed into the Mustang after I unlocked the
door for him, but he didn't comment on my car. I
chalked it up to shock.

Outside his brother's house, cars blocked the
driveway and part of the street. "I would invite you
in," he said, "but I'm sure your own family is missing you."

He closed the car door, leaned over, and waved.
I'd quelled my impulse to pat his shoulder before
he got out; his reserved manner spoke of someone
who preferred a lawyer-client relationship maintained without hugging or mush. What an odd
Thanksgiving.

The narrow road that circled through the Lake's
Edge neighborhood climbs and turns at steep
pitches. The houses sit back off the road, and trees
and shrubbery crowd the drive. Fortunately, I was
creeping around the curve from the Bertram enclave
when I came upon a walker commanding more than
her share of the road. She sashayed along in one of
those multicolored bodysuits, arms akimbo, her
backside to the hood of my car.

As I pulled around her, on the wrong side of the
narrow rutted lane, she stopped, hands on her hips. I
immediately recognized Cissie Prentice, a friend
from high school.

"If it isn't Avery gahdam Andrews!" I could hear every overexclaimed word through the closed car window.

She unlatched the door and swung her long, synthetically covered legs into the passenger seat. "What're you doing in town and not callin' me?"

Cissie wrapped me in an awkward hug and slammed the car door. "You're a lifesaver. Take me over to the Legion field so I can take my walk. You can come, too."

"You want a ride so you can go take a walk?" The Legion field lay about a block and a half's distance from where we sat. But that was Cissie.

"I heard you were back in town. You shoulda called. Why ever you'd want to come back here's beyond me. You gonna stay awhile? If you are, I got some plans for us."

Knowing Cissie and what the tone of her voice implied, the plans were scandalous, but fluid enough that she could write me in—or out—quickly.

I didn't bother to elaborate on my situation. At the stop sign, I hung a right onto the road toward town, then a quick left to the baseball fields.

"Whatcha doin' over in my neck of the woods?" She rearranged the band holding her curly blonde mane in a ponytail.

"Meeting with one of your neighbor's family members. Melvin Bertram. Know him?"

She turned to look at me. Not the self-absorbed, half-cocked attention she usually pays other females. She really looked at me.

"Do tell," she whispered, wide-eyed.

"What?"

She smacked my arm with a backhand. "Girl, don't *what* me. Melvin Bertram? That man killed his wife and everybody in town knows it. And he's a sight too old for you. What's he like? I hear he's got money."

"I'm not dating him, Cissie. It's business."

"Mm-hmm," she murmured. "I know you, Avery Andrews. He's nice-looking, I've heard. In a graying kind of way. 'Course, he killed a slut. What are the odds he'd do that again? Slim to none, I'd say. You hear they found her body? Come on." She waved her hand as she climbed out.

"Naw. I got to get back to the house. I—"

"Come on, Avery. A walk'll do you good. Give us a chance to get caught up."

She slammed her door and crossed in front of the car to my door, pulling down the legs of her high-cut leotard and scanning the parking lot as she walked.

"Come on." She opened my door. "Serves you right for not calling me earlier. And, law, we gotta get rid of some of that turkey dinner."

Where she had hers stored, I couldn't tell. I was thankful I'd discreetly disguised mine under a cardigan sweater and not paraded it about in hot pink and black spandex.

Cissie performed some impressive stretching moves that looked like she was coming on to the hood of my car.

"Cissie, I'm not really dressed for an athletic endeavor—"

Cissie's snort cut me off. "Relax. The walking's

nothing. The really athletic stuff won't start until later, if all goes as planned."

I followed her gaze across the creek to where the walking trail wound into the woods. Rounding the bend out of the woods, a tall man strode, effortlessly swinging a set of hand weights. His hair, thin where he'd begun to bald at the crown, stuck up in damp spikes. He looked like a middle-aged exercise ad.

Cissie rested a warning hand on my arm, waited until he'd begun his next loop around the path, then she started across the footbridge. "We'll pass him a couple of loops. Then you can head on home."

Cissie always approaches females more directly than she does males. I couldn't say female friends— I'm probably the closest she has, and we really aren't friends.

"So, tell me about this Melvin Bertram. He's cute? Not as cute as Michael Driggers." She grinned her barracuda grin.

"So that's his name. What's he do?"

"One of the new engineers up at the nuclear plant."

"Single?"

She gave me a withering look. "I don't hunt down married men."

"Just stumble across them now and then."

"A'vry, honey, if you'd loosen up a little, you wouldn't be gettin' those worry wrinkles between your eyebrows. Did he do it?"

"Huh?"

She snorted, exasperated. "Kill his wife."

"I don't know. We really haven't worked that into the conversation."

"Well, ask him, silly. You're a lawyer. Wouldn't you know if he was lyin'?"

I didn't bother explaining to her that I wouldn't know, which was unfortunate, since all my clients probably lie to me about something.

We walked at an easy pace. I figured Cissie wouldn't want to break a sweat—or be too tired to run her prey to ground should she be forced to drastic measures.

"You goin' out with him? Or is it strictly business? Silly question. Everything's business with you, isn't it?" She poked me with her manicured finger.

"Strictly business, Cissie."

"You gettin' any, then?"

I changed the subject. "You think it's possible she committed suicide?"

Cissie strolled along, uncharacteristically quiet for about three steps. "Possible, I guess. Spread her legs for anything, all the way through high school, what I heard. My older brother knew her. Gawd, I hope not in the biblical sense. Sure surprised everybody when she hauled Melvin Bertram down the aisle. Everybody started countin' months, Kevin said, 'spectin' a bun in the oven. But no—"

Cissie began swinging her arms athletically, but didn't really pick up the pace any. She'd spotted her quarry through the trees where the path curved around the most distant ball field.

As we passed him, she flashed him whatever

indecipherable siren signal women like Cissie know. I couldn't tell if he'd caught it, but I suspected he had. Cissie didn't launch many spars that missed.

After he was safely past, she quit flinging her arms about. "Suicide? I don't know. Would a girl like that kill herself? What do you think, she just drove herself into the lake?" Cissie shuddered. "What a dreadful thought. Seems like there'd be an easier way, duhn't there? I mean, if you were considerin' it at all."

I thought about the rusted hulk of a car, the red-stained water inside, that fright-house skull floating into focus, then disappearing.

"Yeah," I murmured, then just walked for a moment in silence. Finally, to change the subject, I asked, "So, what have you been up to lately?"

Cissie sighed. "You've been gone awhile. You shoulda come home to visit more. My divorce was final a few weeks ago. You handle any divorces? The first one hit me a lot harder. By this second one, I knew what was comin'. And it wasn't so scary. 'Course," she snorted, "this time, there was money comin'. Cleveland had the time of his life while we were married, I can tell you. He had this trick of slidin' his hand down my belly while he was inside me and touchin'—"

"Cissie." I held my hands out to call a halt.

"A'vry, honey, you need to loosen up. You're missin' out on a lot. Cleveland was a pig, but if I can teach that trick to somebody else—you just wouldn't believe."

I shook my head. I was glad somebody else was having some fun; it kept the universe in some kind of balance.

"Okay, Avery, we'll have to visit some other time."

She stooped to adjust her glow-in-the-dark gel shoes, strategically displaying a lean haunch to her prey. I wished I could stick around, take some notes. Cissie always said her all-girls' college experience made all the difference—that's where you learn to hunt men, she said. I'd made the mistake of going to a school where the men were plentiful, and I had thereby failed to develop either skill, craft, or instinct.

I strolled the short distance to the footbridge and my car before I hazarded a casual glance back at Cissie and her engineer. He stooped on one knee, apparently adjusting her shoe for her. And she stared down, her ponytail looped across her shoulder, posed like a predator exulting over its fallen prey. Sheer poetry in motion. I hoped he was ready to learn some new tricks.

The rest of the afternoon at Mom's house passed quietly. Well, as quietly as it can when Clemson wins a bowl game. Following a nap on the sunroom sofa, I ate leftovers, despite the fact that I'd pledged after lunch never to eat again.

That evening, I slung my satchel into the backseat of the Mustang and headed toward North Main and the mountain road.

Main Street took me past my great-aunts' house

and, two blocks down, past the Garnets' house. Where the four-lane divided street narrowed to two lanes, I passed the sign marking the turn to Garnet Mills.

The sun had long before dropped from sight and the mountains loomed ahead, dark and solid, topped with the feathery shading of leafless winter trees against the darkening sky. Surprisingly little traffic moved through town, and the two convenience stores on the north edge of town were dark and empty, closed for the holiday.

Deep in my chest, I felt the percussive thud, like a bass drum. Then I heard the sound. In almost the same instant, my rearview mirror caught the flash of the explosion—a white-hot orange flash, followed by more sound. Or the sensation of sound. I couldn't be sure which.

I took the next left turn, on reflex, not sure what I could do, but certain something had happened. Through the treetops and past a hodgepodge of small houses, I glimpsed flames. I cut back one block and over another street. Garnet Mills. I drove past the first parking lot and loading docks. The flames seemed fiercest at the front of the plant.

The plant sat slightly downhill from the road, so the roof lay visible—or what remained of the roof. A gaping hole full of flames was centered about where I remembered the reception area. Nothing moved, except the smoke and flames.

I seemed to be the only person around. Alone with an inferno. I reached automatically for the place where my car phone had hung in my BMW.

But I cracked my knuckle against the gearshift of the Mustang and remembered I didn't have a car phone anymore. I wrestled with the gearshift and reversed the car in the road, backing onto the shoulder of the narrow lane to go for help.

Then I heard the sirens.

At first, the fire seemed to be everywhere. But, as the shock wore off, I saw that it had confined itself to the one-story office section of the building, attached to the sprawling manufacturing plant. Flames shot out the roof as I pulled in front, and the fire burned bright and hot.

I yelled, but saw no movement inside. The heat kept me at a distance. No cars stood in the small front lot or along the street where the Mustang's headlights shone. Probably no one working on Thanksgiving night.

I backed away, across the ragged pavement, as the fire trucks rocked down the narrow residential street toward me.

The firemen jumped into action. A couple of them I recognized, even under their hats and heavy gear. One yelled something at me. I waved back, gesturing toward the building and shrugging my shoulders dramatically.

He came closer, grabbing my elbow and yelling into my ear. "—see anybody inside?"

I shook my head.

"How'd it start?"

I yelled over the surprisingly loud sounds of the fire. "I just heard a sound. An explosion, I guess. From Main Street."

He turned, shouting instructions as men reeled hoses off the truck.

I walked back to my car, reached inside to click off the headlights, then leaned against the front fender, waiting for my legs to quit shaking.

The firefighters played water on the outside and roof of the manufacturing building. Most of their efforts seemed focused on keeping the fire contained rather than putting it out.

I couldn't do anything to help. After a few minutes, I headed up the mountain rather than watch, feeling helpless. The smell and the sounds and the raw fear and awe stayed with me into the next morning.

Six

I slept late and awoke to the acrid smell of smoke and a raw, burned scratch in my throat. The fire scene from the night before—and my disturbed dreams—hit me with the force of a stream from a fire hose.

I'd dumped my clothes on the porch of the cabin and stood under the shower until the hot water heater emptied. After that, I'd warmed a cup of milk, thinking somehow it would neutralize the taste in my mouth as well as dispel the chill that permeated me.

But the next morning, the smell and the taste singed my every breath. The cabin felt chilly, but I certainly didn't want to build a fire. I bundled on a turtleneck, a heavy sweatshirt, ski tights, and jeans. And I kept moving.

Looking first in the refrigerator, then idly through the cabinets, I couldn't decide on anything to eat. Finally, I grabbed some Fig Newtons and a Coke and headed toward the lake's edge.

My grandfather's cabin sits backward, with the back door facing the gravel and grass drive where I had parked the Mustang, and the front facing the lake. Considering that the cabin had been built for enjoying the view rather than receiving callers, its backwardness made sense. Inside, with one large living area and two small bedrooms tucked to one side, it didn't matter which door one entered. A deep porch ran the length of the cabin's front, the tin-roofed overhang sheltering its rough-hewn lap siding from heavy rain and hot summer sun. A path, scarcely more than a footfall's width, ran jaggedly to the lake, to where an old johnboat lay upside down.

I propped myself against the boat's bottom, hoping I wouldn't disturb any snakes that had taken winter refuge underneath. The blue-black water mirrored the trees around the lake, a soft contrast to the images from the night before. I could still smell the smoke.

I'd set aside today to work on the cabin. The day after Thanksgiving would be quiet around the court-house and, I hoped, the jail and the magistrate's of-fice. If Harrison Garnet wanted to get in touch with me, he had my parents' phone number. Why hadn't he called? He didn't seem interested in my advice, so why had he hired me in the first place? I'd begun to doubt that my trial qualifications or availability had attracted him. Maybe he'd wanted somebody who didn't know as much about him as the local boys did. That was not a reassuring thought.

Keeping busy around the cabin would be no

problem. Narrowing down exactly what I could do—or had the time or inclination to do—was a problem.

Did I reseal the wax ring under the toilet and risk dropping the bolts under the house because I couldn't lift the toilet alone? Rescreen the windows? Or wait until closer to summer? Replace the rotten boards on the front steps and porch? That job would take more time than I had, since I'd have to drive to town to buy pressure-treated lumber and borrow a circular saw.

I settled on replacing the broken windowpanes— five in all—that had been boarded over. Along the porch railing, I arranged the glass, putty, and glazier's points I'd bought earlier in the week, then tackled the window beside the door first. The plywood piece nailed over the hole came off with loud protest, and removing the dried putty required meticulous, mindless chipping.

I could never make a living at this, given how slowly I work. But, when I surveyed my handiwork, I realized I enjoyed a job where I could actually see what I had accomplished. As I worked, I realized that I envy people who could sit back at the end of the day and say yep, I did that.

I couldn't dig out all the stubborn old caulk, but, when I tested the pane, it fit well enough. I'd just started to bead in a line of new caulk when car tires crunched in the gravel drive and stopped out of sight around the other side of the cabin. Carrying the caulking gun, I swung off the porch, an easier path than walking through the cabin.

Sheriff L. J. Peters pulled herself from the front seat of her cruiser, one hand on the top of the door and one on the doorjamb. Extricating all six-plus-feet of her bulk, even from something as roomy as a Crown Vic, required effort. She brushed her fingers through her cropped black hair and set her brimmed hat on her head before she spoke.

"Why the hell you got yourself stuck all the way up here in the middle of nowhere?"

"To personally inconvenience you."

We stood like two gunslingers, L.J. with her .357 strapped to her ample hip, me with my caulking gun dangling recklessly at my side.

"Well, for gawd's sake, why don't you have a phone? Thought I'd come by and see what had happened to you."

"Thanks. A new service of the sheriff's department?"

"Only where the potential victim is a smart-ass lawyer with a client down to the jail."

"Who's that?"

"Thought the promise of a fee would perk your interest. You don't pick your friends too well, though."

She paused for dramatic effect. I waited her out.

"Melvin Bertram," she said.

I tried to keep my face straight, not to give anything away. Why was that such a natural reaction? Because she was a cop? Or because she was L.J.? "For what?"

"Questioning. He won't talk without you. Says

you're his lawyer. Now tell me why he keeps needing a lawyer and him back in town only a couple of days?"

"You tell me." I slid the caulking gun under the railing onto the porch. "And what grounds have you got for questioning him?"

"He agreed to come down and talk about the fire last night. You were there, weren't you."

She wasn't asking a question. So I didn't answer. Glancing down at my clothes, I picked at a smudge of dried caulk on my jeans.

"Give me a sec to change. I'll be right behind you."

On the way in the door, I popped the board back over the window pane. I'd have to finish that later.

I sponged off and pulled on my navy blazer and slacks. No court appearances, so no risk of a judge frowning on my failure to appear in skirt and panty hose. I ran a comb through my hair, pulled it back into a ponytail, then hopped in the car. I tried to apply powder and mascara as I sailed down the winding mountain road to town.

In the now-familiar interrogation room, Melvin Bertram, clad in a yellow cotton sweater and navy corduroys, sat on the edge of a wooden chair, his forearms crossed casually on the table. The presence of worry wrinkles between his eyebrows heartened me. In my limited criminal-court experience, only the guilty are graceless enough not to look worried.

"Avery." He stood to shake hands. I suspected even he wouldn't have been able to explain whether a businessman's reflex or a troubled person's need for human touch had prompted the handshake.

L.J. pushed into the small room with us.

"L.J., you mind if we have a few minutes here?" I asked.

She fixed me with a withering look, but worked her toothpick to the corner of her mouth and left without saying a word.

"Any idea what this is all about?" I glanced around the small room as I took a chair opposite him. It crossed my mind how easy it would be to bug this room. I glanced at the tape recorder to make sure my voice hadn't activated it.

Melvin followed my glance, then shrugged. "They asked about the fire last night. At the mill. The sheriff's tone got a bit belligerent. Brought back some bad memories." The shadow of a grin drew at the corner of his mouth. "So I told her I didn't have anything to say without my lawyer. I hope you don't mind."

I shrugged in turn. "That's what lawyers are for. Why do they think you know something about the fire?"

Even before I finished, he started shaking his head. "I have no idea. My connection with Garnet Mills ended years ago. Maybe I'm just convenient. The new resident suspect." His attempt at humor evaporated behind his sarcasm.

"Okay." I went to the door. "Answer the questions. Don't volunteer anything. And give me a chance to interrupt before you jump to answer."

He nodded, and I motioned down the hall to where a dark-suited deputy stood against the wall, looking like a fleshy potbellied stove.

The deputy summoned L.J. from wherever she lay in wait and, after she addressed the preliminaries to the tape recorder, she began her questions.

"Mr. Bertram, we appreciate you taking time to come talk to us. I know this is an inconvenience, particularly on a holiday weekend."

I refrained from rolling my eyes. L.J. must have just gotten back from a seminar on playing the good-guy cop. Trying to put a suspect at ease came across as an unnatural act for her.

Melvin merely nodded. He still sat on the edge of his chair, his arms crossed in front of him like a barrier—or a restraint.

"Mr. Bertram, could I ask your whereabouts last evening?"

Melvin paused a brief space, with a slight upturn at the corner of his mouth. "You mean after you and I got together yesterday afternoon? I spent the evening—Thanksgiving—at my brother's house. With his family."

L.J. blinked, reminding me somehow of a lizard. Or a Komodo dragon. "Could you describe for me your relationship with Harrison Garnet and Garnet Mills?"

"Now? None. I haven't seen or spoken to Harrison in—oh, probably fifteen years."

"Since your wife—disappeared."

Melvin nodded.

"Please answer aloud. For the tape recording." L.J. gestured toward the little shoe-box recorder, a motion designed to remind Melvin this was no casual chat.

"Since around that time, yes," Melvin said.

"Your wife worked for Garnet Mills."

"Yes."

"But you haven't been in touch with the Garnets since her disappearance?"

"There's been no need."

L.J. settled against her chair back, the plastic seat protesting. "Your father and Garnet were partners, weren't they?"

Melvin paused. "Yes. A number of years ago."

"And you did some work for Harrison Garnet, accounting work. Back when you lived here?"

A deep breath and a careful answer. "Yes. Dacus had no other accountants or financial advisers at that time." He implied that the oddity would've been if Garnet hadn't hired him as his accountant.

"What do you know about the fire last night?"

The crease between Melvin's eyebrows deepened slightly. "Nothing, except that there was one. Some kind of explosion, I understand."

L.J. leaned forward, keenly interested in his reply. Or feigning interest. "Now, where did you hear that?"

Melvin shrugged. "Somebody talking around the house. Or uptown when I stopped to get gas. Or at the post office."

L.J. chewed her bottom lip, studying him, waiting to see what he would add. Melvin didn't oblige her.

"Mr. Bertram." She settled back again, her tone

more conversational. "I hoped you might help me understand something. You ever been involved in or know about a case—as an accountant—where somebody tried to destroy records? You know, by setting a fire they hoped looked accidental, but arranging things so important documents would be destroyed?"

Melvin paused longer than he had for the earlier questions, more wary. "No, I haven't. That area of fraud investigation has not been a part of my practice." Another pause. "If you need an expert of that kind, I have a friend who works fraud investigation for the U.S. Attorney's office. White-collar-crime stuff. A forensic CPA."

L.J. nodded. "Well, thank you. That might come in handy."

Whatever she'd expected, it hadn't been for him to volunteer the name of an expert. But surely she hadn't expected him to scream *I did it, I did it, I blew up that building. You caught me red-handed.*

L.J. studied him a few more seconds, then turned to me. "You were there last night, weren't you?"

She dropped her saccharine tone and didn't waste any of her good-cop questioning methods on me. I didn't point out that, since I sat there as Melvin's counsel, her question was out of line.

"Yes. I heard the blast from Main Street, then saw the glow in the sky."

"Pretty loud boom, I hear. Convenient you were there."

I frowned, meeting her steady gaze. "I don't know. Somebody else called the fire department.

There certainly wasn't anything I could do to help."
I remembered the orange flames. And the heat. And
my sense of helplessness as I reached for a car
phone I didn't have. That wasn't anything I'd share
with L.J. Or Melvin.

"Did you see anything? Or anybody?"

I shook my head. "No. Not anything that made an
impression. But frankly, the damage to the building
looked so—incredible. I'm afraid I couldn't take
my eyes off that. Then I left. I didn't want to be in
the way."

L.J. stared. She wanted to say something smart-
ass. But she knew the tape recorded her comments
as well as ours, so she too had reason to choose her
words carefully.

She picked at a scar on the table, then asked, "Either one of you know Nebo Earling?"

I'm sure my face betrayed my surprise at hearing
that name again so recently on the heels of my
graveyard chat with Aunt Letha.

Melvin shook his head. "No. I don't believe I do."

But L.J. ignored him, staring at me. I shook my
head. "Just by name."

I didn't explain that Aunt Letha had taught him in
school. And I doubted that Nebo's graveyard flower-
snatching prompted L.J.'s interest in him.

"You know he works for Harrison Garnet?"

I shook my head. "I don't believe I did."

She glanced at Melvin. We sat in uncompanionable silence for a few exaggerated seconds. Melvin
maintained the dispassion of a business executive at
a rubber-chicken dinner.

"Thank you again, Mr. Bertram, for taking time to answer a few questions. We have to ask questions, you know. Eventually we get answers. From somewhere. I'll have one of the deputies take you back to your brother's."

"No need," I said, pushing back from the table. "I'll be glad to drop you by, Melvin." The stiffness in my muscles highlighted for me how tense the meeting had been. Or how little I'd exercised over the last couple of weeks.

I needed to spend more time at the walking trail. Without Cissie Prentice and her designer outfits.

"Nice car," Melvin said as we pulled out of the Law Enforcement Center parking lot.

I'd known all along he would come to his senses. "Thanks. It belonged to my grandfather."

Melvin rubbed his palms along the thighs of his corduroys. "I hope this'll be the last ride I have to catch back from the police station."

We both smiled, trying to turn it into a joke.

He studied the five-and-ten store as we stopped at a red light. "You know, I'd actually toyed with the idea of moving back here, setting up an office in Dacus, moving back closer to my family."

I stared at him.

"I know," he said, amused. "Two trips to the sheriff's office in two days isn't quite as inviting as a Welcome Wagon visit."

"No, I guess not." Not knowing what to say, I changed the subject. "What do you do, Melvin?"

He nodded. "Mostly I work as a financial adviser.

On limited partnership ventures, that sort of thing. Which I thought could be done from Dacus as easily as from Atlanta. But now I'm back to rethinking my career options."

I didn't say anything about my own career confusion. The red light changed. How would life in Dacus be for Melvin Bertram?

"Avery, I did have another favor to ask. Before you got there, two of the deputies were talking. One of them—a fellow named Mellin—attended the autopsy. Of the body from the lake." His voice had lost its wry edge. "Apparently he hadn't even had time to fill the sheriff in on the details."

Body wasn't a word that floated first to my brain when I thought of the passenger in that car, with those teeth bumping against the back window.

"—if you could talk to him." Melvin's words floated back into focus. "You know." He paused uncomfortably. "Find out—"

I nodded. "I'll check and see. Who'd you say accompanied the—remains to Charleston?"

"Rudy Mellin? I think that's his name."

Melvin climbed out at the bottom of his brother's driveway. This had become an awkward ritual.

"I'll call if I find out anything," I said.

He nodded and waved.

I turned toward my parents' house. Carlton Barner had closed his office for the day, so I couldn't go there to use the phone. But no point in driving back up the mountain if Rudy Mellin had already returned from the autopsy.

To preserve the chain of custody—or whatever

they called handling a body—and to reduce the number of times the state's few medical examiners must testify in court, cops usually accompany bodies and observe the autopsies. That, I'm sure, adds immeasurably to the attraction of law enforcement as a career.

But such activities didn't explain why cops like Rudy Mellin developed doughnut butts. Seemed to me a steady diet of autopsies would act as an appetite suppressant. But I'd heard stories about them holding a cadaver's liver in one hand and munching on a bean burrito in the other. At least that's the kind of stuff they tell each other.

Neither of my parents was home. I called the sheriff's main number and, after a couple of transfers and lots of holding time, a slurry voice drawled into the phone.

As soon as I heard his voice, a picture of Rudy Mellin materialized unbidden in my brain. I'd run into him in Maylene's a few times over the years. He still wore the same size-34-waist pants he'd worn when we sat next to each other in high school chemistry. Unfortunately, now his actual waist size spanned an additional ten inches, while his size-34 pants sank lower and lower on his hips.

"Hear you drove to Charleston with a friend, Rudy."

"She-ut, A'vry. Truth tell, I never been around bones that stunk like those. Can't get the smell outta my nose for nuthin'."

"Who'd've thought it." I paused a polite interval. "What'd they find? Any word?"

"Shouldn't be by now, but there is. It's Lea Bertram, all right. Car was hers, so I carried her dental records with me. Perfect match."

"Any sign what killed her?"

Rudy snorted rudely. "Hard to check for lake water in her lungs, bein' as she didn't have any lungs."

"Right." *Har, har.*

Rudy smacked on something. Chewing gum? "No broken neck or trauma visible on the bones, though. Doc went over those with a magnifying glass. Said sometimes bullet or stab wounds actually nick a bone and are visible long later. But nuthin'."

"What was that stuff on the face?"

Rudy made a gagging sound. "That's what still stunk after all these years. Doc called it grave wax. Looked like Grandma's tallow soap to me. Which Doc said it kinda was. Bodies that rot in damp places, sometimes their proteins change into fat. 'Hydrolyzed something.' Sounded like the ingredient list for potato chips."

Cop humor.

"Could they tell how long she'd been down there? Would that stuff have lasted very long?"

"Hard to say for sure. But Doc—she got so excited, she had to go to her office and pull a couple of humongous books off the shelf while she dictated her report—she said some cases have been reported ten or fifteen years later with that stuff. She called it adipocere." He pronounced it *addy-po-sear.*

"That long? But don't bodies decompose faster in water?" I'd been an avid *Quincy* fan, mostly because of a kid-size crush on Jack Klugman.

"Sure, but the little fishies couldn't get to her to nibble her up. And she certainly didn't float to the top as the gases bloated her. Nope, she stayed down there a decade and a half, sealed up in her own little soap-making factory."

Ick, I thought. But I wouldn't give him the pleasure of my squeamishness. "So everything points to her dying about the time she disappeared."

"Yep."

L.J. and company had sense enough to send Lea Bertram's dental records to the autopsy, so I knew they'd have been digging around in the old files.

"So what do you think happened, from what you know so far? Did she just drive off into the lake and drown?"

Rudy snorted. "And pigs fly. S'pose anythin's possible. But how do you accidentally drive down a boat ramp and end up eighty feet from shore?"

"Could she have committed suicide?"

"Hard to read her mind, A'vry. Despite the time me and her spent together on the way to Charleston."

"Did your records indicate what she was supposed to be doing the day she died?"

"Yep. According"—he paused to make a couple of smacking sounds—"to a coupla witnesses, she'd planned to drive up the mountain. Do some painting. You know, pitchers."

"Um-hmm." *And I'd thought for a minute she'd taken up house-painting, you goober.* "So, did you find painting stuff in her car?"

Smack, smack. "A plastic box, with some metal tubes inside. Prob'ly anything else would've rotted."

"How about some little metal cylinders, like the bands around paintbrushes? Or—"

"Yeah, A'vry. We dug around in amongst the rusty seat springs and rust-covered floorboards looking for rusty cylinders that would probably turn to powder soon as we touched 'em. Like everything else in that spook-show wreck."

"Oh."

"The hood, whole parts of that car just crumbled away. Dangdest thing, that it'd hold together all this time, then just crumble."

Had it crumbled away faster, they would've had nothing to pull Lea Bertram to the surface in. Her wax-covered bones would've scattered and sunk in the muck of Luna Lake. And nobody would be hauling Melvin Bertram to the sheriff's office for questioning.

"Why is L.J. asking about Nebo Earling? He have something to do with the fire?"

"Well," Rudy drawled, "there's been some speculation about that. But not by anybody that knows Nebo. Nebo's one dumb shit. Hadn't got sense enough to strike a match without singeing his eyebrows off. Naw, they reckon he might've seen something."

"At Garnet Mills?"

"He 'uz sort of a watchman. Not that I'd set him to guard my doghouse without expectin' to find the dog's collar gone and him hungry."

"So, is the ME running tests on the bones from the car? Or—"

"Tests on what? On commercial uses for that cheesy stuff growing on her face? Come on, A'vry."

"Well, how about a bone expert of some kind? Or—"

"A'vry, this is Camden County. The autopsy on that weirdy sack of bones already cut into our budget bad enough. This itn't some fancy-britches law firm. This is a little county with a little law enforcement budget. Hell, they got us on a paper clip ration here. We gotta pay for experts. And for what? We already know who she is. Maybe Sam's bloodhounds could come chew on those bones and render us an opinion."

"Okay, okay. But what about Mr. Bertram? He's still got a cloud hanging over his head. And—"

"What makes you think he wouldn't still have a cloud, even if some kinda gahdam expert dicked around with those bones? Huh? My thought, he'd be likely to have a murder warrant hanging over his head, 'stead of that halo you'd have us hang there."

"Rudy—"

"You ner nobody's gonna convince me that little girl decided to kill herself by drownin' herself in a car. And if it's an accident, it's one of the damdest I've ever seen."

"Rudy, cars drive off into creeks and ponds and rivers all the time. Who knows how many people just disappear and nobody knows—"

"Scant few, if I had my guess. The way I see it, you've gotten yerself snookered by a wife-killer.

He's probably just lookin' at ways to get better at gettin' away with it."

"Thanks for your advice, Rudy. I can't tell you how much I appreciate it."

"Any time."

"Will the ME issue a report?" I didn't know how these things were handled. "Can I get a copy?"

"When I get one. Sometimes takes 'em a while. Depends on how many people die in peculiar ways over the holiday weekend. I'll send you a copy. Or you stop by and pick it up, how 'bout?"

Rudy managed to invest that last sentence with a clear-intentioned leer.

"Sure, Rudy. Thanks."

I called Melvin's brother's house. The kid who answered the phone went screeching through the house in search of Uncle Melvin, then Melvin's measured voice came on the line.

"Melvin. I just wanted to let you know." I paused. The words came harder than I'd anticipated. "It's—it is Lea. I'm sorry. The dental records confirmed it." As if a medical opinion somehow sanitized the news.

He didn't speak for an uncomfortable number of seconds. "Thank you, Avery." Another pause followed, but when he spoke, his voice didn't waver or show any emotion. "When will they release the—body? For burial. Did they say?"

"I forgot to ask. I'm sorry. I'll call and let you know." My words tumbled over themselves. How stupid to forget the need for funeral arrangements. Of course a grieving husband would be concerned about that, even fifteen years later. Would a murdering husband think of that so quickly? Perhaps, especially to get it over with, maybe escape the guilt if it could be buried deeper than the car had been.

I'd spent too much time the last couple of days with suspicious cops.

"Thank you, Avery. For everything." He should have been a radio announcer, with a phone voice like that.

When I called the sheriff's number again, Rudy had already left the office. The fellow who answered the phone couldn't tell me anything about the release of the remains. So I left a message for Rudy to call me.

When the phone rang, I didn't screen it with the answering machine, thinking maybe Melvin or Rudy was calling back. Jake Baker's mush-mouthed Charleston slur took me by surprise.

"A-ver-ee, darlin'. Ah'm so glad I caught you in. This is Jake Baker down in Charleston. How you doin'?"

"Just fine, Jake. How 'bout you?"

"Be a lot better if you'd return my calls and tell me you're fixin' to come down here and work with me."

"Jake, I told you when you first called, you can't turn an insurance defense lawyer into an ambulance chaser. That defies the laws of nature."

Jake chuckled right on cue. "And I tole you, Averee, the only reason I call most insurance lawyers is to get 'em to write one of my clients a check. But you, you're worth savin'. You're one helluva trial lawyer. You just went astray temporarily, fell in with a bad crowd, those defense lawyers. But I'm the one can turn you from the dark side."

I had to chuckle in return. That summed up the opposing camps of civil trial lawyers as well as anything—each saw the other as lured away from the paths of righteousness by unfathomable evil.

"Jake, I can't change my spots. You know that."

"Avery, pardon me for bein' blunt, darlin', but what the hell you plannin' on doin' with yourself? After Winn Davis at the Calhoun Firm gets through trashin' you, no stuffy, staid defense firm in the state'll let you in the delivery entrance. And a cracker-jack litigator like you would shrivel and die stuck in some padded boardroom doing corporate transactional work."

Those last words he drawled out with an audible sneer. "You read the want ads? What the hell's transactional work? It'd bore me so bad my dick'd shrivel up and fall off. And it'd bore you too, Avery. Admit it."

"I'm exploring other options, Jake. I appreciate—"

"She-ut, Avery. With your now-tarnished reputation, fighting for the rights of the little people is probably the only option you have left. Nobody who pays big salaries for legal counsel likes to take risks. Hell, if they liked takin' risks, they wouldn't be workin' by the hour for some corporation or defense firm. They'd get real jobs."

"Fighting for the little people? Don't you mean

fighting for big settlements that you grudgingly share with the little people?"

"I can see my work's cut out for me. But that's okay. It'll take time to deprogram you. But hell, this may be the only employment option left for a lawyer with a questionable past. Joe Six-Pack who got crushed in the machinery at work won't care that you've been blackballed at the country club."

"Now, Jake, not all plaintiffs' lawyers have dark pasts. Even I know that, watching 'em from the other side of the courtroom."

"Yeah, but how many of those plaintiffs' lawyers live in an honest-to-God historical mansion in downtown Charleston and drive a Lamborghini to the beach on weekends?"

"Not many, Jake. But you didn't say anything about being able to sleep in that mansion of yours. You have any problems doing that?"

He laughed. "Not a bit. I found if you fuck good and hard a couple of times before bedtime, you sleep like a baby. And fortunately, my dick's not fallen off from boredom. What about those weenies you worked with down at the Calhoun Firm?"

"Jake, honey, you're a piece of work. I've got to go."

"Come do me anytime, sweetie. I'll be in touch. Standing offer."

"Thanks, Jake."

To keep from dwelling on Jake's assessment of my employment options, I considered stopping by the Builder's Supply for some pressure-treated lumber. I could borrow Dad's circular saw. But I hadn't measured how many board feet I'd need—or estimated how much the rotting porch would cost me to fix.

I delayed deciding what to do next by rummaging in Mom's refrigerator for something to augment my long-past Fig Newton breakfast. I grabbed a cold chicken leg off a plate of leftovers and poured a glass of ice tea. My mom brews it right—steeped, never boiled, with loads of sugar cooked into the hot water until it's sweet as syrup.

I was gnawing on the chicken leg and reading the cartoon page when Mom swung in the back door.

"You're here! Is that all you're having? There's some leftover lima beans and mashed potatoes. You could just heat those up."

"This is fine." I draw the line at eating cold limas or mashed potatoes. And I was too lazy to put a plate in the microwave.

Mom set the armload of files and papers she carried on the countertop. "Lucky you're here. Something came up this morning. You might be able to help."

"Sure."

"How do you do a criminal background check?"

My mother's blunt but dramatic questions ceased surprising me years ago. "What do you need to check for, exactly?"

"Oh, I don't know. Just stuff in general." She sighed and pushed a strand of faded red-gold hair off her forehead.

I just looked at her, waiting. She knew she'd have to do better than that.

"Okay." She shuffled through the load of papers she'd shed, organizing them into stacks as she spoke. "You know the new Economic Development and Planning Board for Dacus? Your father serves on the board now."

That was news.

"And they've hired a new director. Sy Bonifay. He came from downstate somewhere, I think. Maybe New Orleans or Tennessee before that. Anyway . . . ." She paused in her paper shuffling, as if searching for the next sentence. "Well, this sounds stupid. But his eyes just don't look right. They remind me of somebody. And—well, they just need to check him out."

"Surely they did that before they hired him." I sipped my ice tea.

Mom gave me one of her "oh, Avery" looks. "Sure, they read his résumé or whatever. And they interviewed him. And they probably even took time to call whatever references he provided. But that's the key, isn't it? He provided them."

"Well, what doesn't look right? About his eyes," I asked.

Her blue eyes focused on me over the gold-framed half-glasses perched on her nose. "They just look too big for his face."

"So what's got you worried?"

She flapped a file folder on the countertop. She didn't direct her exasperation at me, but at her inability to articulate what felt wrong. Considering some of the projects she takes on, her instincts come in handy. But sometimes it takes a while for her to know exactly why somebody strikes her the wrong way. She says the good Lord protects her. I say anybody else would've been found dead in a ditch a long time ago.

"Avery—I don't know. Just—how do you do a criminal check?"

I shrugged. "L.J. ought to be able to run one for you, if it's important."

"So the sheriff can just plug in his name and find out—what?"

"She'll need his social security number. And maybe his birth date. But the national system should turn up any felony convictions."

She frowned. "Only convictions? Not arrests?"

I shook my head. "And no misdemeanors."

"Such as?"

"Most of those, you likely wouldn't care about. You know, jaywalking, traffic fines, that sort of thing. Trouble is, sometimes more serious things get pled down to misdemeanors."

She raised an eyebrow. "Such as?"

I shrugged. "Sometimes a case that a prosecutor can't quite prove for some reason will get bumped down to a lesser charge, in exchange for a plea agreement. The guy pleads guilty to something, and the county avoids the expense of a trial it might not win."

"What kind of cases?"

"Depends. Maybe something like arson, which is

often hard to prove. Or drunk driving. Or child abuse or sexual assault."

Her frown deepened, and I hastened to explain. "That's usually cases where the victim is too scared to testify or wouldn't make a good witness for some reason."

The valley stayed between her eyebrows. "So how can you find out about misdemeanors if they aren't on this national system?"

"You could ask L.J. to make sure. I think you still have to do a county-by-county search of the records. And then sometimes neighboring counties. Sounds like this Sy Bonifay has lived a lot of places, though. That'd take a lot of time and money to do a thorough search."

Mom nodded, thoughtful. "It's probably nothing. I'm just curious, is all. He—maybe I just need to get to know him better."

I didn't press her any further. She'd tell me when she got ready. Or she'd keep her mouth shut. Not much I could do to push her one way or the other.

Seven

I loaded Dad's circular saw in the Mustang's trunk and stopped by the builder's supply for a few boards and nails just to get started on the porch.

As I turned toward the mountains, the cloud cover that had opened the day began to lift. On cool days, the mountains that shelter the north of town turn a striking cobalt blue as the clouds lift. The scene always takes my breath, a deep, looming blue, with its overshadowing gray-bottomed clouds.

I drove, leaning with a practiced memory into the curves, the car's tires burping only slightly as I pushed the accelerator in the depth of each curve. A melancholy enveloped me. Before I'd left my parents' house, I'd called Melvin to pass along a message from Rudy Mellin. Lea's body wouldn't be released immediately, since the investigation was ongoing.

Ordinarily I hate talking by telephone, mostly because I can't read the person on the other end. But even without visual clues, the despair in Melvin's voice sounded palpable, an emotion too strong to bear in person. I felt an odd gratitude for the separation that technology provided, the simultaneous insulation and intimacy of wires and distance.

How had Melvin dealt with the disappearance of his wife? Had he loved her? Something about his reactions now, the quiet, sad calm, spoke of a depth of feeling that had a calm surface but had not grown shallow over the last fifteen years. What would it be like if someone you loved just disappeared? To not know how. Or why. Or where. To know the whole town whispered. And to have the police looking nowhere but at you.

What must the last fifteen years have done to him? After fifteen years, he could finally grieve, formally and openly—but still under suspicion. And still with no body to bury.

The cool air off the lake gave me energy I wouldn't have had otherwise. The work on the porch progressed surprisingly well. I didn't slice off any personal appendages, drop any glass panes, or hack off any key support timbers on the porch. A couple more windows were winter tight, and I'd repaired enough of the porch to walk to the front door without falling through to the clammy dirt underneath. Before I bought more supplies, I'd have to sit down with my checkbook and take a serious look at my financial reality. And I still needed to decide what I'd do about that reality.

I hadn't thought much past coming to Dacus. A couple of weeks ago, I'd simply run away from Columbia. I still had no idea what, if anything, I should run toward. I'd never imagined coming back to Dacus to stay. Yet somehow, with everyone else assuming I'd come here to stay, I found myself mentally trying it on for size.

Even given the charity of my family, it cost a lot to merely exist. But I currently spent a whole heck of a lot less to maintain my lifestyle now than a month ago. Amazing what you could do without, once it has been ripped from your grasp.

The sun began sketching deep shadows from the house to the water's edge. That prickle of someone staring, a sense that someone stood nearby, tickled the back of my neck. I'd been so engrossed in prying off, measuring, measuring again, sawing, and nailing down, I don't know how long she'd stood there, watching me.

"No doubt about who your granddaddy was," she said.

She wore a blue down vest with a plaid shirt and jeans. A thick braided pigtail reached halfway to her waist, with a soft halo of gray curls fuzzing around her face. Standing near the porch, she gave the impression she stood eye level with me, a large woman who seemed to fill up more space than she actually required.

"You knew my grandfather?"

"Sure did."

Something about me, the cabin, or life in general amused her.

"Sure did," she repeated. "Your granddaddy and I went back a ways. He knew my daddy. Used to play on that porch where you're standing when I was a little girl. While they talked men talk." The crinkles near her eyes deepened.

"I'm Avery Andrews."

I stood on my newly repaired step to offer her a handshake, which she cupped in both her strong, rough hands. Like her hands, her face was large but not fleshy.

"I'm Sadie Waynes. You must know you look like him."

I smiled. I didn't want to say no, I had no such idea. My grandfather had been a tall, gaunt man, old when my mother was born. I, on the other hand, at five foot two, was anything but tall and gaunt.

She must have read in my face what I didn't speak. "A'course, when I say folks look like somebody, not too many would agree. Depends on what you choose to see, I always say." She didn't elaborate. "You're named for your granddaddy."

I nodded.

"You're the one who went to law school. He was rare proud of you. You back to stay?"

I was disconcerted by how much this big-boned woman who came out of the woods knew about me. Rather than answer, I asked, "Do you live around here?"

She gestured past my cabin, over the hill away from the lake. "My family's place is up Back Creek Cove."

I'd never been struck before by how odd it sounded to call a landlocked draw a cove. Odd, now that I could see my growing-up place through distant eyes. Sadie Waynes studied me as she might someone who'd come from a distance. I found myself studying her in much the same way. Even in a place as small as Dacus, we didn't know each other, but some of the mountain people maintain an isolation from Dacus proper.

"So you knew my grandfather," I repeated for lack of anything better to say.

She nodded, hooking her fingertips into her jeans pockets. "For as long as I can remember. A wonderful man. Suffered no fools gladly." She kept eyeing me as if she planned on buying me.

"What brings you over to the lake?" I asked, trying to move the conversation—and her study—on to other things.

She indicated a croaker sack in a heap at her feet. "Diggin' 'sang."

Ginseng, the much-prized forked root used in herbal remedies and health potions, grew in the hollows. Digging it required patience and a constitution given to long walks, sharp looking, and patient stooping.

"Hadn't been here in quite some time," she continued. "Stopped comin'." She half turned to look across the lake, her profile to me. "Law, been some time. A decade or more, now that I think on it. This lake carries a deep mist."

The water lay clear and bright under the dimming sun. No mist that I could see.

She kept looking across the lake to the darkened trees on the opposite shore. "Hear they found her."

I nodded, but she didn't notice.

"Maybe that's what had things here clouded. Had to come see. A sad place, for sure." She sighed. "I wisht I'd known. Something went akilter here, but who could've known."

What could I say to that?

She turned. "You were there when they found her." She didn't ask; she told.

I nodded. "By accident."

"This lake's hidden other things. Things aren't always as they seem. You see some things one day all clear. But you can't know what they were like somewhere else, earlier, before you knew them. Or what they are where you can't see. Places are like people. But all keep marks, of who they are, what they've been. I had to come."

I shivered. The air grew noticeably cooler as the sun peeked through on its way down behind the trees.

She inhaled deeply, as if waking from a sleep. "Good to meet you, Avery Andrews. If there's anything you need, you let me know. I'll be here." Her sack held carefully at her side, she disappeared into the trees at the side of the cabin.

The next morning, shadowy memories of Dacus dreams clung like wisps to the edges of my brain. My dreams included Sadie Waynes. And my grandfather. And a guy I'd known in high school that I hadn't thought about in years. Much to remember— and to learn—about this place I thought I knew, all swirling around in my head.

I popped the top on a can of Coke, munched a half-dry bagel, and perched on the porch railing, watching the lake. For some reason, when autumn bares the limbs, I can't quite remember what the trees look like in summer. Then, in summer, I can't quite imagine the bare limbs.

I didn't hear the car pull up on the other side of the cabin. But Deputy Rudy Mellin let out a holler that carried well ahead of him.

"Around here," I yelled back. He appeared, the weeds beside the cabin brushing against his dark uniform pants.

"A'vry. Why the hell you holed up up here? Hidin' out from the law?" He har-harred and tugged his pants up around his doughnut-padded belly.

"Not very well, apparently. You found me."

"Yep." Rudy manages to hide his insecurities behind a blustery, macho self-confidence. Well, not hide, exactly. They stick out in myriad manifestations, including his leering drawl and a belt loaded with phallic-shaped cop stuff. But he's a pretty good cop.

"So what brings you up here? Care for a Co'Cola or something?"

He wrinkled his bulbous nose at my choice of breakfast drinks, then settled one big boot on the porch step.

"Got some preliminary information on that fire." He leaned back against the railing so he could study the lake.

"That's good." Though I couldn't figure out why he'd tell me.

"Not for somebody, it wadn't."

I waited him out.

"Yep." He hitched up his pants and fished a toothpick out of his shirt pocket. "Not good for somebody."

I still didn't respond, knowing he'd tell me more if I didn't seem too anxious. He went on. "The state sent some fire investigators in from Columbia. The insurance company had a fella in, too. All the way from near Chicago." He waggled his toothpick around. "They started sifting through things, soon as what was left cooled down enough."

"Makes sense they'd have to wait," I said non-committally.

"Yep. Found enough to convince 'em it's arson."

"Arson?" Not such a surprise after L.J.'s not-so-subtle hints about the accounting records.

He nodded. "Yep. Somebody wanted that building to go. And maybe a bit more besides." He paused. "They found a body."

I sat my Coke can on the porch railing. I didn't want him to see the quiver in my hand. "Oh, dear Lord."

"Yep. In a little room in behind the offices. Haven't ID'ed him yet. Whoever it was, he's a reg'lar crispy critter now, all bowed up like he 'uz fightin', the way they get."

Rudy probably wasn't trying to disgust me as much as purge his memory of what he'd seen.

"What makes them think it's arson?"

He pulled the toothpick from his mouth. "Natural-gas pipe running to a space heater, low down to the ground, has been cut."

"Who'd cut a gas line and not expect to get blown sky high?"

"Naw, not like that. A firebug'll turn off the gas, saw a slash in the pipe low down in the room somewhere. Then he'll set an igniter, something that'll do the trick after he's had time to leave and the room's plenty full of gas. Then, *kaboom.*"

"Who else you questioning on this? Besides L.J.'s obligatory pass at Melvin Bertram, that is."

Rudy shrugged. "Looking at a couple of guys."

"Like who?" The memory of the flames and the choking smoke and the sounds flashed in my memory.

Rudy spit out part of his toothpick and shrugged. "The good news, sheriff's 'bout decided your boy likely didn't have anything to do with it."

"My boy? Melvin Bertram?"

He rolled his eyes. "Who else might I mean?"

I didn't volunteer that my only other client was Garnet Mills. That would likely dry up the faucet of information that stood before me mouthing a toothpick.

"How much of the mill burned?"

"Sprinklers did some water damage in part of the plant. Lucky they had those, though, what with all that wood and sawdust and who knows what. Mostly just the office area burned. Thing blew the roof up and it collapsed back into the building. It actually smothered some of the fire, they said."

"The office area, huh? So they'll be able to get production up and running soon."

"Yep. I reckon. Get those fellas back to work, that'll be good. I don't reckon old man Garnet pays shit. Can't believe that dump's still in business, truth told."

"Why do you say that?"

"Shit. You seen that place? When I got outta high school, they were barely paying minimum wage then. Some'a them guys worked there their whole lives. Bad when you can't get a job in a textile mill and working at a place like Garnet is the best you can do."

The plant hadn't looked all that prosperous. And neither had the folks working there.

"I guess they'll do an autopsy," I said.

"Yep. Glad I'm not the one taking it to Charleston. Watchin' that'd put you off eatin' barbecue for 'bout the whole rest of your life, I reckon."

"They finish processing the scene yet?" I asked to change the subject.

He shook his head. "That insurance guy looks like he's moved in to stay. I 'magine he'll be around awhile, tryin' to lock down a way to keep his company from havin' to cough up any dough."

I nodded. I needed to call Harrison Garnet, the sooner, the better.

"Rudy, I appreciate you coming all the way up here to tell me my client's off the hook. Frankly, I couldn't figure out why he was on it to begin with, but . . ." I shrugged.

Rudy snorted. "Sooner or later, L.J.'ll hang

something on that a-hole. He might've gotten away with murder once, but that don't mean L.J.'s given up on him. He looks like one of her new permanent favorites."

"That's harassment, Rudy." I tried to keep a playful tone in my voice.

"Yeah, well. Your boy'd be wise to pack his bag and head back to whatever hole he crawled into fifteen years ago. When L.J. takes an extreme dislike to somebody, it itn't a pretty sight."

I nodded. So that's what he'd driven up here to tell me. That, and to have somebody to share his mental pictures of the fire victim with—somebody who wouldn't give him a bunch of macho-cop bullshit.

"Can't imagine why he'd want to hang around, Rudy. Can you?"

"Nope." He glanced across the lake as he turned toward his car. "Well. Need to head out. Take care of yourself, A'vry. Why the hell you stayin' way off up here, anyway?"

I shrugged. "Place needed some work. And I needed something to do."

"Shit," Rudy snorted. "Hang around your office and create lawsuits outta thin air. Itn't that what you lawyers usually do? You be careful up here," he continued in a gentler tone. "Not too many folks around this time of year. Popular spot for kids lookin' for easy drug money. Lotta break-ins."

Hard to believe there weren't many people around, considering how many visitors I'd had this week. "Appreciate it, Rudy. I'll be careful."

As soon as Rudy backed his cruiser down the rutted track toward the road, I closed up the cabin and followed at a safe distance.

The little store sat on the main road—a country store, not to be confused with anything like a convenience store. But it had proved plenty convenient for me, complete with everything from charcoal briquettes and wasp spray to Butterfingers.

The guy who ran it—we'd never exchanged names—rarely met my eye. But he had begun offering a routine nod, a curt acknowledgment, whenever I came in. Which was probably as friendly as he ever got. He had run the store as long as I could remember, and he obviously didn't give a flying flip about building repeat business on the basis of warm customer relations. I bought a Coke and got some change.

The pay phone hung on the outside wall between the rust-crusted ice machine and the air compressor. Fortunately, it sat sheltered enough from any cars whizzing past on the two-lane road that I could carry on a reasonably intelligible conversation.

Surprisingly, the Dacus phone book listed Harrison Garnet's home number. A woman answered. "Mr. Garnet isn't home right now. May I help you?"

"Mrs. Garnet?" I hadn't recognized the measured tones at first, until she started flattening her *r*'s. "This is Avery Andrews."

"A-va-ree," she drawled but without any true welcome in her voice. "Harrison's not here right now. He's down at the plant, dealing with all those people about the fire."

"That's why I called. Just to see if there was anything I could do to help. I—"

"I'm sure Harrison will appreciate your concern." Her drawl deepened in that dangerous way magnolia mouths have. "Especially since you've already been so much help."

"Mrs. Garnet, I—"

"Avery, you must know exactly what you did. Things have gotten all out of hand now, and your cute little trick with that environmental boy has landed Harrison in considerable difficulty."

"What trick? And what—"

"Avery, Harrison tells me everything about his business. He always has. We have that kind of marriage. And of course I feel deeply responsible since I was the one who suggested he contact you in the first place. Doing a favor for old family friends and all. And now this."

"Mrs. Garnet, I—"

"Avery, you might protest with some people and have them believe it. What I can't figure out was what you thought you would accomplish by ordering that little environmental fellow to leave. Were you just being cute? Or were you purposely trying to do Harrison harm?" She no longer even tried to disguise the venom in her voice.

My blood boiled, but I had to acknowledge a tiny fear behind my anger. "Mrs. Garnet, I can assure you that terminating the interview with that inspector was, in my opinion, in the best interest of your husband's company. If circumstances have changed because of the fire, I haven't been informed. And I resent—"

"All I know is that Harrison has been at the plant since early this morning. He's got fire inspectors and insurance investigators, police officers, and who knows what crawling all over the place, asking him all sorts of questions. What with that death, this thing has just turned into a nightmare. And you, with your snippy attitude toward that inspector, have made them all suspicious. They're looking for somebody to blame for all sorts of things, and by upsetting that fellow the other day, you practically drew arrows pointing them right to Harrison."

"Mrs. Garnet, I can assure you that was not my intent. No one could have foreseen that our discussion Wednesday with the inspector would have anything to do with this fire investigation. But I—"

"Perhaps it would be best if you just stayed out of things now, Avery. You obviously didn't know anything about what you were doing. I feel so responsible for what I've done to poor Harrison. His health just won't take much of this. I thought I was helping him out by suggesting he call you. I should have listened to the stories I'd heard—"

The phone felt hot against my ear. Rather than try to crawl through the phone to decapitate her, I gave her a clipped "Good-bye, Mrs. Garnet," and hung up.

I tried to calm myself with the thought that she must be distraught. Or grieving, trying to find somebody to blame. I'd counseled enough clients to recognize that sort of anger, and give her some benefit of the doubt.

Deep inside, though, I feared her accusations might be striking a little close to home. What had happened?

The canon of professional responsibility included something along the lines of "Thou hast a duty to refer cases thou hast no expertise to handle." Had I screwed up? I mentally shook myself by the scruff of the neck. True, I'd never handled a regulatory inspection before. But I'd done my homework. And I'd handled dozens of lawsuit negotiations with big money on the table. Leaving the Calhoun Firm didn't mean I'd lost my edge.

And I shouldn't trust Sylvie Garnet's take on things. After all, she might not have fully understood her husband, while he shared the intimate details of his business dealings over a breakfast of pink grapefruit halves.

I leaned against the side of the ice machine, letting the slight hum of its compressor massage my back. I needed to change out of my jeans and Red Adair sweatshirt before I drove down the mountain to see Harrison Garnet.

Eight

The scene around Garnet Mills looked like the movie set for a disaster film. The wan winter sun couldn't penetrate the blackened area that had been the office. But sunlight glinted off the red and chrome fire truck and the fire marshal's wagon and off the bald head of Harrison Garnet, who sat at the center of the aimless activity.

Nobody seemed to be doing anything. They stood in small clumps or stirred around like the last autumn leaves in a weak breeze, apparently waiting on something or someone inside the charred hull of the building. In a flash of déjà vu, I transported back to Luna Lake and the directionless urgency of the lake search.

Two men stood with Harrison Garnet, their backs to me as I approached. One, in a uniform shirt with epaulets, talked down to Harrison Garnet in his wheelchair. The other slumped off to the side.

I hung back, not wanting to intrude. Mr. Garnet saw me out of the corner of his eye, but gave not even a wave of acknowledgment.

The epauletted one abandoned Garnet as two

men in soot-streaked coveralls, carrying flashlights
and a camera, walked out the now-missing front entrance. I watched as they conferred. One of the men
in coveralls talked as much with his hands as he did
with his mouth.

Left sitting alone, Garnet maneuvered a half turn,
nodding me over.

"Avery." He extended his hand and shook mine.

"Mr. Garnet, I'm sorry. About the fire." This felt
as awkward as a funeral. What should I say? I
wasn't sure how much they'd told him yet about
their arson suspicions. Rudy probably hadn't come
by to gossip with him.

"It's hard to take it all in," he said, glancing back
at the charred hole in the front of his building. "It's
hard to even remember what it looked like before, or
even that a door stood there. And windows and
desks."

The man in epaulets returned, saving me from
having to respond.

"Mr. Garnet, the fellas will be here awhile longer,
double-checking everything and finishing the pho-
tographs. They've found evidence of arson." His
tone carried an undercurrent of accusation.

Harrison Garnet ignored any undercurrent. "Mr.
Simms, I'd like you to meet Avery Andrews." He
sounded like the membership chairman at a country
club brunch. "Avery does some legal work for me."

Simms acknowledged me with a slight nod, but
neither of us offered to shake hands.

"Exactly what is this evidence your boys found?"

Harrison nodded toward the guys in streaked coveralls as they returned to the shadows of the dripping, dark building.

"I'd be happy to show you, but it's hard to get back in there." Simms glanced at Garnet's wheelchair. "Maybe your attorney would like a firsthand look."

"Certainly." Harrison volunteered for me. "Perhaps you could give me a *Reader's Digest* version first?"

"A small natural gas–fueled space heater located at the front of the office area looks to be the point of origin."

Garnet nodded.

"The pipe leading into the heater came through the wall and ran along the baseboard for a distance of approximately eighteen inches and linked into the heater. Following a common method, the bug turned off the gas, sawed a slit in the pipe, then turned the gas back on."

I had a whole new appreciation for Rudy Mellin as a source of inside information.

"While the room filled with gas, rising and filling the room from the top, he apparently proceeded to decorate the office area with an accelerant. Probably used some kind of sprayer, since we haven't found any pooling pattern. Then he set his initiating device, designed to blow things after his departure. A nicely planned job. Not the most sophisticated thing I've ever seen, but certainly not something a junior high kid came up with in a wet dream."

He paused, studying Garnet. Garnet seemed oblivious to the attention Simms was giving him. He just stared into the black cavern in front of him.

"So someone definitely set this fire. Deliberately," Harrison said, his voice hollow.

"Absolutely. There's more, but that's it in a nutshell. Know anybody who has it in for you, Mr. Garnet?"

Garnet jerked his head up and stared at Simms. "No, Mr. Simms. I can't imagine who'd do this." He sounded bewildered, disbelieving, and, to me, believable. But I can be gullible.

"Anything at all that you could think of, it'd certainly help us in our investigation, Mr. Garnet. Any disgruntled employees? Any threats? Anybody with business or money problems who would benefit?"

Something in Simms's unbroken stare telepathed the message he wasn't willing to speak: *Any reason you'd torch your own building?*

But Harrison Garnet apparently didn't hear the unspoken message. "No," he said slowly, staring at what was left of his building.

Simms's expression was too guarded to reveal whether he believed Garnet as he turned his attention to me. "Well, Ms. Andrews. Would you like a closer look?"

The challenge in his voice squelched any reservations I might have expressed. "Certainly, Mr. Simms."

He studied me, all the way down to my feet. I noticed that he didn't wear the protective coveralls the other investigators had on, but he did have on thick-soled work boots that looked much more substantial than my leather flats.

"We'll confine ourselves to the open areas," he said. "Watch your step here." He pointed to the jumble of brick scattered over what had been the front walk.

"The parapet—the brick facing—collapsed here, which would be expected in a fire in this type of brick-and-wood joint construction. The plant itself," he pointed to the adjoining manufacturing area, largely untouched by the fire, "is the old heavy timber construction often used in textile mills a hundred years ago. Thanks to those thick beams and the sprinkler system, that sustained almost no damage."

"So they should be able to get people back to work soon."

He shrugged. "That would be up to Garnet. Step carefully. Those shoes of yours won't protect you from exposed nails or hot spots."

We stood just inside what had been the reception area. "See the distance the brick rubble has fallen from the front of the building?" He pointed out toward the sunlight. The sparse lawn between the building and the sidewalk lay buried under rubble. A few bricks had scattered across the rough asphalt of the parking lot.

"The normal collapse pattern of a brick parapet would've been up to the full distance of the height of the wall. The parapet began just above the lintel that ran over the front windows here." He pointed overhead to a smudged steel beam. "The windows here were constructed like those in a storefront, with the beam over the windows and a freestanding wall overhead."

I remembered the line of old-fashioned metal-framed windows, like those of an old elementary school, stuck in the brick face of the building. Only buckled metal bands and glass shards remained.

"The distance those bricks flew indicates an explosion, rather than a simple collapse of the building as a result of the fire."

I nodded but said nothing. After he pointed it out, the wide scatter-pattern of rubble became clear, though I certainly would've made nothing of the jumbled bricks without his explanation.

We moved farther into the building. Simms pulled a flashlight from his pocket and, even though he wore heavy work boots, he chose his steps as carefully as I chose mine. The water on the floor glistened in black pools and began to seep in the edges of my shoes.

"The space heater sat here, apparently to supply additional heat to the ladies working at these desks." His wandering flashlight beam picked out the shell of the small heater box and the skeletons of office furniture, including fire-blackened filing cabinets and the metal legs of office chairs.

I became acutely aware of the constant sound of dripping water throughout the cavernous room. The air felt noticeably colder than the sunlit air outside. Somehow, I hadn't expected so much cold and water, the muffled wet sounds, and the overpowering, nose-eating stench of burned wood.

"Sometimes it's difficult to discern what damage has been caused by the streams of water used to fight the fire and what has been caused by an explosive incident that preceded the fire."

Simms obviously enjoyed his role as fire scene tour guide, a magician who liked to amaze his audience. Despite the mucky water squishing in my shoes with each step, I found the view through his eyes fascinating.

"The alligatoring of the wood here," he pointed to an interior wall joist blistered into charred squares, "indicates the burn pattern, up from this section of pipe. From the pattern and depth of charring, we know we had a gas jet burn here. See the V pattern?"

He motioned with both hands, indicating an area of more severe damage radiating up the inside wall. "That's something we always look for, to indicate the site of origin."

Cops—and apparently fire investigators—always use such arcane language. Surely there was a casual way to say this stuff without sounding like a military manual.

"The explosion likely didn't do the damage the bug expected it to. Most folks don't realize how hard it is to get materials—even paper—to burn. But this guy had enough experience to know that he'd have to help it along."

He took a couple of steps toward the remains of an office desk. After a brief mental calculation, I realized this would have been Rita Wilkes's desk. The sodden jumble on top was almost unrecognizable. Something that looked like a picture frame, twisted and black, glass shards around it, lay facedown on the floor.

"He knew enough to add fuel to his fire, so to speak. Due to the absence of pooling, I imagine he used something like a garden sprayer to mist fuel around the room. Saw a case like that in a tobacco warehouse downstate a couple of years ago. Fella there damned near blew himself up—filled the place with fumes, then threw a match. 'Bout burned his own pants legs off, with him in 'em." He shook his head, allowing himself a tight smile at the memory.

"Our bug here proved a bit more sophisticated. Haven't personally seen one with this MO, but that's okay. Somebody will have heard of somebody who set something this way before. They learn as they go."

He pointed to a V-shaped piece of metal lying in a puddle, about where the door to Harrison Garnet's office once stood. "Unless I miss my guess, that's the transformer from a neon sign."

I raised my eyebrows but refrained from asking, *Huh?*

He continued explaining the puzzle pieces. "Igniting flammable vapors, such as a concentration of natural gas, propane, even gasoline fumes, is tricky. The air has to contain a certain ratio of air to gas, since a fire requires oxygen in order to sustain itself. You can't just toss a match and walk off by the light of it without risking blowing your own eyebrows off. On the other hand, setting a delayed-ignition device is tricky. If it sparks too soon, before enough vapor is present, no go. If it ignites after too much vapor is concentrated in the subject space, no go.

"Our boy genius used a continuous spark. A horn gap. Something like you'd see in Frankenstein's basement, with an electric arc crawling up between two metal prongs."

Understanding must have registered on my face, because he continued. "I've heard about that type of ignitor but, to be honest, it's the first time I've seen one. I've seen articles in those underground anarchists' publications on how to prepare a bomb shelter and blow up your own neighborhood."

"That's scary."

"You can say that again. It's particularly scary if you're the firefighter called to the scene at a creaking old hull like this. Who knows which way a piece of junk like this will fall when it goes?"

He stared upward, where part of the roof had disappeared, either in the explosion or in the fire. The creaks and drips took on a more ominous meaning for me. I couldn't quite decipher the sounds in the cavelike darkness. The sunlight, visible through the missing roof sections, couldn't penetrate the gloom.

"Fortunately, no one tried to be a hero here. Give me a fire in a sturdy old barn like that any day." He nodded in the direction of the factory building. "Those heavy old timbers hold until they're too hot to get close to. You don't have to worry about them coming down on your head.

"Of course, with so much evidence left behind,

we gotta wonder who's desperate enough to do something this stupid. And this dangerous."

He fixed his stare on me. I stared back. How had he gotten a smudge of soot across his forehead? He hadn't even touched anything, that I had seen.

When he saw I wasn't going to respond, he nodded toward the remains of Rita Wilkes's desk. "This is where things get really interesting. Don't touch anything." He held his arm out as if I might lunge toward the smelly mess on the desk. "See those tented items?"

Once he pointed them out, I saw quite clearly what they were. Along the top of the desk, someone had propped heavy books open facedown on the desk, three or four spines forming jutting peaks.

"Classic pattern," he said. "It's one of the first things an arson investigator looks for in a commercial enterprise."

His tour had changed directions, and his tone told me I wouldn't like the direction we were headed.

"Records, particularly ledgers and other bound materials, are amazingly hardy, extremely difficult to ignite. Smart bugs—or those who think they're smart—make sure the filing cabinet drawers are open and the ledger sheets are exposed and ready to burn."

I glanced back at the misshapen outlines of the filing cabinets standing sentinel a few feet away. All four drawers on all three cabinets stood at least partially open.

"You can see why the insurance investigator has

requested SLED's document examiner come gather up what he can. They do amazing work getting ashes to talk to them. What they can't handle in Columbia, they'll send to the FBI lab in D.C."

"That's—very interesting, Mr. Simms," I said after an uncomfortably long pause, which he refused to fill. "Have you discussed any of this with Mr. Garnet?"

"Briefly. He maintains that he has no idea who would've had any reason to do such a thing." Water dripped in the background. "Perhaps, Ms. Andrews, you can discuss this further with your client. Once we get this material into the lab, it will have a lot to tell us. Much more than you might expect. And it'll speak loud and clear to the FBI and the environmental guys."

My surprise didn't escape his notice. "Oh, yes. They showed up bright and early this morning, only a few hours after the investigator from Mr. Garnet's insurance carrier arrived. This is the kind of feast they really enjoy."

I refused to acknowledge his threats, preferring to keep up the pretense that this was a purely informational tour. "The body you all discovered in here? Any indication who it might be?"

"They discovered the body there, in what apparently served as a small storage room." In the small room lay a mass of twisted wire, the innards of a coil mattress.

"From what you've said, you don't think he's a suspect."

"Extremely doubtful that he set the fire, if that's what you mean. A bug caught in his own trap wouldn't have been lying peacefully asleep in bed when his rig exploded. The body was partially burned, charred into the fetal position we commonly find in fire death."

"Who was he?"

He shrugged. "Hasn't been identified yet."

He watched me closely for my reaction to the twisted metal and the stench. "As Mr. Garnet's counsel, you should advise him of the provisions in the *South Carolina Code* under which an explosion or fire causing death or serious bodily injury moves the charges from third-degree arson to first-degree arson. He should be aware there's no difference between the guy who set it and the guy who hired him. The good news is that the maximum penalty for first-degree is only twenty-five years."

He was goading me for a reaction. I didn't give him one. The more he talked, the more I learned. "An autopsy should be able to show how he died," I said.

"If he died of smoke inhalation, that's one thing. But," he said, "if anyone harmed the guy before he crisped, that would add to the charges. Fire damages the outside of the body, but evidence of internal trauma is still visible at autopsy. And the organs, even the vitreous fluid in the eyeball, can usually give them a blood alcohol content. They can learn a lot from what's left of that body."

I kept my voice steady. "The more information, the quicker you can get to the bottom of this whole tragic incident." I wasn't certain enough of my client—or my relationship with him—to venture a more aggressive defense at this point.

Simms's jaw muscles bunched tightly as he clenched his teeth. "You can fill Garnet in on all this," he said, then turned toward the building's missing front wall. Picking our way back through the rubble proved easier with the sunlight in front of us highlighting the puddled water and blackened obstacles.

After a curt farewell, Simms rejoined the guys in jumpsuits near the red van. I walked over to Harrison Garnet.

"Well?" He held his hands loosely entwined, his elbows resting on the arms of his chair.

"As he said, there's every indication someone deliberately set the fire using a gas buildup and a delay device. Business records were deliberately burned. This wasn't done by a bunch of high school kids with a book of matches."

He gave no sign he heard me. His gaze was fixed on the charred building.

"They're looking for similarities with other fires, trying to discover any link or pattern that could lead them to who started this. And they'll perform an autopsy on the body they found inside."

He started to say something, looked puzzled, as if he couldn't think of the words, then shrugged his shoulders. "We'll deal with that when we need to. We've got some more immediate problems." He nodded, indicating somewhere behind the factory. "There're fellas back there. They showed up this morning waving a search warrant and asking a bunch of questions."

"Search warrant?"

"That little environmental boy brought some of his friends. His hard-ass supervisor and a fella in an FBI windbreaker."

"They're here now?"

He nodded. "Since early this morning, when they served that search warrant you seemed so anxious for them to get. Seems they showed up with chips on their shoulders and suspicious minds. I've always found you gotta be very careful around suspicious minds, Avery. People have a way of seeing what they think they'll see."

His voice lacked the shrill accusation his wife's had carried in our phone conversation earlier. But the implication rang clear nonetheless.

"You should have called me," I countered. "This is what you asked me to help you with. Where are they?"

I took one step toward the factory but he held up his hand. "I don't think that'll be necessary. They're going to do what they want to do. There's not much I can do about that now."

"Mr. Garnet, you really shouldn't let them wander about your premises alone, search warrant or no. There are procedures."

Mentally I ticked off the suggestions from the law library articles I'd read. Any point in educating him? But Harrison Garnet continued to try to stop me. "Avery, I think you've done enough already."

His tone was tired, resigned, without the venom of Sylvie Garnet's earlier tongue-lashing. But I'd observed the social niceties long enough. "No, Mr.

Garnet, I haven't done enough. I started doing my job earlier this week when we met with that inspector. Now it's time for me to carry through with that job. What kinds of things have they specified? What have they asked to see?"

"Avery, they're loaded for bear. Asking that little twerp to bring back a warrant ticked him off. Now that there's been a fire, they've moved to some not-so-veiled threats about a cover-up. Avery, the shit has hit the fan and I don't like where you've put me."

"I didn't put you anywhere. Let me finish the job I started. You need to know what they're looking for and what they find. You won't learn that letting them traipse around your property while you sit here." I found myself leaning toward him on the balls of my feet, my voice rising angrily.

"I'm going around back to have a chat with your visitors."

He broke our stare first with a glance over my shoulder at the fire scene. Then, with a sigh, he said, "Whatever, Avery," and gave a dismissing wave.

As I crunched along the brick and glass scattered on the sidewalk, I realized my fists were clenched. I strode along the length of the factory building, turned the corner, and found myself alone.

Other than the heavy stench of burned wood, this end of the building showed remarkably few signs of the fire. And no signs of life. I scanned the trees that edged the far side of the rough-paved lot. At least two—no, three—men stood just inside the line of trees.

I crossed the football field–size parking lot. The

men waited as I crunched across the gravel at the edge of the lot and onto the cushion of pine needles.

"Mr. Smith," I said, my hand outstretched in Jason's direction. "Good to see you again."

In the South, civility is the base-level requirement for any acceptable interaction.

"Ms.—Andrews?" He took my hand, his grasp loose and slightly damp.

I nodded and turned to Jason's companions. I offered my hand to a rumpled, heavyset fellow with wiry gray hair. "I'm Avery Andrews."

He made a motion as if cleaning his hands on the sides of his khaki pants, then stuck his right hand awkwardly toward me. "Dawson Smith," he said. "From Environmental Control. This is Agent Burke, with the FBI."

Even without the navy windbreaker with the insignia, Agent Burke would never be mistaken for anything but a cop. A very large, serious cop.

"Mr. Smith. Agent Burke," I responded. "I'm not sure Mr. Smith here"—I nodded toward Jason— "has had a chance to brief you. I do some legal work for Harrison Garnet." Maybe that was safer than claiming to be Garnet's counsel.

Dawson Smith nodded. Agent Burke simply narrowed his eyes.

I continued. "I happened to stop by on some other business and Mr. Garnet told me you fellows were here executing a search warrant." Maybe it would help if Harrison Garnet and I both sounded like innocents with nothing to hide.

Agent Burke studied me in that way cops have,

memorizing distinguishing features so he could spot me in a lineup, a mug book, or on a darkened street corner in a questionable part of town. But he didn't speak.

Dawson Smith took a step closer to me, breaking the imaginary circle that bound him to Burke and Jason Smith.

"We've received a complaint and are, of course, obligated to investigate." He smiled and ducked his head almost apologetically. "You understand, we can't tell the hollow complaints from the real scare stories unless we come look."

I nodded. Dawson Smith looked like he'd be at home on Luna Lake with a fishing line dropped off the end of the dock and a couple of beers in a cooler. His short gray buzz cut spiked a bit and his barrel chest strained the buttons on his light denim shirt. He was shorter than Agent Burke's six-two, and kindlier and more befuddled-looking than young Jason. At the same time he conveyed an air that said he was in charge.

"If we can answer any questions for you, Miz—Andrews, is it? Please let us know. Otherwise, we'll just go about our business here." He smiled and dismissed me with a turn.

"Mr. Smith, first, I'd like to see a copy of that warrant." I tried to keep my tone polite but insistent.

"Um, sure," he said absentmindedly. "It's in my case. Just a sec. Jason, take that still camera and grab some shots of that."

Dawson pointed at a spot on the ground, then scribbled something on his clipboard. Out of the corner of his eye, he watched Jason fumble around setting up the shot while he shambled toward a nylon satchel propped against the base of a pine tree. I watched him as he watched Jason. I couldn't see anything worth photographing. Jason had shed his suit coat, but in his taupe trousers and designer tie, he was overdressed for the day's activities.

"Did I remember to give you back that ruler for size markings?" Dawson said, his tone helpful as he stooped over his satchel.

Jason started, looked around, then fumbled in his hip pocket, from which a banana-yellow ruler stuck conspicuously—in plain sight of Dawson Smith.

I looked at Dawson Smith with more respect. He made sure the job was done right, without unduly embarrassing Junior.

As Dawson rifled through the papers in his satchel, I ambled over beside him. The stand of trees started where the ragged edge of the asphalt lot ended, and sloped easily toward a slow creek with flat banks. The creek, broader than many around here, lay about five feet wide, slow and shallow. Mountain and foothills creeks tend to cut deeply, so that flat banks were an oddity.

Something whacked me on the shin. For a brief moment, I thought I'd caught my leg in a hunting trap. "Aoww!" I whistled breath out my nose to keep from cussing.

"Be careful there!" Dawson Smith was beside me in a bound, trying to disentangle my foot from a metal hoop I'd upended from the dirt.

"Jason, come get a shot of this. Do you mind, Miz

Andrews?" He held me by the arm so I could step back from the half-buried hoop. "Would you just stand there so your legs can give the photograph some perspective?"

Jason hunched down, fiddling with the camera's focus until I wanted to jerk it out of his hands and take the pictures of my own feet.

"What's your interest in a rusty metal ring?" I asked, stepping clear of it after Jason clicked a few shots and Dawson let go of my arm.

Agent Burke, who had wandered farther into the trees, rejoined us. He stared soberly at the spot where Jason focused his camera. But he still didn't speak.

"That rusty metal ring," Dawson said, watching Jason closely, "is what's left of a buried barrel." He looked up at me. "The administrative warrant spells it out, if you'd like to see it." I took the papers he offered me. "The complainant alleged that the parking lot and this area served as a waste disposal site for a number of years. What we're seeing here indicates that there's—"

He stopped talking, his attention drawn by Burke's movement. Burke had turned toward a man in denim overalls who was crossing the creek. He'd appeared out of nowhere and seemed to walk on top of the water. With a loose-legged gait, he strode the few yards to where we stood. His boots had not a spot of water on them.

"Glad to see you fellas here, fine-ly." He spoke carefully around a chaw of tobacco.

Two long-eared bluetick hounds took that oppor-

tunity to splash across the creek along roughly the
same track the newcomer had taken. They joined us
with their noses to the ground, jowls hanging and
eyes full of sad. Water glistened on their spotted
coats.

"I'm Born Wooten. Euborn Wooten to the IRS
and the social security. Just born to ever'body else."

Putting an age on him was impossible. His much-
washed overalls puddled onto the top of mud-red
work boots. With his eyes sunk deep into weathered
wrinkles, he peered at us over his beak like an eagle.

"I take it yore the environmental guys. I called
and called and like to give up on you ever comin'."

Dawson Smith made the introductions all around,
including me. At the mention that I was a lawyer
and working for Harrison Garnet, Born Wooten
spent a bit more time studying me.

"I myself worked here at the plant, nigh on forty-
five years. Retired a couple of years ago." He nodded back across the creek. "But still live right there."
What he actually said sounded like *rat tar,* but only
Jason Smith, junior G-man, looked like he didn't
understand the old man.

"See ya found one'a them barrel tops. Can't tell
you how many hundreds a'them things we're
standin' on top of. I been livin' across the crick there
long as they been plantin' 'em here. Longer'n it
took those slash pines to grow. You reckon them
things had some kinda pie-zin in 'em?"

Dawson Smith responded by joining Born
Wooten in studying the ground at his feet rather than
eyeing him directly. In so doing, he communicated

volumes to Born Wooten. Mountain folks usually avoid eye contact, except as a challenge.

"We can't rightly say just now, Mr. Wooten. We'll be taking some samples of the soil around in here. Maybe you can show us some places we should be certain to check."

"Shore can." Born Wooten nodded and carefully aimed a stream of tobacco juice away from the group.

"You worked at the plant. Any idea what might have been buried in those barrels?"

Born Wooten shrugged his shoulders, the puddled overalls on his boots rising, then falling. "Stuff from the plant. Makin' furniture, you know the kinds of stuff you have. Varnishes, stains, glues. Rags soaked in that kind of stuff, we threw in barrels, capped, and hauled out."

"For how long?"

"Law, years. Long as I worked there. Some years back, they got a lot more careful about how they got rid of stuff—you know, gov-mint regulations and all. But we still kept glue-rag barrels. Right up to a few years ago."

"How many years?"

"Can't rightly say. You know how years"—he pronounced it *ya-airs*—"all run together, without you have some sort of markin' event. Somebody birthin' or dyin' or somethin'."

"Any idea how far they go through here? Or how many deep they're buried? Or anything else that might help us?"

Born Wooten, with his signature slouch and his

hound dogs stretched at his feet, surveyed the wooded patch toward the creek, then looked back across the crumbly asphalt parking lot.

"Not too deep, best I remember. 'Course, didn't have to dig too deep, with this much space." He swung his arm to encompass what we could see. "Startin' in the 'fifties, they 'uz putting barrels in 'bout where that line of pines stands." He nodded across the creek. "Then they worked their way back. Sometime in the sixties or so, they paved over part of the dump. Needed more parking places as folks got more cars, I reckon. I know folks, all of a family, that work here and ever' one of 'em drives their own car to work." He shook his head.

"So the barrels in this part"—Dawson Smith indicated the wooded area where we stood—"they've been buried long enough for these trees to grow?"

Born Wooten nodded. "Yep. Right here in the center, they weren't no trees 'cause they used equipment in here to bury trash. 'Course, back then, no big trucks'd come to haul stuff off. Had to take care of it on your own. Why, I got me a trash heap back'a my place older'n that. Got ever' can'a beans and beer I ever ate or drank buried in my backyard. Well, least until they opened the recycling centers 'round the county. That's a more"—he paused—"responsible thing to do, don't you think?"

Dawson Smith nodded.

"I'll tell you who might know and that's ol' Nebo Earling. Mr. Garnet hired him to do some work on the parking lot and I know for a fact he buried

some'a the glue-rag barrels 'long in here. 'Fore he
upended that backhoe in the crick. Down there
where the bank's steeper." He pointed a few dozen
yards downstream from the crossing to his house.
"Nebo'd know."

For a mountain man, Born Wooten sure talked a
streak. Nebo Earling's name made no discernible
impression on Dawson Smith. But he'd sure popped
up in a lot of casual conversations lately.

"Mr. Wooten, if you knew all these years that
stuff's been buried here, why'd you decide to call us
now?" Dawson asked.

Born Wooten shrugged, his overalls rising and
falling again. "Mostly 'cause that stuff started end-
ing up on my property," he said. "And I been reading, over to the library. Articles about aquifer
contamination."

That didn't sound like a *National Enquirer* lead
story. *South Carolina Wildlife* maybe. Or the
Smithsonian.

"On your property?" Dawson Smith perked up at
that. "How, exactly?"

Born Wooten spit discreetly to the side and said,
"The creek moved."

Dawson Smith turned to face the creek. Through
the trees and underbrush that grew thickly on the
other side of the creek, I could make out the rough
outline of a white clapboard house with a small
front porch.

When we looked puzzled, Born continued. "The
creek moved," he said simply. "Leaving me with

some kind of slime and a buncha those rusty tops trashin' my creek bank." He pointed to the metal ring at my feet.

Dawson Smith nodded. "How many have you found?"

Born Wooten shook his head. "Don't know for sure. But you're welcome to come count 'em for yourself. Or what you kin see."

Dawson Smith nodded, but paused, as if deep in thought. "Glue, you say." He said it as if to himself.

"Yessir."

"What kind? Or kinds? Do you know?"

"Nope. Sure don't. Glue's glue, when they tell you to stick two pieces 'a wood together."

Dawson offered a fraction of a smile. "I reckon so. Do you mind if we come have a look at your creek bank? Maybe take some samples? A few pictures? That'll help us get a better idea of the extent and nature of the problem."

"Sure. Any time. That's what I called you fellas for. Never did think you 'uz comin'."

"We have to take things in order," Dawson said. "But now you have our attention and we're anxious to get to work."

Born Wooten nodded and jammed his hands deeper into the cavernous pockets of his overalls.

"The sooner, the better." Born glanced at his pocket watch. "Gotta go."

With that, he crossed the creek, again looking for all the world as though he walked effortlessly on water. He climbed the bank toward his wood frame house without breaking stride, his hounds trailing and scouting to either side.

"Jason, make sure to note on the grid you've done the site of each photograph or soil sample. We'll almost certainly find phthalates. And likely other contaminants as well—"

"What?" I interrupted. That sounded like something an environmental offender's lawyer ought to know about. Just in case she remained the lawyer for said offender.

"Phthalate," he repeated. He spelled it; I mentally marked that it began with *ph* and hoped I'd be able to find it in a reference book of some sort.

"And that is?"

"An EPA priority pollutant and a suspected carcinogen. Fortunately for your fella over there"—he nodded toward the plant—not an acute one. But certainly of concern for its long-term damage potential in groundwater. Jason, we'll likely need to have some test wells dropped. That's something Mr.—" he consulted his clipboard—"Garnet may have to pay for. Once we get those soil samples analyzed, we'll follow up with him." He made that last remark for my benefit.

I nodded. "Please let us know," I said politely, handing him back his standard, noncommittal administrative search warrant. Might as well keep everything businesslike. Thanks to Born Wooten, Dawson Smith wouldn't have any trouble holding Garnet over one of his own barrels.

"Oh, don't worry. We'll be in touch." If he'd been

wearing a hat, he'd likely have tipped the brim at
me, to complement his John Wayne drawl.

Agent Burke had wandered away from our merry
gathering to study the ground along the creek's
edge. Jason, juggling clipboard, camera, markers,
sample bottles, and other paraphernalia, was too
busy for social proprieties. So I merely nodded to
Dawson Smith and turned back toward the plant.

As I headed toward my car, I didn't see Harrison
Garnet anywhere. I didn't know what kind of car he
drove, so I couldn't tell if he'd left. Come to think of
it, I didn't know if he was able to drive. I guessed he
could. He got around okay with crutches.

After watching Dawson Smith and his faithful
flunky Jason and the brooding cop, I better understood Sylvie Garnet's ire. Those bulldogs would
keep coming until they found what—and whom—
they were looking for. I had an icy suspicion that
Harrison Garnet had no idea his glue-rag barrels
constituted an environmental hazard; as Born
Wooten said, glue's glue. When those inspectors finished with Garnet, losing a chunk of his business to
fire and finding a body inside would be the least of
his worries.

While I was tempted to go set Sylvie Garnet
straight about her husband's business practices, she
really wasn't interested in reality. She had decided
to blame his troubles on me. True, the inspectors
had returned with a vengeance, but even Jason
would've stumbled over those barrel hoops eventually. The fire had just brought Dawson Smith sooner.
And the dead body and sabotaged records would

keep him longer. I still didn't know if Harrison Garnet was a good actor, a good liar, or sadly naive.

So much for breaking into the low-risk world of in-house corporate counsel. Maybe Jake Baker was right. Joe Six-Pack wouldn't be quite so judgmental when it came to my past.

As I unlocked my car door, I chided myself for being petty. *Some poor fellow died in a fire and you're feeling sorry for yourself, Avery Andrews. Very mature. And compassionate. Now why don't you drive by the nursing home so you can tell them what poor health you're in.*

I did a double-take at my reflection in the rearview mirror. Black soot streaked my cheek. I looked like a harlequin—or an urchin. And Dawson Smith had made businesslike conversation with that face and hadn't mentioned it.

Back at my parents' house, I had the place to myself. I found a dry pair of shoes, washed my face, then checked the answering machine, thinking Mom or Dad might have left a message.

"Please tell Avery that Melvin Bertram called," the voice on the machine said. "I'd like to see her this afternoon. Or evening. If she has a chance. Thank you. She has my number in town."

Nine

When I called, Melvin's brother suggested I could find Melvin at Runion's, a barbecue joint outside town. Melvin already had a half-empty beer bottle in front of him when I got there. From his slurpy hello, I judged that wasn't the first he'd drained.

"A'vry, glad you got the message. Glad my brother told you where I'd be. Glad I knew where I'd be. What'd you like to drink?"

"Some ice tea would be great. Thanks."

He leaned over the table and pushed the ladder-back chair across to me.

This Melvin, I hadn't seen before. I studied him as he flagged down the waitress. What seemed so different about him? A sprig of sandy hair stuck out over his ear, as if he'd slept crooked. He slumped, both elbows propped on the table, studying the salt shaker he held in both hands. Red barbecue sauce streaked the white plastic shaker.

"We'd better get something to eat," he said. " 'Least, I'd better. Haven't eaten much today."

When the waitress returned, we ordered barbecue plates with slaw and onion rings. Melvin asked for a glass of water and another beer.

"Thanks again, Avery."

"For what?"

He shrugged. "For coming. I don't have any claim on your time. But heck, I'd be glad to pay you."

"For having dinner with you? Naw, that might put me into a whole 'nother profession. I'll stick with the one I've got now."

He ignored my attempt at humor.

"Will you be able to come to the memorial service tomorrow? Body or no, I decided to get it over with."

"Sunday? Sure."

"At Baldwin and Bates's new emporium. Have you seen that thing? The pseudo-Georgian brick monstrosity with acres of free parking and those outsize lights perched along the sidewalk? You can't miss it. Must be a lot of money in buryin' dead people."

"I hear there is. What time?"

"One o'clock. Gives folks time to get out of church. Probably didn't leave enough time for 'em to make it to the cafeteria, but . . ." He shrugged.

"I'm awfully sorry, Melvin. I know this can't be easy."

I never know what to say in the face of grief. If that was, in fact, what sat across from me.

He blinked rapidly several times, but when he spoke, his voice had the same wry bite to it. "You're certainly not the one with anything to be sorry about." He rolled the stained salt shaker between his palms. "Did you know her?"

I shook my head. "Only by name."

"She'd have been a bit older than you. Of course, she was always a good bit older than she should have been. I've never stayed this long on a visit" he went on. "It's always been hard, coming back. Reckon now it'll be easier?" He paused. "I doubt it."

He gazed toward the restaurant's entrance, but he wasn't looking at the age-stained light fixtures and the old advertising slogans plastered on the walls. "I used to look for her, seemed like all the time. Not just here. Wherever I was. A street corner in Atlanta, the T in Boston. I'd find myself looking at faces, thinking I'd run into her. Sometimes I'd have that knot in my stomach. You ever get that when you're waitin' on somebody, scannin' a crowd, waiting for them to appear?"

I nodded. I'd had that sensation, that expectancy. But never, of course, for someone who'd been missing for years. He didn't expect a reply.

"I once ran a block and a half after a woman in New York City. Dodging through the crowd because she had Lea's hair. I grabbed her shoulder and spun her around. But it wasn't Lea's face. What a shock." He allowed himself a small chuckle. "Lucky I didn't get maced. That was one P.O.'ed Yankee lady."

"I bet so."

"Another time, I saw a woman in a restaurant. Something about her smile and the way she held her head brought Lea to mind so vividly. But, you know, you forget what people look like. You don't think you will. You think you'll always know them. But no matter how often I stared at her pictures, I could feel her slipping from my memory. I couldn't hold her memory anymore. I kept staring at that woman, wondering, is that her?"

He paused. "It's a wonder that woman's boyfriend didn't stomp the mud outta me. He considered it. He hesitated only because he thought I was crazy. Which I was, I guess." His sigh seemed to rise from deep inside him. "Do you suppose I'll stop looking for her now?"

The painful melancholy of that statement hit me hard. "That's what memorial services are for," I said. "So you'll realize a person's gone."

He nodded, the top of his head toward me as he studied the salt shaker's holes. "Sometimes I have trouble going to funerals. I never know whether it's better to go shock myself with the sight of that waxy, pretend person in the box, or just not go at all, so I can sometimes trick myself into thinking he's still alive. Of course, there won't be any waxy, pretend person to haunt me this time, will there?"

I swallowed. A vision of that waxy-faced skeleton lying in cream satin didn't set well with the stale-beer and cigarette smells in Runion's.

The waitress picked that moment to plunk two steaming platters in front of us, loaded with chopped pork and assorted deep-fried things. Since I rarely let queasiness get in the way of eating, I picked up my fork. Melvin abandoned the filthy salt shaker to pick up a hush puppy, which he didn't eat. He absentmindedly rolled it around on the edge of his plate until it landed in the strawberries and limp cantaloupe he'd ordered instead of barbecued beans.

"Lea couldn't eat fruit." He poked the cantaloupe with his fingernail. "She'd swell up like a poisoned pup. Allergies. Doctor said it could kill her, she wasn't careful. Funny how something so healthy for most people can be so deadly for somebody else."

Not that fruit had killed her. Maybe a change in topic would keep him from sinking further into his grim fugue.

"Melvin, I'm curious. What drew you away from Dacus?"

I hoped he'd start talking so I could just nod and eat. The barbecue smelled wonderful.

He pursed his lips and fished his hush puppy out of the fruit. "Nothing drew me away. After I left Garnet Mills—"

"Garnet Mills?"

He nodded. "Yeah. I started there before I even finished college. A sort of intern. Hired on as an accountant, then quickly became CFO—chief financial officer. Which isn't as grand as it might sound. I was still just a glorified bookkeeper, but with a lot more responsibility if something went wrong."

"I didn't know you'd worked there full-time."

"Sure did. My first introduction to the real world of business. Taught me that, in business, all's not always what it seems. Some people succeed in spite of themselves. And others have an amazing capacity for self-delusion. All important life lessons."

He toasted me with his fresh beer bottle and took a gulp. "Left there, headed to Atlanta and from there to California. Did some work for a couple of start-up Silicon Valleys—one was a particularly good investment. Now," he shrugged, "I have a little freedom to decide what I want to do. Toyed with the idea of heading back to Atlanta. I'm not rich, but I could afford to live out my life holed up in a shack somewhere back in the mountains."

"Doesn't sound bad, some days, does it?" I said.

He looked as if he'd forgotten he was talking to me. I didn't try to explain that I would welcome not having to practice law. "So what are you going to do?"

He shrugged. "I don't know. Float around like a piece of lint for a while. You ever try things on? In your head, I mean. To see if they fit?"

Little did he know.

"That sound crazy? I keep tryin' on all sorts of things. Like going to the Ringling Clown College. Or riding as a hobo. Or opening a bookstore. Or going to law school."

I shook my head. "I'd advise against that last one."

He gave me a crooked smile. "I know. Nothing quite seems to fit. I can't seem to do anything but what I've been doing. Maybe I'm too old. Or not adventuresome enough."

At least his options evidenced more adventurousness than "Welcome to Wal-Mart." Or high-dollar ambulance chasing with Jake Baker. I changed the subject. "What exactly is it that you do?"

"I don't even know. I mean, when you say you

practice law, people have some idea what that means. Granted, probably a wrong idea. But a better idea than when I tell people I do analyses for venture capitalists."

I nodded. Politely, I hoped, since I had no idea what that meant.

"Do you think about how you don't really produce anything in your job? I don't mean you don't work hard. I mean, I think about that. I don't do anything. With my hands. I don't have anything to show for my work like I would if I assembled steam irons or grew vegetables or welded metal. Something tangible."

I'd thought about it. But I'd always thought it too weird to talk about out loud.

Melvin didn't dwell on its weirdness. He flagged down the waitress with his half-empty beer bottle, signaling for a replacement. How many had he had?

"You know the one thing I think people want in their lives more than anything else? Something that lasts. Something they can hold on to, feel passion about. The truly deep heartbreaks are when you find out that thing you planned to cling to never really was yours to begin with. That it wasn't at all what it seemed. That's the saddest thing. To find out it was never truly yours. No matter what the pledge."

He swigged from the long-neck bottle of Heineken. "You'd think it'd've stopped hurting by now. But it hasn't. Fact is, right now, it hurts as bad or worse than it ever did. Maybe it's having her float to the surface again."

He giggled. Out of character, and getting more so as he drained his bottle.

"Your wife?"

"My wife." The words came out thick and uncertain. "My wife. I haven't said that in a long time. At first, I said it a lot. It sounded so—strange. 'My wife just called. My wife is picking me up after work. My wife is having her hair done. My wife is having an affair.' At first, you say it a lot. Then—" He didn't finish his sentence. He stared intently at a water ring on the red-checked plastic tablecloth.

I was torn between curiosity and embarrassment. To avoid looking at him, I glanced around the restaurant. It seemed odd, after being in Charleston and Columbia, to see so few blacks. Until I'd lived downstate, I'd never realized how white the hill-country folks are. Odd how being away could teach you about home. I tipped my glass and watched the ice cubes melting inside.

We sat in an uncompanionable silence for far too long. Then Melvin shook himself, reminding me of a dog after a dip in the pool.

"A'vry, when I decide what it is I want to be when I grow up, I'll let you know. You'll be one of the first."

"You do that, Melvin. It might give me some guidance."

His giggle faded into a small burp.

"Melvin, you ready to head home?" I waved away the waitress, who should have known better than to offer him anything else, and laid out money to cover the check.

I think he nodded. At least he seemed willing

enough, with some help, to sway out to the parking lot and into my grandfather's prized Mustang. If he threw up in it, I'd have to shoot him.

We made it to his brother's house without incident. "Melvin, this is getting to be a habit, me bringing you home."

I reached across him as he slumped in the front seat and unlatched the car door. He blinked in the glare from the dome light.

When I nudged his shoulder, he started and swung his legs out onto the driveway.

"I'll see you tomorrow," I said.

He didn't say anything. I last glimpsed him disappearing into the opened garage door. Not until I had backed out and driven away did I think to worry that he might wander into the pond behind the house and drown. But I talked myself out of turning around to find out and drove on up the mountain.

The cabin stood dark and quiet, with none of the raucous racket of tree frogs that echoed and swelled all summer. No water lapping quietly in a boat's wake. Just silence. And stars and the stark outline of trees darker than the dark sky, more solid than the rippled black water reflecting the security lights scattered around the lake.

I swung open the back door to the cabin—the one closest to the weedy drive—and slammed it shut behind me, the noise too loud. I threw the deadbolt home and scanned the cabin. Maybe Melvin's melancholy was contagious. Maybe too many people had reminded me how alone I was up here.

"Get a grip," I said aloud. The sound of my voice dispelled some of the monsters.

Filling a tumbler with water and ice, I tried to wash the smoky taste of cigarettes from my throat. I'd have to shower the smell of smoke and fried grease out of my hair before I could go to sleep.

I pulled the curtains to block out the darkness, and filled the sitting room with lamplight. The sofa, musty from humidity and age, sat next to a battered empire library table. The cabin had collected, over the years, the worn, lumpy, faded castoffs from the many families that had used it. Nothing anybody had to fuss over or worry about. Balancing my water glass on my tummy, I reached over and pulled from the table drawer a cracked leather book.

My grandfather's journal. I'd found it tucked behind a shelf of dusty Reader's Digest Condensed Books I'd thrown away in my cleaning frenzy. I hadn't been able to bring myself to read it then. But tonight, after witnessing Melvin's painful trip down memory lane, maybe I could purge some of Melvin's past with some of my grandfather's.

I'd glanced through it when I first found it. But I'd found myself reluctant to read it, as if, through the arching, sharp scrawl, I would find an entrance into my grandfather's most intimate space—a space he'd never invited me into.

Or anyone else, as far as I knew. But I kept coming back to it, with a guilty curiosity. I'd known my granddad as an adoring granddaughter does. And I'd had the uncommon pleasure of knowing him as a mentor. He'd stood in my corner and cheered me on through college and into law school.

I'd never gotten to sit in his courtroom when he served as judge—he'd hit the mandatory retirement age before I hit kindergarten. But I'd seen him in the courtroom, on into his seventies, stooped but tall, distinguished in a silver-haired, slow-talking way. And, to my eyes, infinitely wise. And funny.

Granddad often displayed his bitingly sarcastic sense of humor, though never at my expense. He tended to target folks who took themselves too seriously. Or others too casually. In him, I saw a man who focused intently on others, who usually left people smiling, but who seemed to genuinely enjoy solitude, strolls down Dacus side streets or paths alongside a trout stream, the quiet of this cabin. And the thinking of his own thoughts.

I fingered the dry leather of the book, aware that I intruded on what held those thoughts. Would that intrusion have been unwelcome?

I thumbed open the journal to a place in the middle. He must have written with a nibbed pen, the letters varying in thickness, the pages slightly embossed with the pressure of his strokes. I just paged through, watching the precise lettering move like a stereopticon.

Aunt Vinnia's name caught my eye.

May 27, 1958. Vinnia had her friend Olivia Sterling over for supper tonight and the girls played bridge on the porch. The weather al-

ready has too much of the hint of what's to come to suit me. My dear sister Vinnia, as usual, has taken Olivia under her wing, trying to cheer her. Sometimes, watching another suffer the pangs of lost love, one is struck with the awkward melodrama of it. Until one remembers, with a painful catch somewhere deep in the chest, the intense pain of one's own losses.

What's it been now? Too many years. No point in counting. Surely I'm old enough for the pain to be duller now. But I still walk into the kitchen and, somehow, I'm surprised that she's not there. Or the morning sun will catch the dressing table mirror just right and I'll swear she's sitting there, brushing her hair.

Ah, that incredible chestnut hair. I used to bury my face in it, to smell it, to be closer to her, lost in her. Ah, Emmalyn. How silly you would think me. And how desperately I wish I'd let you know then how silly you made me feel.

That's probably my deepest regret. I'm certain I was too busy being your masterful protector, I couldn't let you know that the very thought of you could turn me to jelly. How silly. Who am I to begrudge Olivia Sterling her melodramatic broken heart?

I pinched my fingers tight across my upper lip, to fend off tears. Crying gives me a headache. My grandmother Emmalyn had died when my mother was very young. Granddad had never remarried. And he'd never moved her dressing table from in front of the window.

I turned to the end of the journal, so I wouldn't think about it anymore.

> *June 17, 1963. Today I put on my judge's robes, climbed up behind the bench, and sentenced Lew Crowl to life in prison. "Lew Crowl, you will be surrendered to the South Carolina Department of Corrections to serve a life sentence."*
>
> *No matter how many times I must repeat those words, I hope they'll always have a profound effect on me. For always, something tragic beyond the normal ken has to have happened. And all manner of people, from policemen to the solicitor to twelve men good and true, have wrestled with the enormity of that tragedy. And then I do my part.*
>
> *Why I think it matters to Lew Crowl where he spends the next twenty-five years of his life, I couldn't say. Lew hasn't paid that much attention to where he spent the last twenty-five years. And he likely told the truth, by anybody's measure, when he told us that he hadn't meant to kill her.*
>
> *He and Lilann had been doing what they always did on weekends—drinking too much and fighting too furiously. When he held that World War II relic to her head and she spit at*

*him and tried to slap it away, it'd gone off.
Several of the jurors—the usual good number
of Baptists—didn't hold much truck with
drinking. And him screaming, in earshot of
two witnesses passing by on the road, "You
spit on me, I'll kill you, you bitch" like as not
made the difference.*

*Not everyone on the jury could know that
she was a bitch. Not that Lew ever pressed
charges the times she'd beaten him blue. But,
in his own way, I think he misses her. And
probably preferred the verdict and the sentence he got. And the finality of it likely affected no one but me.*

*What dramatic turns lives can take on the
heels of the simplest change of direction.
And, given only a half turn in perspective or
lot, what outcome might have altered?*

*Judges aren't allowed the luxury of phi-
losophizing—except in the bounds of their
private thoughts. Sometimes I stare at myself
in the mirror, wondering whom I see. And
what other people see. And how much of
other people we can know. Perhaps I need
more the mettle of a Sylvie Garnet.*

*Drove by Cabe's place after court today to
check on those pups. Hoped, I guess, the
smell of manure would dampen the clamor in
my head. And there stood Sylvie Garnet,
hands on her hips, ordering some young vet
to put down her horse. "He's perfectly
healthy, Mrs. Garnet." "And he threw my*

*son. You'll put him down now. Or I'll put a
pistol between his eyes myself."*

*I tried to intervene but she looked angry
enough to put the pistol between my eyes.
Can't say that exchange helped balance my
day in court. I certainly couldn't confess it to
anyone, but I actually felt sorrier for that
horse—a fine bay—than for Lew Crowl. The
horse likely was smarter. That young vet was
almost in tears.*

*I had to leave. I didn't know the whole
story—perhaps the horse did present a danger. Perhaps her son—what is he now? Two?
Perhaps he'd been badly injured. Shouldn't
make judgments without all the evidence.
Hard enough to make judgments when you
know more than you want to know.*

I wanted to cry about that damned horse. My
grandfather must have used up all his sense of humor in his interactions with people. He sure didn't
save any of it for his journal.

In the front of the journal, he'd penned *1958 to
1963*. The last date had obviously been added later;
the handwriting and ink differed from the first date.

I hadn't even been born yet.

Had he kept other journals? Maybe being a judge
had motivated him to record some events for poster-
ity. Or maybe he just needed somewhere to vent his
frustrations, his angst. Cheaper than therapy. Not
that that would've been an option for a judge in the
late 1950s.

I wonder what he wrote about my being born. About my growing up. I was thankful this journal didn't include that. That would've been too—intimate. Too intrusive. I'd never thought of my grand-dad as pained. Or introspective. Or torn about his job. He'd always seemed too wise, too much in control.

Everyone must wrestle demons. Do I appear to contain my battles? No, surely everyone could tell I didn't have a clue where I was going or what I should do.

Sometime around midnight, I fell asleep on the squishy old sofa, still clutching the soft brown book.

I didn't wake until the next morning when a deputy I didn't recognize came to tell me Donlee Griggs had killed himself.

Ten

A stringy mist rose off the still water of Cane Creek. A few hundred yards upstream from where the creek plunged into a rocky pool at the bottom of Cane Break Falls, a full contingent of Ghouly Boys crowded the bridge railing. They propped, leaned, and slumped over the metal railing, staring intently into the shroud of mist caught by the leafless branches that sheltered the creek.

The creek, only a few yards wide, flowed shallow. The rocks under the bridge had long been a favorite summer wading spot for those who liked a hint of danger. The falls seldom posed much risk, though, unless the wader had been drinking too much. Which probably described Donlee Griggs last night.

I didn't see anybody I recognized, so I silently joined the onlookers. A guy sporting exuberant muttonchops recognized me as a newcomer and obliged me by providing a lecture on what we were witnessing.

"Yep, looks like they're getting that guy-rope tied down now, that there line run from that pine right at

the head'a the falls. They'll use that for rappelin'.
Down the side there, I 'magine. Did some'a that
rappelin' myself, back in the Rangers. Can't say I'd
go outta my way to fling myself off a slickery-wet
rock in this weather. No, siree."

He crossed his arms over his thin chest and rocked
back and forth on the heels of his cowboy boots. He
didn't directly acknowledge me as his audience, but
the tubby kid standing on the other side of him had
turned his ample backside toward us. He'd apparently heard enough Ranger exploits to do him awhile.

Behind us, cars crept past along the bridge. The
line of cars pulling off the shoulder on either side of
the bridge continued to grow.

After a few minutes more without anyone volun-
teering to fill me in, I asked the whiskered fellow,
"Know what happened?"

He rocked back, then forward. "Fella jumped
off'a the bridge, they said. There's a spot'a blood
right there. That deputy is makin' sure nobody leans
up into it or messes with it. See there?"

He pointed about ten feet from where we stood. I
saw some smudges on the metal railing and on the
concrete, but couldn't have sworn it was blood.

"Isn't the creek pretty shallow? Why would
somebody jump off here?"

He shook his head. "Don't rightly know. I heard
tell two guys 'uz fistfightin'. Started down to Tap's.
They ended up out here sometime last night or this
morning."

I leaned cautiously over the railing for a better
view. A couple of fellows in a johnboat sat next to

the bridge pilings. But most of the activity focused on the top of the falls.

"Good thing we've had a couple of freezes already this year," I commented. "That creek bank's usually choked with poison ivy."

"Yep."

"So this guy fell in, then went over the falls?"

"Yep."

"Wouldn't he have broken his neck, falling in? It's so shallow." I leaned over again, watching the water eddy lazily around the bridge piling.

"Don't rightly know," he said. "Had a good bit'a rain lately, so creek's running a little high."

"Can't they get to the pools a lot easier from the bottom of the falls?"

"Yep." He kept talking out over the edge of the bridge, acknowledging my presence with his words, but never with a glance. "They think he lodged up on one'a them ledges under the falls. So they're comin' down from the top."

"They think he might be alive?"

"Can't rightly say. Wouldn't want to take a chance on a thing like that, would they?"

"I suppose not."

We passed a few more companionably silent moments before I asked, "They think it was Donlee Griggs?"

He turned to look at me for the first time, his rosy lips sucked back behind his beard. "I don't rightly know. Is that who they say?"

He seemed surprised that I had any gossip to share. Or that he'd missed out on some.

The damp chill seeped down the neck of the sweatshirt I'd pulled on with my jeans. I'd neglected to put a turtleneck under it, or to grab a scarf or hat or bra.

I wondered if the men in the wet suits were the same ones who'd been up at Luna Lake last week. I shivered again as the vision of murky water and that rusty car floated across my memory. I wouldn't be in a chilly place near water again without thinking about that.

As I watched the painstaking preparations at the top of the falls, part of me wanted to dismiss this as just another harebrained Donlee stunt. But this gathering had a different feel from the one at Luna Lake—more subdued, maybe. Or more intent. The bystanders conducted themselves more like bird dogs on point than folks who didn't have anything better to do early on Sunday before church.

Damn Donlee's hide. If that big idiot had jumped off the bridge, I'd—what? Look him up and give him a good swift kick in his dumpling-shaped butt?

About the time I'd worked myself around to some serious righteous indignation, I spotted a familiar face in the crowd. Pee Vee Probert's signature squat-legged swagger caught my attention. But when he saw me, I could've sworn he deliberately ducked behind somebody. And disappeared.

I left my whiskered commentator rocking on his boot heels and dodged through the crowd. Onlookers had spilled off the narrow edging and started to fill one lane of the bridge. Passing traffic was forced to navigate the bridge single file.

Craning my neck to catch a glimpse of Pee Vee, I bounced off a guy whose belly stretched his *Damn, I'm Good* T-shirt all out of shape. Then I careened right into Deputy Rudy Mellin.

"Have you seen Pee Vee Probert?" I asked.

Rudy hitched his pants up and nodded, not trying very hard to wipe the grin off his face. "Don't tell me you've thrown poor ol' Donlee—pardon the pun—over for that shrimp."

"Rudy."

The reprimand in my voice penetrated his sarcasm enough that he dipped his head slightly before he answered. "I was just questionin' Pee Vee. He rode over here with me, so I reckon he's still around."

"Questioning him? About what happened here?"

Rudy studied the activity downstream before answering. "He knows something, all right. Trouble is, whatever it is, he's lyin' about it."

"And my guess is, Pee Vee's not a very good liar."

Rudy pursed his lips in agreement. "So what do you think happened?"

"What would I know? L.J. mentioned that Pee Vee and Donlee took off together yesterday afternoon. I half expected a call from the drunk tank. I sure never expected this."

Rudy didn't say anything, just stared downstream. I couldn't help notice that folks gave us a wider berth when they strolled past. A couple of kids stared back over their shoulders at Rudy. Probably admiring his gun.

"You really think he jumped?" I asked.

Rudy heaved his shoulders in a shrug. "Don't know. Donlee's not what anybody'd call bright on his best days. Drunk, who knows what he'd do. He might've jumped. Or been pushed."

"Pushed? What—you don't mean Pee Vee?"

He shrugged again. "He's lyin' about something. He twitches, his eyes blinkin' and flittin' around, keeps sayin' 'You gotta believe me' and 'If I'm lyin', I'm dyin'.' Anybody spends that much time insisting he's telling the truth, he's gotta be lying. I just can't tell about what."

"Well, neither one makes any sense—jumping or getting pushed. How could Pee Vee get the better of somebody Donlee's size? How'd you find out about this, anyway?"

"Call came in to the nine-one-one dispatcher. From a pay phone down next to the auto repair shop." He nodded toward town. "Wouldn't give a name. Said he'd seen a big guy, a guy he knew as Donlee Griggs, throw himself off the Cane Creek Bridge. Said he was drivin' by. And to hurry. Then he hung up."

I hesitated before asking, "You think this is another hoax, one of Donlee's pranks?"

His expression was serious and, to his credit, Rudy didn't take the opportunity to give me a hard time about Donlee and the Luna Lake incident. That same chivalrous restraint didn't apply, unfortunately, to Pudd Pardee.

"Well, A'vry. Fittin' that you should be here." Pudd had rolled up behind us, the crowd parting around his rescue squad truck. "What a tragic end for unrequited love. Kinda like Romeo and Juliet, it-n't it? Young love denied. Well, not so young, maybe."

One flabby arm on the window frame, he leaned half in and half out of his truck.

"Yeah, but Juliet killed herself," I said. "Not the head of the county rescue squad. So that'd be another difference."

Pudd probably detected a tinge of sarcasm in my voice. He caressed his steering wheel and turned to Rudy.

"Rudy, you seen Willy up here? We need him down under the bridge. He's got dive experience and they need help mannin' those guy-ropes they're using."

Rudy shook his head. "Haven't seen him. Sorry."

"Don't reckon you could help us out there, A'vry. You bein' the cause of Donlee's tragic end and all. It'd make a nice photo opportunity for the newspaper." He guffawed as he raised his hand to wave at a weed-thin fellow with two cameras hung around his neck.

The photographer barely nodded, intent on worming his way up to the bridge railing. The crowd had grown to carnival proportions, with Pudd cast as chief clown. Before he could dazzle us with any more repartee, he tapped the accelerator enough to lurch forward, narrowly missing an elderly fellow in overalls. "There's Willy." He'd spotted somebody farther along the bridge, and inched off through the crowd without so much as a fond farewell.

"I'd better be going, too," I said to Rudy. A

glance at my watch told me I'd already missed Sunday School and, no matter how quickly I moved, I'd be late to church.

I stepped into the pew and stood beside Dad as the organist finished the chords introducing the "Doxology." The hair on the back of my neck still felt damp, but I had managed to find both halves of the same pair of shoes at my parents' house.

Across the aisle, Aunt Letha leaned around Vinnia so she could give me a meaningful stare.

During the lengthy pastoral prayer, the preacher—a newcomer to Dacus First Baptist and barely older than I am—refrained from dramatic references to any local events and, instead, focused on dramatic references to national events: crime, political hot spots, unrest, the recent elections.

I whispered a prayer for that big dumb weirdo Donlee Griggs. Part of me fumed, certain that he'd either gotten drunk and done something stupid or stayed sober and done something stupid. The other part of me felt guilty for fuming.

"Our Scripture lesson today comes from James's letter to the New Testament Christians, the New Revised Standard translation." The preacher—what was his name?—grasped the lectern with both hands and gave us a reading.

Aunt Vinnia caught my attention from across the aisle by surreptitiously waving her hand until I noticed the movement. Of course, by then, half of three pews had noticed.

"Lunch?" she mouthed, her eyebrows raised.

I darted a glance at my parents. Dang, I'd forgotten to mention it to them. I shrugged and nodded. Aunt Letha leaned forward with another, sterner look. I faced forward before she decided to come over and rap my knuckles.

" 'They are like those who look at themselves in a mirror; for they look at themselves and, on going away, immediately forget what they were like.' May God bless the reading and hearing of His Word."

I lost the context he'd planned for those verses as Granddad's journal entry came flooding to mind, his observations about how little we know of other people. How do other people see me? If I stared at a mirror, what would I remember when I walked away? If I knew so little of myself, how in the hell could I hope to know anything about anybody else?

What about folks I knew well now—what had they been at other times in their lives? If I'd been my granddad's age, would we have liked each other? When he was a young lawyer, how much of the old lawyer and judge had been there? Would he like the grown-up I'd become? Would Aunt Letha and I have been chums?

I must have shuddered at that thought because Dad turned slightly to look at me. He caught my attention and winked.

The service closed with one of my favorite hymns: "Count Your Many Blessings." But the organist must have forgotten to take her Geritol. The enthusiastic young mother singing loudly in front of me nearly hyperventilated from holding the first word on each chorus.

The usual crush headed to the door to shake the preacher's hand and beat the Presbyterians to the cafeteria. Aunt Letha caught up with my parents and pulled them along in her undertow.

When I got to my great-aunts' house, I parked on the street behind a battered gold Nova that belonged, it turned out, to a widower living in the elder-care apartments across town. Mr. O'Hara, who smelled faintly of mothballs and Old English furniture polish, didn't say much. So he fit right in between Vinnia and Hattie, where he quietly smiled around at everyone and ate his mashed potatoes, which didn't all manage to stay inside his mouth.

As the bowls of potatoes, gravy, coleslaw, oven-fried chicken, rolls, apple salad, and vegetables circled the table, Vinnia asked, "Avery, so how was your meeting with Harrison Garnet? Has he hired you to be his attorney? What does he want you to do? Make sure he pays you a lot. He's richer than Zeus. And what about that awful fire?"

"Well—"

"Vinnia, for heaven's sakes," Letha said, "you can't expect Avery to go around violatin' her attorney-client privilege. And Harrison Garnet didn't get rich by givin' his money away, I can tell you that. The only one in that family who's allowed to spend money is Sylvie Garnet. That's why she married him, and that's why she's kept him around all these years."

"Aletha." Hattie handed her the butter dish. "Now

be careful. Let the sermon stick to you just a little while."

"And just what did I say? Nothing that wasn't the word of truth."

Hattie didn't miss a beat. "Preacher must be saving the part in James about taming the tongue for a later sermon."

Letha pursed her lips and slathered butter on a hot biscuit, but didn't say anything else.

"What happened to Mr. Garnet," I asked, "that he's in a wheelchair?"

Vinnia made a *tsk-tsk*ing sound. "The saddest thing. He's developed some kind of circulatory problem. He can walk some, but it's certainly changed him a lot. He used to be such a vigorous, active man. He seems to be taking it well, though."

"The legs are the first to go," Letha said. "Bud's started having trouble getting up and down."

"Letha, I hardly think you can compare Harrison Garnet with your dog," Vinnia said.

"Don't know why not. They've both got bad legs. They both can't get up anymore without help. And they've both been known on occasion to wander after bitches in heat."

"Aletha," Hattie scolded. "You're digging up old history and I don't see—"

"You're right. Bud hasn't done that since I got him fixed."

"Those stories about Harrison Garnet are ancient history, and never were worth much credence."

"How can you say that? You know good and well

he was engaged to Olivia Sterling when he started keeping company with Sylvie Jones."

Her sisters should know better than to preach to Letha about minding her tongue; it just encourages her.

"Aletha, they've been married forty years. Isn't it time to put it to rest?"

"And Olivia's been single that long, practically left at the altar. Not that that's such a bad thing, mind you."

"Well, it is bad, if for no other reason than that Olivia minded so much." Vinnia sighed. "It devastated her. And to think, the whole thing was a cruel ruse."

"What?" I asked before another sermonette from Hattie squelched what sounded like a juicy tidbit.

"It just breaks my heart every time I think about it," Vinnia said. "I so worried about Olivia at the time. Feared she might do herself harm, she was so distraught."

"Olivia Sterling was engaged to Harrison Garnet?" I knew Olivia Sterling as a family friend and as the high school secretary. Tall and willowy, she'd finished Winthrop when it served as a girls' school training teachers and secretaries. She'd always been, for me, the quintessential career woman of that era. This painted her in a dramatically different light.

"Engaged and weeks away from the wedding," Vinnia said. "There'd been parties. Harrison's dad had a house, one he usually rented out, for them to live in. The bridesmaids' dresses were being made.

She had her wedding gown all ready. Then Harrison Garnet shows up at her parents' doorstep sheep-faced. Says he's sorry, he hopes she'll understand, but he just can't marry her. Then he stumps off down the sidewalk and disappears into the cool spring evening." Vinnia sighed.

"Only to reappear days later with Sylvie Jones on his arm," Hattie added.

"Well, I guess those things happen," I said, though I couldn't see choosing Sylvie over Olivia Sterling, given the choice.

"No, those things seldom just happen." Letha snorted. "At least not to Sylvie. No, more likely those things are well engineered. 'Course, Harrison Garnet's like most men—gullible and egotistical in the same, confused mix. Sylvie took him by the nose—or something—and led him down the prover-bial path. Idiot fellow didn't have sense enough to question her claim that she was pregnant. Reckon he figured out she lied to him when it took Harry Junior another four or five years to be born."

"She lied about being pregnant?"

"That was rumored." Hattie's tone said she thought such rumors best not encouraged. "But, of course, Sylvie never said anything to anybody."

"Didn't have to," Letha countered. "That hang-dog look Harrison Garnet wore around town told everybody he'd jumped the fence. Serves him right, he found himself penned up with a she-dog a right-thinking man would've avoided."

"Letha—"

"Sylvie Garnet made up a story like that to trick a

man into marrying her?" I thought that cheesy ploy
had been invented for soap opera audiences.

"Sylvie Garnet would've stuck a firecracker up
her butt and shot herself in a flaming arc across the
sky if she thought it'd land her a man with money,"
Letha pronounced. "Sylvie always knows what she
wants and she always manages to fix things so she
gets them. If I had my guess, she'll get that son of
hers elected governor or God himself'll be explaining why."

"Harry's really considering a run for governor?"
I said.

All three of my aunts and both of my otherwise-
quiet parents nodded. My dad, obviously relieved to
have the conversation shift, said, "Apparently some
of the political powers think a fresh, new face can
make a run against the traditional state machine."

"Well, if it's a fresh face they want, that's Harry
Garnet." I knew Harrison's son. A brain, no. I'd always figured Harry to be damned lucky to have a
daddy with money. He'd tried several business ventures around town, leaving a string of disasters and
questionable dealings behind him.

"And speaking of jumping fences," I said, "how
do the political handlers plan to deal with Harry's
lively history? Just think who'll be coming out of
the woodwork, dying to talk to the newspapers."

"Avery, now . . ." my mother cautioned.

"Emma, you know good and well she's tellin' the
truth," Letha said in my defense. "Nuts don't fall
very far from the tree. Harrison Garnet didn't learn

from his mistakes and neither did his son. Randy as goats, both of 'em."

"Letha," Vinnia said, "you have no way of knowing that for certain."

I started to volunteer my friend Cissie Prentice as a reliable source on young Harry's history, but decided that might raise embarrassing questions about how she knew so much. After all, she based everything on one brief interlude after a Dacus Dance Club Christmas party, on the pool chairs at the Ramada Inn.

"Don't get so prim on me, Vinnia," Letha said. "Everybody in town knows about it. Why, he ran around with that little Lea Hopkins, even after she married."

"Harrison Garnet had an affair with Lea Hopkins?" I said, confused.

"No, no. Harry. Sylvie Garnet 'bout had a cow. You can imagine how she reacted. White trash, and married white trash at that." Letha reached in front of Mr. O'Hara for another biscuit.

"Now, Letha, just because Lea was a little wild doesn't mean she was trash."

"Okay, then, a tramp."

"Was their affair common knowledge?" Being back home made me realize I'd missed out on a lot of good stuff over the years.

"No. Not really. I knew because Sylvie and I were working together on something about that time. She mentioned things she thought cryptic, until you put 'em together with other things being talked about around town. Then you were left with a pretty clear impression that something naughty was going on."

Letha paused before taking a bite of her jelly-slathered biscuit. "Come to think of it, the police asked Harry a few questions when she disappeared. That'd make interesting campaign material: a former murder suspect presents his crime bill proposal."

"My," said Vinnia, ignoring Letha's sarcasm, "think what must be going through Sylvie's mind now that poor girl's body's been found. She probably rejoiced when she disappeared. Think how bad she must feel now, knowing that Lea was dead and in Luna Lake all that time."

Letha snorted. "Feeling bad? Sylvie's only regret is that, had she known sooner, she could have figured out how to walk on water so she could dance on the watery grave."

"Letha." Hattie's voice said clearly she considered the topic exhausted. "Harry's married now and settled down. Some smart young lady from Charleston."

Under Hattie's guidance, the conversation took a less catty turn. I excused myself before they cut the pecan pie—which required a tremendous act of will. The funeral started at one.

The crowd at the new Baldwin and Bates Funeral Home, built on a hill overlooking the new commercial bypass, outstripped the Georgian brick's capacity to handle it. I arrived early, but the closest parking spot was in the grass beyond the back lot.

Amazing how many friends a woman missing for fifteen years still has, I thought wryly.

"Amazing how many ghouls and vultures live in a town this small," Cissie Prentice said, appearing at my elbow and magically reading my thoughts. "Present company excepted."

"I had a personal invitation," I smarted back.

"From a skeleton. Sure you did. Or did you find out how cute the grieving husband is? A bit old. But much in need of consolin', don't you think?"

Cissie signed the family book and handed me the pen. She still drew little circles over the *i*'s in her name.

Cissie had chosen a deep-burgundy dress that clung to her like kitchen wrap—her idea of appropriate mourning attire. Even I stared as she sat and crossed her legs.

"How do you walk in those heels?" I whispered.

"Hell, I can balance a cup and saucer on my foot while—"

I tried to forestall any more graphic details by leaning across Cissie to greet Mr. Earnest, the barber. We said polite hellos in properly subdued funeral-home tones while Cissie grinned at me maliciously.

I glared at her as I settled back. She replied by carefully recrossing her legs, giving Mr. Earnest more of a show than he'd bargained for at a funeral.

The organ set up a wheezy, high-pitched whine, mournful in a way the organist likely didn't intend. She'd cranked out several measures before I recognized "Amazing Grace."

The flower display stood directly in front of us.

At funerals, I always hear my granddad's voice: "Nothing sadder than a funeral with no flowers." The organist modulated into "The Sweet By and By," piercingly shrill on the high notes.

I leaned over and whispered into Cissie's ear, "You ever hear anything about Lea Bertram and Harry Garnet?"

She gave me a boy-are-you-out-of-it look, eloquently spoken with one raised eyebrow.

"Me and everybody else," she whispered. "They were one hot item for quite a while."

"When?"

She shrugged and leaned toward my ear. "Sometime after she married. But it ended before she disappeared, for sure."

"So she and Bertram had been married, what? Two or three years?"

"I guess."

"Was Harry the only one?"

Cissie shrugged again, the effect on her mourning attire drawing Mr. Earnest's attention. "Probably not. They were spotted together often enough that she'd have been hard put to work anybody else into her schedule. But don't you remember her scandalizing everybody, riding around with one of those motorcycle guys? Said she was just catching a ride to work." Cissie's raised eyebrow questioned that claim.

I settled back onto the wooden pew and chewed on the inside of my lip. Cissie had always been a precociously well informed gossip, but she was a high school kid at the time. If she'd known about Lea, plenty of adults had, too.

Had Melvin Bertram known? Did he follow Lea up the mountain one day, expecting to thwart a tryst? Or had Lea accidentally rolled her car into the water? Had somebody been there with her? Somebody who'd kept his mouth shut all these years? Maybe somebody who, with a gubernatorial race ahead of him now, would especially want to keep things buried in red mud and silt? Or was I jumping to too many conclusions? I hadn't seen any of the Garnets in the funeral crowd. I guess an employer's social obligation expires at some point.

The rich copper gleam of the casket picked up the golden tones of the russet-tipped roses blanketing the top. The sight of the casket surprised me. Maybe they'd released the remains after all.

Reverend Brown, from the Presbyterian church, read from a small white Testament. The words floated around us like a soothing, somber comfort. " 'Neither death, nor life' "—his voice resonant and warm—" 'will be able to separate us' " . . .

Fortunately he skipped the ashes-to-ashes part. No ashes, just mud-stained bones. And those grinning teeth.

I shut my eyes, bowed my head, and let the sounds wash over me: the quiet rustling of paper programs, the creak of wooden pews as mourners squirmed. The funeral chapel was packed, although the only actual mourners were probably Melvin Bertram and a thin, blond fellow sitting beside him. Lea's brother? Melvin's brother?

The rest of the watchers were looky-lous. Folks like Cissie—and me—who'd been drawn by a morbid fascination. Quiet sniffs and snuffles were notably absent. Few tissues would be sacrificed to false emotion today. And, tastefully, the Reverend Brown didn't whip out a eulogy designed to elicit those tears.

From where I sat, I couldn't see Melvin's face until the congregation stood. We sang a couple of verses of "Peace Like a River" while the family filed out. Melvin didn't scan the crowd to see if anyone he'd invited had come. Hard to tell the difference between a hangover and deep mourning. And hard to describe what made him look off balance. He had dressed in a conservative navy suit, white shirt, and subdued tie. Not a hair lay out of place. His gaze stayed on the red carpet runner all the way up the center aisle.

Melvin left, escorted by the fellow who'd been sitting with him and another slightly built man who would have looked more at home at a Little League game. No one stopped them by reaching out with a comforting hand or a murmur of condolence. The attendees stood around more as audience than mourners.

No graveside service had been announced, so most folks strolled to their cars, enjoying the lazy, cool Sunday afternoon.

"Cissie," I said to draw her attention from the limousine disappearing down the winding drive. "How certain are you that Lea Bertram had an affair with Harry Garnet?"

Her ponytail flipped sassily over her shoulder as

she turned to face me. "Well, why don't you ask the cops? They believed it enough to question Junior at some length when Lea disappeared. Of course, they didn't look too seriously at anybody but Lea's husband. From what I remember, Junior's mama saw to it that the sheriff's attention stayed focused somewhere else. Sylvie Garnet apparently raised holy hell when they came sniffing around her baby." Cissie paused, glancing at the line of cars streaming out the exit and down the hill.

"Reckon what led them to question Harry?"

She shrugged. "Guess cops follow up on gossip. And there was plenty. Even I remember it. I guess because Lea hadn't been out of high school that long. And she'd been a cheerleader."

Cissie had also been a cheerleader. They must maintain some sort of cult relationship, binding across the years. Of course, Cissie had been asked to leave the squad her senior year for conduct unbecoming to a cheerleader. Whatever that was, we'd never talked about it. "Seems like," Cissie said thoughtfully, "I remember somebody said they saw him in her car? No, somebody saw his car—I remember he drove this boss silver Cadillac—following her car up the mountain road. But he must have had some explanation." She shrugged, her dress straining dramatically.

"Or the eyewitness made a mistake," I added. "That happens more often than the times an eyewitness sees it straight."

"Looks like the parking lot's cleared out enough.

I'm heading home for a nap. I have to catch up on the sleep I missed last night." She grinned slyly. "Stayed up late to see the comet. You seen it yet?"

"No, not yet." And I probably wouldn't see it from the vantage point she'd had. "Does the *Kama Sutra* recommend anything special for comet watching?"

She smirked as she climbed into a glowing white Lexus sedan and closed the door.

"Like the new car," I mouthed as she turned to wave.

She waggled her fingers in reply and swooped down the winding drive. My faded Mustang cranked right up, and I followed.

As I turned onto Broad Street, the flapping red, white, and blue banners and miniature flags lining the walk caught my attention. The billboard-size *Garnet for Governor* signs made it clear this was no used-car lot.

On a whim, I pulled into the parking lot beside what had been a car dealer's showroom. *Experience: for a Change* banners festooned its circled glass windows. Experience at what? Harry probably hoped few voters asked, with his string of business failures and aborted get-rich-quick schemes.

Movement amid the patriotic posters inside the showroom windows caught my eye and I climbed out of the car.

"Hello?" I called as I pushed open the unlocked glass door. "Anybody home?"

At first, only the fresh chemical smell of newly

printed posters greeted me. Then a head topped by a soft corkscrew afro popped around the door frame of one of the old sales offices lining the back of the showroom.

"Uh . . . yes?" Her eyes round in her milk-chocolate face, she looked startled at having visitors. "May I help you?" Her hands smoothed the sides of her denim dress.

"I just noticed your headquarters. And I knew Harry years ago—in school. He's not around, is he?"

What were the odds of that? Pretty good, as it turned out. Harry appeared behind the elf-life black woman, his white shirt unbuttoned at the neck, his cuffs rolled up a notch or two.

He looked puzzled for a few seconds too long, then he blinked in recognition. "Avery? Avery Andrews. Is that you?" I got the distinct impression I'd interrupted something.

He stepped around the clutter of boxes, his hand extended. *Bet they'll lock the door next time.*

"Sorry to interrupt, but I saw your new headquarters here. Pretty exciting, Harry."

The young campaign worker hung back in the doorway, not intruding but not returning to the office, either.

"Yep," Harry said, reflexively running his hand along the waistband of his pants, tucking in his shirt. "Had no idea how much work was involved, running for statewide office." He fixed me with a smile that looked like he popped it out of a can and pasted it on as needed. The smile never quite reached his eyes.

"I'm sure. Isn't this a bit early in the campaign season, though? Next November's a long way off."

Harry shook his head. "I thought so, too. But not according to the calendar the party guys keep. They assure me there's plenty to keep us busy."

His eyes scouted around me, as if he were searching a crowded room for a more deserving audience. Must be a politician's reflex, because only the sun-bright windows stood behind me.

Before the lull in the conversation got uncomfortable, a newcomer joined us. I saw the slender, golden woman approaching outside the windows before Harry did. But she had eyes only for him—storm blue eyes, expensively enlarged by artful makeup. One eyebrow arched in a sharp question.

"Glad to see the door's not locked." Her husky voice dripped acid. "Hello, Lori."

The young woman bobbed her curls in a nod and evaporated out of sight into the office.

The slender woman with the golden hair and the golden suit then turned to me. The eyebrow arched again as she studied me from head to foot.

Harry, who'd stood frozen like a possum in traffic, recovered the social graces his mother had no doubt pounded into him.

"Lindley, I'd like you to meet Avery Andrews. We grew up together. You're—a lawyer now, aren't you, Avery?" His receiving-line smile occupied only part of his face.

"I sure am." I extended my hand and grasped Lindley's long, cool fingers. She finished her physical examination, finally looking me in the eye, her eyebrow still slightly cocked.

"Avery, this is my wife, Lindley Duncan Garnet."

Of the Duncans and Lindleys, I half expected him to say.

"So nice to meet you, Lindley. Helping Harry on the campaign trail, I see."

She graced me with part of a smile. Her direct gaze testified to her low-country roots more volubly than her round, mushy vowels. "It's so nice to finally meet some of Harrison's friends."

It took me a blink to realize that she meant Harry rather than his dad. So much for the folksy touch of campaigning with your childhood nickname.

"Since Harrison and I met in graduate school at Carolina—we were both getting our MBAs—we haven't spent much time here in Dacus." She talked now on autopilot while she studied Harry. Probably a useful skill for a politician's wife, to talk cheerfully about nothing while keeping a sharp eye all around.

I knew I should be feeling sorry for her, having to keep Harry's leash so short. But I found myself feeling sorry for shallow, stupid Harry. And for cute little Lori. And whoever else got between Lindley Duncan Garnet and whatever she had her eye on.

"I know you folks must be busy. I just stopped in on my way home. From Lea Bertram's funeral. Did you all attend?" I hoped I looked innocently wide-eyed.

Harry gave the reaction I expect in a witness uncomfortable with the direction of a cross-examination. He licked his lips, glanced quickly upward to his left, and looked like somebody who wanted to lie.

"Um—no. No, we didn't go. We—"

Lindley glided the few steps to Harry's side, touching her hand to his shoulder blade, cutting him off. "No, we didn't attend. Harrison's candidacy doesn't mean he has to appear at every morbid circus that comes to town."

I smiled sweetly. "Oh, I wasn't really thinking of Harry's candidacy. I was thinking of Lea's relationship with Garnet Mills. After all, she had"—I paused—"an employment relationship with the Garnets."

Lindley's hand on his back and her puppet-master posture couldn't control the flush that crept up past Harry's unbuttoned shirt collar and across his tanned, fleshy cheeks.

Lindley kept speaking for him. "Harrison isn't Garnet Mills or its representative," she said smoothly. "Joining a display like that funeral would serve no good purpose."

The flush on Harry's face began to recede. Harry, bless his heart, had found himself quite a handler.

"Well," I said, "I didn't mean to take up so much of your time. I know you all have plenty to keep you busy." But Lindley seemed up to the task.

Harry resumed his role of the jovial host and escorted me to the door. Lindley turned into the office where Lori had taken refuge.

What were the words to that old song? Something about marrying a girl just like the girl who'd married dear old dad? Poor Harry.

I drove directly to the cabin, relishing the occasional squeak of a rear tire when I pushed it too hard in a curve. I also relished the silence of the cabin, which seemed an odd reaction, following a funeral. But, after the polite small talk and strained emotion, the unbroken silence comfortably held me.

I changed into jeans and took the Sunday paper I'd filched from my aunts out to the back porch. The sun warmed the porch this time of day, and the rickety wooden rocker facing the water would allow me to soak up the silence.

Unexpectedly, the deafening roar of what sounded like an angry invading army of giant hornets shattered the quiet.

Eleven

The sound of the motorcycle engines grew from the first faint buzz in the distance. By the time they'd reached the end of my rutted driveway and what passed for the cabin's backyard, even the shelter of the cabin couldn't protect me from the din.

The thundering reverberations—so at odds with the Sunday quiet—chilled the skin on my arms. I have to admit I wanted to crawl under the porch and hide. But it offered precious little cover.

I slipped inside the screen door, retrieved my .38 pistol from its hiding place in a canvas bag, and slipped it into the back waistband of my jeans.

In books, the hero or heroine always makes that sound like a simple maneuver. But my jeans were too tight from too many home-cooked meals. And no one ever mentions how cold gun barrels are. Or how heavy guns are. On second thought, good thing my jeans were tight or they might have slid around my knees under the weight of my arsenal.

The cold metal felt reassuring—until I slipped

around the side of the house to spy who had come calling.

When I saw what sat in my yard, the gunmetal felt suddenly hot against my skin. I stood in the shadow of the cabin, trying to figure out my options. I had nowhere to run or hide. I had no idea how to get to Sadie Waynes's house. If I crossed either of the side yards toward the woods, I'd be on open ground. The still expanse of lake lay at my back. The cabin had no closets and I couldn't fit under the bed.

With no flight possibilities, I opted for a casually amused lean against the side of the cabin, watching two of them clump up the steps to my back door.

The one with a bandanna do-rag wrapped over his blond hair almost forgot to duck under the porch roof. He recovered and hiked his pants up from his beefy hips while his companion pounded on my door with a fist that threatened to splinter the weathered boards.

Then Do-Rag spotted me. I nodded curtly. Not the sort of greeting I'd give if the Frank Dobbins circle came calling. But a proper greeting. And wary.

Do-Rag thumped his companion on the arm and motioned to where I stood looking up at them. They were both big suckers.

The meat-fisted one sported a wiry mud-brown beard that filled his shirt front. His beard might once have reached to his waist, but his waist had grown off and left his beard high and dry. Both men carried a lot of extra weight—linebackers gone to seed. But I would put money on either one of them in an arm-wrestling match.

I touched my shirttail to make sure it covered the gun grip, then asked, "May I help you?"

"You A'vry Andrews?" Do-Rag asked.

"Mind if I ask why you're looking for her?"

"That's her," Ham Fist said. "Jodo said she 'uz a skinny, mouthy thing with reddish hair."

I prefer to think of my hair as burnished blonde, but since I had no idea who Jodo was, I likely wouldn't get the chance to explain.

"Max'd like a word with you." Do-Rag swung off the steps toward me.

"Max," I said.

Do-Rag cocked his head toward the assembled motorcycles. The gleam from the chrome bikes enlarged the perception of how many big men on big motorcycles sat in my yard.

"Well, tell Max to come on over and state his business."

I still stood at the corner of the cabin, with the yard and the lake at my back. How far could I swim in November water before hypothermia sapped me and sent me to the bottom? To the place Lea Bertram had recently vacated.

"Max'd like to talk to you there." Do-Rag jerked his head. He reached, as if to take my arm, but I made a little step back, then around him.

"Well, by all means. I didn't know he couldn't get off his bike."

Do-Rag spun and sandwiched me between him and Ham Fist, and we approached the circle of motorcycles like supplicants to a throne.

At the center of a loose circle of a dozen or so

bikes sat a thin-chested man with a heavy handlebar mustache and wild, dark hair. And even wilder eyes. He sat astraddle a Harley chopper, his arms crossed on his reedy chest.

"Hear you're friends with Sheriff Peters."

Odd introduction. "I've been accused of worse. But not lately."

Wry humor was wasted on this crowd.

"And you're old man Garnet's lawyer." He stated fact, no questions.

I kept my gaze level and struggled to keep a small smirk at the corner of my mouth. But I acknowledged nothing. What the hell was he after?

We stared at each other a moment more. "Need to get a message to the sheriff," he said. "Since it interests Garnet, thought you could pass it on."

"Why don't you just call L.J. yourself?"

That, they considered humorous. Smirks and snorts rippled mildly through the audience.

"L.J.," he said mincingly, "and I aren't on a first-name basis. And this information is best passed through somebody else. Somebody more—impartial."

He sat studying me, his arms still crossed. "We voted," he announced finally, emphasizing each word. "Unanimously." As if I understood—or cared.

A sense of unease seemed to move through the bikers. Which certainly didn't comfort me any.

"How do we get—what d'ya call it? Attorney-client protection."

"Privilege. Attorney-client privilege," I said, then winced inwardly at my schoolmarmish tone.

"Attorney-client privilege."

"By hiring an attorney. One who doesn't have a conflict of interest from representing another party involved in the matter. Which means you can't hire me if it has something to do with Harrison Garnet or Garnet Mills."

He pursed his lips. I don't think he'd blinked once the whole time we'd talked. "Okay. You can do this for free, then, since you don't represent us."

Ouch, hit a starving lawyer where it hurts.

He smiled. Or gave what I supposed passed for a smile—two buck teeth appeared beneath his handlebar mustache.

"I'm not sure I'll be able to—"

"Does Harrison Garnet want the cops to find the guy who torched his factory?"

That got my attention. "I'm sure he would." Assuming he hadn't done it himself.

"Well, tell L.J. that Noodle Waitley is in a house trailer up Crossover Road. Been holed up there since Thursday night. Sheriff's been looking for him, but don't know where he's at."

"Will the sheriff know which trailer?" Trailers have a way of reproducing quickly and easily if left in close proximity to one another and unsupervised for long enough.

"Only one after the fork in the road past the old Mitkin dairy."

"And what makes you so sure L.J. wants to visit with this Noodle?"

Something I said angered him. His careless slump straightened. "Because that bitch sheriff's been nosing around us ever since it happened. Can't get anything done without her or some pencil-whipped idiot sniffin' our butts like lovesick dogs."

"So you decided to do your civic duty."

His jaw muscles worked so hard his mustache twitched. His voice grew quiet, but I had no trouble hearing him. "Don't misunderstand me. Members don't rat each other out. What I'm doing here would ordinarily mean a death sentence for me. That's why the whole club came. Noodle's offense endangered the entire club. And for his own gain. He really left us no choice. We're just taking care of business."

"So this is sort of like the black spot, huh?"

Maybe he hadn't read *Treasure Island* in his mis-spent youth. Or he'd forgotten it in his misspent adulthood. He must have thought I'd made fun of him, because that jaw muscle started working again.

"Just pass it on to the sheriff."

"You still haven't told me anything that would help the sheriff. Why's she targeted you all, anyway? And how do I know you're not setting up me or my client—or even this Noodle fellow—for something?"

He leaned forward slightly onto the handlebars of his bike. "The sheriff's targeted us, as you say, be-cause Noodle was dumbshit enough to be seen at the wrong place at the wrong time. He'd taken to hang-ing around Garnet Mills drawing a lot of unneces-sary attention. We can't seem to reason with the sheriff."

I nodded sympathetically at that. I'd known L.J. since the third grade. Nobody could reason with her unless he got her attention first—maybe with a croquet mallet. "Hanging around doing what?"

"Collecting on debts from some of the workers. Don't make sense we'd burn that plant down to get to one deadbeat." He shook his head sadly.

"That's what L.J. thinks? That you killed a—client—and burned the plant?" Why was I cataloging the scenario for a possible hit? Especially since Max didn't look pleased.

"Lot of our steady customers work at that plant. Customers can't spend their paychecks doing business with us if they ain't got paychecks. We're not stupid. We're businessmen."

He didn't even try to choke out the word *legitimate*. Businessmen who ride Harleys, wear do-rags, chains, and full beards, and who likely sell drugs, women, and whatever else isn't nailed down. I didn't ask him for a sales brochure.

"Just so you can check what I'm telling you, tell the sheriff he used a garden sprayer. It's one of his trademarks. Dumbshit probably has the thing with him up at the trailer."

I hoped my face didn't give away too much at his mention of the garden sprayer.

"So you've all agreed to turn him in," I said. "To take the heat off the—club."

"And because he did it. Man went out on his own, doing his own shit. Now he's like a bad stink comin' back on us. Can't have that."

He crossed his arms to punctuate the finality of that statement.

"I'll call Sheriff Peters."

"Done." He nodded and stood to kick-start his bike, then paused. "Just a word of advice, lady. You always this much of a bitch to get along with, you gonna have one hell of a time making it in the lawyering business around here."

The roar of a dozen engines drowned out any reply I might have made. I gave a salutary wave as they spun their bikes in a complicated ballet around my yard. Too bad. Those were probably the only members of the criminal element in Camden County who could afford to pay for legal counsel. And I'd alienated them.

I went into the cabin through the front door to pull the .38 pistol out of my waistband. The trigger guard had cut a biscuit out of my rump.

With my knees shaking just a bit, I grabbed my car keys and drove to the country store.

I had to admit, painfully, that the biker's parting words stung a bit. How long would the bitter taste of being fired from the Calhoun Firm last? Was I hard to get along with? Was that my fatal flaw—or at least a symptom of it? True, I'd lost my patience with an important trial witness—a witness who'd turned out to be not only a renowned physician, but a liar and a perjurer.

I'd certainly tested the patience of my supervising partner, who'd been a crude and abusive womanizer. In introspective moments, I considered filing a formal sexual harassment charge. The statutory 180-day filing period hadn't yet expired. Witnesses to his abuse were plentiful, and many were victims themselves.

Making him and the Calhoun Firm squirm would be a delight. But filing a complaint would seal my fate; never a hope of another big-firm partnership.

And it was still too close in time and pain. I knew what a lawsuit entailed, the psychic energy it sapped. I could only imagine what my clients had endured, having their lives examined under a microscope in front of a roomful of people they didn't know—strangers, news reporters—or worse, people they cared about. I certainly didn't want any of that for myself. Better to focus on the future.

At the store, I called L.J. Even sheriffs and their deputies have to take time off, I know. But I wish they wouldn't leave idiots to take messages when they go. It doesn't leave me feeling particularly safe.

The junior G-man read my message back to me in a whistley voice that didn't sound as if he had reached puberty yet. He promised to call L.J. at home. I trusted that he would call because he sounded excited—and more shrill—when he heard the name Noodle. I took that as a sign that the sheriff's department had actually been looking for Noodle. Where does a biker tough pick up a nickname like that? I probably didn't want to know.

To reward myself for my civic good deed, I counted out the change in my jeans pocket, just enough for a banana Moon Pie. Even without an RC Cola, Moon Pies are one of nature's most perfect foods.

I gunned the Mustang down the winding few miles back to the cabin, enjoying the scenery flashing past and the stiff, almost unmanageable wheel in my hand. Surely no one who hadn't grown up in Dacus could appreciate its prickly charm. Coming home to a place I'd been all too anxious to leave affected me in powerful but indecipherable ways. Most of my friends had left for college when I had and most had never come home. I certainly hadn't planned on ever coming back. I couldn't remember even an instant in my life when I'd mentally tried on the idea of living in Dacus, and certainly never a time when I thought the idea fit.

The way the roads dipped and turned, disappearing and reappearing in the distance, the red clay soil, the rusted house trailers with yards full of red-stained kiddie cars and hound dogs, the way people studied whoever walked through the door of Maylene's for lunch, the solemn stares of greeting—all assaulted me, both with present impression and past memory. Something resonated deep within my breastbone that sometimes made breathing an exercise I had to focus on, impressions that wouldn't have registered had I not been away, then come home with things to compare them to.

In such a short time, I now thought of "downstate" as a distant, alien country. And this odd place, nestled into the lush and brooding Blue Ridge, with its solemn, distant people, felt welcoming.

By the time I'd pulled into the yard, the shadows had lengthened beyond dusk.

Squatting, I flipped the boat onto its bottom and studied the inside for any crawling life-forms. A lone spider scuttled down the side.

One foot inside, I struggled to balance and shove at the same time. I felt like a hog on ice. How silly to feel so awkward doing something I'd done dozens of times before, in this same boat off this same grassy bank.

My muscles eventually remembered what my mind had forgotten. When I let my instinct take over and quit trying to force the rhythm of the paddle in the water, things went more smoothly.

Had I been more practiced, I would have checked the bottom of the boat for leaks. Several yards from shore, I remembered, then tentatively peered into the darkened bottom and slapped my sneaker around, listening for the telltale slosh. Nothing.

The boat slid smoothly toward the center of the lake, never quite reaching the place where the moon's reflection lay, but always gliding along the drawing light it cast. I laid the paddle beside me, the loud thud announcing my stealthy bobbing to anyone listening. Amazing, how water supports boats. I lay back across the seats, my rump suspended above the boat's bottom. Not a comfortable position, but one that brought floods of memory.

I listened to the water lapping the boat on either side of my head. The stars overhead were countless. Not a city sky, but a dark sky painted bright by pinpricks of light. I twisted slightly. I spotted the Big Dipper, and there, like a smudge of light, was the comet. And its tail. Was that an optical illusion? Did it really stretch back across the sky that far? It looked as though someone had taken a finger and smeared a long, faint streak across the sky.

I lay suspended between sky and water, between the dark, painted bright sky showing off its smudgy visitor nine million miles away and the dark, lapping water. Water that showed off its secrets only occasionally—only when it wanted to or only after a fight, when they were wrestled loose by a storm. Or a wrecker winch.

With the lapping sound came the image of water churning around the rusted sheet metal of the car. The car that had sat submerged in the very water where I floated, sealing its secret in murk and mud for fifteen years.

Had I floated on this water, in this very boat, somewhere over that silent, horrible crypt? How many people had swum and fished and picnicked and made love floating on this still, dark water while she floated below, sealed in her rusting two-toned Thunderbird?

Panic seized me. Spooked, I sat upright, wobbling the rickety boat dangerously. I fumbled with the paddle, my fist a white-knuckled ball around the handle for fear I'd drop it as I paddled toward shore.

Flailing toward shore more aptly described my progress. One of the perversities of water is that slow, steady movements are always more effective than powerful assaults. But unreasoned fear never learns.

I dragged the boat as far onto the grassy bank as I could but didn't take time to flip it upside down. A shot of adrenaline electrified the hairs on the backs of my wrists.

I ran to the sheltering porch. As I reached for the doorknob, a low voice came from the shadows of the porch.

"You left your door unlocked."

Twelve

At the sound of the voice, I tried to yelp, but my terrified bolt across the lake and the yard didn't leave my lungs enough air. I couldn't see who sat in the shadows.

"Sorry," the voice said, the speaker certainly able to see my fright. "Didn't mean to startle you. Came over to check on you."

Sadie Waynes. I didn't know whether to hug the woman or slap her. I merely nodded, my hand on my chest. In the gloom, I couldn't make out her rawboned face or the thick gray braided club of her hair.

"Heard them motorcycles earlier. Didn't think much about it. Thought they 'uz just passin'. Till I heard 'em start up again after a bit."

The rocking chair where she sat creaked once. "I come straightaway, but you 'uz gone. Got right worried. Then I saw the boat out there. Moon's bright."

I nodded, trying to soften my huffing.

"So I decided to wait." She didn't say anything about my frenzied paddling or my mad dash from the boat. Which probably meant I'd looked really stupid. Maybe if I'd dashed into the bathroom or something, I could have saved a little face. Doubtful.

"Thanks for checking on me. I really appreciate it. My motorcycle visitors were a scary bunch. Glad to know you were there."

"Yep. Caught sight of 'em down the road, as I came over the hill."

"I'm sure glad to know you can hear stuff that happens here. You know. Back up at your house."

"Been hard to miss a dozen souped-up 'cycles," she said matter-of-factly. " 'Course, lots goes on up here that it's best to keep an eye on."

Her rocking chair set up a slow, measured creak. "Not that folks always want to know what you've seen," she added.

The steady creak came as an invitation. I pulled the other rocking chair across the porch, scraping it over the rough boards, and joined her in the gloom. Sadie didn't seem in any hurry to leave, now that she was here. And I couldn't very well leave; it was my porch.

We spent a few minutes rocking, watching the moon streak the lake with pale color. To make conversation, finally I said, "I got to admit, being on that lake tonight spooked me a bit."

She didn't say anything.

"I got to thinking about that car, with that girl trapped in it, under the water for all those years."

Gentle creaking came as the only reply.

"Were you living up here then? When she disappeared? Did they look for her around here?"

"Yep. I 'uz here, all right. Lived here all my life.

Before there 'uz even a lake. And yeah, they looked for her here. Found some of her painting stuff left on a picnic table near the lake. Not a sign of her anywhere."

She paused long enough that I thought the story had ended, but then she added, "They even drug the lake looking for her."

"How could they miss a whole car?"

I sensed rather than saw Sadie shrug beside me. "Had divers and boats and big iron grappling hooks. Spent a coupla days. Hard to imagine missin' a car in a little puddle of water like that. But the fellas said at the time that the visibility 'uz so bad, they wouldn't know if the *Titanic* had sunk in there."

I studied the lake. I knew from swimming in it that the water stayed murky and red-stained, particularly after heavy rain churned the muddy bottom.

"'Course, they weren't lookin' for a car. Only a body. They thought her car'd been stolen and her dumped in the lake. Nobody really expected to find a car under there. Maybe if they'd listened at the time. But then, even I 'uz surprised."

"Listened?"

She took a pause before she answered. "I seen her. That day. I told 'em."

I turned to face her. "You saw Lea Bertram up here the day she disappeared?"

In the reflected moonlight, she nodded. The angles of her large-boned face were solemn.

"Nothin' that mattered, a 'course. But still. Her family musta been upset, not knowin' for so long. But they wouldn't listen."

"Her family?"

"No, no. The po-lice. They had it figgered that she ran off with somebody. But the somebody I saw her with didn't make sense to them. Guess even then, I 'uz just a crazy old mountain woman. What did I know?"

"You saw her up here with somebody? And they wouldn't listen?"

"Oh, they listened to me. But they listened louder to his mama. 'Course, who'd know best where her son was—me, what saw him with my own two eyes, or his momma?"

"Who'd you see, Miss Sadie?"

She rocked for a few beats. "I have to be accurate. Don't go listenin' to an old woman who lets her stories get a step ahead of the truth. If I 'uz full honest, I didn't see him that day. Only his car. But I seen him plenty enough times, just like that day. And her with her paintin' stuff sittin' on the table while they 'uz entertainin' themselves inside that big Cadillac. And that's what I told the po-lice."

"Whose car did you see, Miss Sadie?"

"That Garnet boy's."

"Harry Garnet?"

"As sad as it is, yes'm. His daddy's big silver Cadillac, the one he always drove up here to play in."

"To meet Lea Bertram?"

"Um-hmm."

"Did the cops ask about that? Did she ever meet other men up here?" My questions spilled out, except the one I couldn't ask: *Did her husband know?*

"I don't rightly know. Seems they started comin'

up after the summer folks packed up and went home. And it 'uz always that big silver Cadillac. Does seem her husband'd notice that she went away to paint a lot but never had any paintin's to show for it."

Now that she mentioned it, that part of the story had bothered me. Granted, I had known Lea Hopkins Bertram only by reputation, but she'd never sounded much like the dedicated-artist type.

"The cops questioned Harry Garnet. He must have had a plausible story."

The sound Sadie made wasn't quite rude enough to be a snort. She rocked a few creaks before she said, "Or a daddy with money and a momma with a sharp tongue."

I nodded a silent acknowledgment. The Garnet name would have been formidable protection. Now, launching a statewide campaign, Harry Garnet wouldn't want to be harvesting any long-planted wild oats.

We rocked with our own thoughts. That quiet lake—never more sound than the occasional lapping of tiny waves on mud banks—that lake must know so much, I mused. Surely the sheriff would've listened to Sadie Waynes, the quiet lady who knew so much.

Who had Sadie Waynes been fifteen years ago? Maybe lines on her face and gray in her hair lent her more authority now than she'd had then. Maybe the cops had seen someone far different than I saw now; the strong, watchful woman from over the ridge.

Even she admitted that she hadn't actually seen Harry Garnet that day. Only the car he usually drove. But surely Sheriff Jacobs had followed up on that.

Maybe what Sadie knew of the story had become shaded by time—or by the distance she felt from town people. Not even Harrison Garnet's position could have protected Harry if there'd been any serious suspicion that he'd been involved in Lea Bertram's disappearance.

But that was the key, wasn't it? Lea Bertram had simply disappeared. Run off with another man, so the story went. Would the sheriff have had a different take on Sadie Waynes's story if he'd known that Lea had run no farther than the bottom of Luna Lake?

I shivered slightly. "Miss Sadie, can I get you something to drink?"

Her rocking chair gave a mighty creak as she rocked forward, both hands planted firmly on the chair arms. "No. Thank ye. I gotta be going."

"Well . . . um." What was the protocol with a would-be rescuer? "Could I—give you a lift home?"

"Nope. You know how the roads run here. Take you longer to drive than it'd take me to walk. 'Preciate it, though. That's your granddaddy's car," she observed as we walked together around the side of the cabin.

"Yes'm. My dad fixed it up for me to use." I didn't try to explain more than that.

"Yep. I remember when he got that. Like a tomcat with a brand-new tail. He thought for a while folks'd think him an old fool. Not that what folks thought sat long with your granddaddy." She gave what sounded almost like a chuckle.

"Are you sure I can't give you a ride home?"

She waved my words away. "Moon's almost full light."

"Miss Sadie, thanks again. For checking on me."

She turned to face me, staring until her gaze became almost uncomfortable. "Somethin' about you reminds me of your granddaddy. He 'uz one fine man. 'Bout the best I've ever known."

I nodded, not knowing what to say. She turned and walked into the woods, waving once when I called a last thank-you before I lost sight of her in the darkness.

She'd never asked what the motorcyclists wanted.

Not until I'd brushed my teeth, getting ready for bed, did it dawn on me that I hadn't heard what happened to Donlee Griggs at the waterfall.

For half a second, I toyed with the idea of driving back to the pay phone to call the sheriff's office. But the idiot answering the phone likely didn't know—or wouldn't remember, if he did know. Besides, the sheriff's department should be out hunting down Noodle, desperado arsonist.

I'd wait until morning to learn the fate of Donlee. If he hadn't actually succeeded in killing himself—or at least doing himself some grievous bodily harm—maybe I'd volunteer to do it for him out of sheer exasperation.

I wandered into the office the next morning a little after nine. When I'd practiced in Columbia, I'd usually been one of the first ones into the office and one of the last ones to leave. That way, I'd found nobody much questioned where I spent the rest of the day.

Now, nobody questioned anything I did. Except Lou Wray, who seemed to question my very presence in her universe. We exchanged a smile for a cold shoulder, and I ambled back to my office. I'd brought the Atlanta and Greenville papers, a week-old *Newsweek,* and a thermal mug of iced coffee. I didn't want to presume upon her kindness by partaking from Lou's coffeepot.

I figured I'd read the papers, drink my coffee, maybe call to find out about Donlee. Then rearrange the pencils in my desk drawer.

Before I finished the comics, the phone startled me by ringing—twice before I fumbled around and picked it up.

"Avery Andrews's office." I tried to mimic the purr the Calhoun Firm's senior secretaries always used.

"Avery, honey, is that you? You probably don't remember me, but I know your mama. And, of course, her aunts. And—well, your whole family. I saw you at the Frank Dobbins circle meeting last week and, well, I decided you were just the one to help. You bein' a lawyer. And you bein' at that meeting to hear the outrage for yourself. I've stewed about this for the better part of a week. Then I decided, who better to handle this than a lawyer? And who better than Emma Andrews's little girl? That man must be stopped. The outrage of it all!"

Her voice built to a crescendo, then silence. She must have stopped for a breath.

Uh-oh. I should have paid better attention to the

lecture at the circle meeting. I'd obviously missed the good parts.

"Avery, you still there?"

"Um, yes'm. I'm sorry. I didn't catch your name."

"Geneva Gadsden, honey." She repeated it slowly, as if to a half-witted child who had trouble taking a message for her mother. *"Ge-ne-va Gads-den."*

"Yes, ma'am." I knew the name, but couldn't put a face or a body with it. "Miz Gadsden, if you have something you think I could help you with, perhaps we could set up an appointment. You could come in and we could talk about it."

"What's there to talk about? All you need to do is think of some way to stop that man. He's an outrage. He must be silenced. By any means necessary."

Maybe she mistakenly thought she'd reached the *Soldier of Fortune* hit man hotline. "Miz Gadsden, I seem to have missed something. Perhaps if you could start at the beginning. So the notes I'm taking will be more complete."

An exasperated sigh rushed through the phone line as I pulled a legal pad and pencil from the desk drawer. They weren't hard to locate, since the drawer held nothing else.

"You were there, Avery. You heard him with your own two ears. Surely even God would find him a blasphemer and an abomination. Weren't you listenin'? How could he say such things about Katie Hope? Surely, if nothing else, that's defamation of character. So sue him or something."

Katie Hope? The Civil War Confederate spy that

fellow had talked about at the circle meeting? What had he said about her? How could I tell Geneva that no, I hadn't heard what he'd said? Geneva Gadsden sounded wrought up enough, she might throw a blood clot.

"Miz Gadsden, it wouldn't be possible to sue because somebody defamed a dead person. You see, the law requires—"

"I don't give a gnat's kneecap what the law requires. That-man-must-be-stopped." She punched each word. "The things he said. He called her a traitor. Claimed that she was a Yankee sympathizer. That she—that she had *relations* with both Yankee soldiers and Southern boys and passed on information. I never!"

The Three Stooges' salacious "we-ell, I can see why" popped unbidden to mind.

"Miz Gadsden, perhaps if you'd come into the office, you could outline for me your exact complaints. If, in his book, he's made any misstatements of fact, then perhaps—"

"Misstatements of fact, my grandmother's knickers. Avery, if you're worried that I won't pay you— of course, my husband is close with the family budget. But he knows what a passion I have for preserving our local history. I can assure you, you'll be paid. As long as you aren't trying to take advantage."

"Miz Gadsden, I'll be happy to have an initial consultation free of charge. If there's any reasonable avenue we can pursue, we can talk about fees at that time. But—"

"Free, you say? What time would be good for you?"

So as not to appear too desperate, which I certainly wasn't, particularly since she likely would never pay a cent, I said, "How about tomorrow morning? Around ten? I have an office in Carlton—"

"I know. Your aunt Letha told me. Ten o'clock, then. Good-bye."

I'd better check on this Katie Hope scandal, find out from somebody what that fellow had said at the meeting or in his book. Maybe I needed a couple of burly guys with a straitjacket and a syringe to greet Geneva Gadsden tomorrow morning.

When the intercom on my phone buzzed, it took a second to register. Then I couldn't figure out how to respond. My initial instinct was to stick my head out the door and yell down the hall. But, on a hunch that it might work like the system at the Calhoun Firm, I picked up the phone receiver and said, "Hello?"

Nothing. Even with some button-pushing, still nothing happened.

I trundled down the dingy hall to the receptionist's office. Lou Wray turned slowly when I asked, "Excuse me, did you buzz my office?"

She didn't have a phone receiver in her hand. Maybe she'd given up while I fruitlessly punched buttons. She gave me the fish eye, then said with deliberation, "You have a visitor."

She didn't offer to introduce me to my visitor, as I'd seen her do with Carlton Barner's clients. And that failure proved awkward when I stepped across the hall to the waiting room. I had no idea whom I should ask for.

On the camel-back sofa sat a girl who looked too young to be the mother of the two children playing around her feet, though, judging from her laconic indifference, she probably was. She'd likely come to divorce their dad or to enforce a child support agreement.

A man in a blue work shirt, his greasy boots planted firmly on the fake Oriental rug, clutched *Field & Stream* with his grease-blackened fingers.

A plump woman in a print shirt and lime green polyester pants filled the armchair in the front window. Although *plump* wasn't the right word. *Doughy,* maybe.

Before I could turn and saunter across the hall to ask Lou Wray to tell me who the hell had come to see me, the large woman in the window spoke up.

"Miz Andrews?"

I nodded and smiled.

She smiled back and struggled out of the armchair. "Miz Andrews, I'm Nila Earling. I'm sorry to trouble you on such short notice, but I 'uz in town takin' care of some business and—well, I hoped you might have some time to see me."

Against her stomach, she clutched an oversize handbag with a tarnished gold clasp. Cardboard stiffener showed through the cracks in the strap.

"Certainly. Won't you step back to my office?"

I glared at Lou Wray as we passed her office—for

all the good it did, since she sat with her rigid back to us.

"Have a seat." I motioned to the chair closest to the door while I took the other one in front of the desk. I thought sitting together might put her at ease enough that she'd relax. But she gripped her handbag in a two-fisted clutch against her midsection and smiled at me.

Her skin sagged, eggy sallow, and the pockmarks looked like half-formed bubbles on a partially cooked pancake. Her eyes looked like two pale blueberries that had been pressed into the batter.

She continued to smile, a bland, permanent smile that likely didn't evidence pleasure as much as it did a tried-and-true method for coping with the world. She smiled. And clutched her purse in front of her.

"How may I help you?"

"Well." She took a deep breath, preparing to launch into a tale. "I 'uz hopin' you could help me get some money. For my brother. For his buryin'."

"Yes, ma'am?" I nodded encouragement.

She smiled. "Well, he's dead. Or so I'm told."

"Yes, ma'am?"

She blinked. Her expression said she thought I should be catching on quicker.

"Well, it just don't seem right. He's dead. And they ought to pay. Don't you think?"

"Perhaps you could fill me in on some of the details." I reached for my notepad and pen.

My note-taking seemed to encourage her. She

heaved another deep breath. "Well, Nebo, he died? In that fire? Over to the mill?"

She read the surprise on my face and paused.

"I'm sorry, Miz Earling. Nebo was your brother?"

She nodded, smiling.

"I didn't realize—I mean, that they'd identified him as the victim. I hadn't heard. I'm sorry."

She bobbed her head once, accepting the condolence, then she seemed ready to move on.

"Well, that's my point. It 'uz hardly his fault he died in that fire. And they should pay. Don't you think? Least for his buryin'. And perhaps," her eyes cut to one side, then back to me, "a little somethin' for his family's grief and sufferin'. Don't you think?"

I studied my legal pad a second, as if it held the answer. How to work past the fact that, last I knew, her brother had been wanted for questioning in the arson fire that had apparently killed him?

"Miz Earling, have the police been to see you about your brother's death?"

She nodded, frowning slightly. "That big deputy came. Askin' questions about Nebo and Mr. Garnet and what kinda work he did for the mill and such. And I tole him. Mr. Garnet 'uz good to Nebo. Why, gave him a job drivin' that back loader. 'Course, that 'uz years ago and Nebo had to quit that soon after. Bad back, you know. Got the workman's comp for that.

"But Mr. Garnet, he 'uz good to Nebo still. Let

him stay over at the mill sometimes. 'Specially if it 'uz cold. Times I wouldn't let him stay, if he'd been drinkin'. Give him odd piece work to do. Him on the disability and all, findin' piece work 'uz hard sometimes."

I nodded. I made a note about the worker's compensation claim.

"So what exactly do you need help with today?"

"Why, talkin' to Mr. Garnet. Seein' if he won't he'p bury Nebo. That fella down to the funeral home, he's talkin' numbers so big they don't make sense. I can't see why it'd cost Nebo more to be dead than to live. But they want more for the box to plant him in than my house trailer cost. That don't seem right. And it don't seem right, Nebo dyin' in that fire. Mr. Garnet ought to pay, don't you think? It bein' his building and all. And Nebo gone and my only kin."

She sniffed faintly. "I'd like to see him with a fittin' burial. He'd had such a hard life. We 'uz all each other had."

Her smile returned, a bit fainter.

"Miz Earling, if you'd tell me how to get in touch with you, I'll make some calls, then get back to you."

"Sure. I knew you would. That deputy said you 'uz Mr. Garnet's lawyer. I figured if anybody could get some money, you could."

"Miz Earling, I can't promise you anything like that. I just said I'd make some inquiries." Why did I start using bigger words the minute I thought I needed something to hide behind? "But I will get back to you."

Her smile didn't dim or waver.

"Do you have a phone number where I can reach you?"

She leaned over to watch me write it down as she recited it for me.

"That's my neighbor? But she'll come get me if-f'n you call."

"Fine. I'll be in touch as soon as I can tell you something."

Even as I stood to show her out, I wondered why I'd agreed to help. Here I was, acting again as a messenger, first for the biker boys and now for Nila Earling. I couldn't picture asking Harrison Garnet to pay the funeral expenses for Nebo Earling, grave flower thief.

And how does one bill for this sort of errand-running? Always before, I'd had well-defined client relationships and a secretary with a drawerful of our "standard agreements." Lou Wray wouldn't even loan me a sharpened pencil.

After Ms. Earling ducked her head as a farewell and waddled down the hall, I decided to go see L.J. If I admitted it, curiosity was the real reason I'd promised to look into Nila Earling's request—and some intuitive sense that it wasn't good business to get a reputation for being high-handed with people who came asking for help.

After all, if I decided to practice permanently in Dacus—now, that was a scary thought. Who was I kidding? Potential clients the likes of Geneva Gadsden, Nila Earling, and Donlee Griggs made chasing ambulances with Jake Baker a rosy option indeed. I needed to start looking for a real job.

To postpone that, I picked up the phone to call L.J., then thought better of it. I had enough trouble reading L.J. in person. I'd see if I could catch her in her office before lunch.

Thirteen

Yep." L.J. waggled her toothpick to the other side of her mouth. "The ME in Charleston ID'ed Nebo Earling. Or what the fire left of him. Don't tell me Nebo was one of your brand-new clients. You accumulatin' quite a list of losers."

"Not a client, but thanks for your concern."

She nodded.

"You figuring Nebo for the arson?" I figured we'd toy with each other a bit.

Her desk chair gave a frightening squeal as she leaned back. She eyed me over the tops of her black brogans, maybe trying to decide how much to tell me. After a wait, she spoke.

"Naw. Can't really see it. Nebo might start a fire by dint of sheer stupidity. Nobody'd be surprised by that. But settin' out to destroy records and all. That don't ring quite true."

She sucked on her toothpick as she studied her shoes. "I reckon somebody could've hired Nebo to torch his records for him." She dangled an opening for me to leap in and protest Harrison Garnet's innocence, but I didn't oblige her.

" 'Course, let's face it, nobody with good sense'd hire Nebo to walk a dog."

Couldn't argue with that logic.

"And the settin' of the fire. That was a sight too sophisticated for Nebo Earling. Imagine him sawing into a pipe to start a gas leak. No way that boy'd have sense enough to turn off the gas first. We'd've found him spattered in droplets all over that place."

Descriptive. And accurate.

"So who do you have figured for it?"

She shrugged, sending another protesting creak through her chair. "You tell me. I need somebody smart enough to rig that blast without blowin' himself to kingdom come—or at least scorchin' his eyebrows off. And I need somebody with a reason to destroy Garnet Mills' company records." She raised a questioning eyebrow.

"What records were targeted? Enough left to tell?"

"Shit, yeah. Hard to burn books. Did you know that? I have to say, I really didn't. You'd think a book, it's paper, it'd go right up. But they don't. That guy outta Columbia said it's hard to get enough oxygen to the pages. Close together, you know."

Fun facts to know and tell.

"You got my message about Noodle, didn't you?"

Her lips tightened around her toothpick. "Yeah. Later I may be askin' you how you come to know so much. But right now, I got alligators up the ass."

"You find Noodle?"

"The investigation's ongoing."

I took the hint. Time to change the subject.

"L.J., I had an interesting conversation last night. You probably know the story, but it came as a bit of a surprise to me. You know Sadie Waynes? Lives up on the mountain near Luna Lake?"

L.J. pursed her lips, then shook her head.

"She lives over the ridge behind my granddad's old cabin. She paid me a visit last night. We were talking." I didn't quite know how to get into this story. "Had you heard—or does the case file mention—any reports about Harry Garnet being seen regularly up at Luna Lake with Lea Bertram?"

L.J. didn't register any surprise, just gave a non-committal sniff. "There's some mention of them keeping company."

"Any mention that Sadie Waynes saw Harry Garnet up there the day Lea disappeared?"

The chair protested mightily as L.J. thudded her feet to the floor and leaned across the desk to face me, her eyes narrow slits. "You in here tellin' me how to do my job? Get your story straight, Counselor. Sheriff Jacobs's case file reports that a car fitting the description of the Garnets' silver-gray Cadillac Seville was seen parked near the picnic tables the last day Lea Bertram went to the lake to paint. However, Harry Garnet had a solid alibi. As did his father, just in case you were wondering."

I hadn't wondered, which gave me a new appreciation for the deviousness of L.J.'s mind.

"Sheriff Jacobs probably reached the same conclusion I would have—that the witness was mistaken. It happens. Happens more times than they're right, if you must know. So that doesn't take the heat off your boy Bertram."

"So Lea Bertram was seeing Harry Garnet?"

L.J. fiddled with the magnetic paper-clip holder on her desk. "Not much doubt about that."

"And others?"

She looked over at me. "Let's just say Lea Bertram had a lot more extracurricular activities than most young married ladies did."

"Any other names?"

"And if there were, what would make that any of your business? Seems to me, the more boyfriends you find, the more reason you have for Melvin Bertram to go over the edge."

I gave her an exasperated look. "That'd be one way of looking at it, I suppose. Seems like talking to Harry Garnet again wouldn't be a bad idea, either."

She smirked around her toothpick. "Thanks for all your helpful advice."

I stirred around, reaching for my purse as if ready to leave. "Out of curiosity, L.J., what did the ME determine about Nebo Earling's cause of death?"

L.J. had to know that question came from more than idle curiosity. On the off chance Nebo had died of natural causes before the fire started, the charges would be limited to two to twenty years, rather than a possible death penalty case.

"Clearly died of smoke inhalation. The heat got

to him later. Crisped him good. But no sign of additional trauma."

She shuffled through file folders and papers stacked on her desk. "Here." She pulled out a thin stapled sheaf of paper. The stack on the edge of her desk threatened to topple, then settled onto itself.

"Must've let one of the med students handle this one. Got awful chatty in the report. You'll enjoy this." She arranged her toothpick so she could read to me.

" 'Generalized charring left skin a uniform black color, though uncharred portions found underneath the victim's belt indicate he was Caucasian.

" 'Characteristic pew—*pugilistic* or boxer's attitude of the arms and hands and legs shortened the length measurements of the victim. However, his height is estimated at five-six to five-eight."

" 'Sealing of the lips by the intense heat largely preserved the teeth from thermal damage. The teeth exhibited poor maintenance care; several were missing, as noted below. While no dental records were available for comparison, the victim's right front incisor was exceptionally long and protruded in a pronounced overbite. The left front incisor was missing; wear patterns on the teeth indicated this loss occurred well in advance of the fire. The end of the right incisor showed minor signs of heat exposure where it protruded slightly through the lips.' "

L.J. looked up from her monotone reading. "Now, how many guys you know in Dacus got a right front fang poking out their mouth?"

"Given its clinical tone, not a bad description of Nebo, that's for sure."

L.J. bent over the document and resumed her recitation. " 'The skin of both hands had peeled off in a characteristic glove. The glove was delivered intact and in a state of preservation, allowing finger-prints to be taken. The fingerprint card was initialed and delivered to the attending deputy.' "

L.J. added, "Lester Watts matched 'em to Nebo. He was arrested about five years ago on a minor theft charge."

"Guess that cinches the ID."

L.J. made a show of flipping to the next page and kept reading. " 'Cause of death,' " she announced. " 'Soot particles were observed in the nostrils and mouth and into the upper airway branches of the lungs, indicating that the victim was alive when the fire started.

" 'No external trauma inconsistent with esti-mated temperatures and duration of exposure were observed.' What in the hell does that mean," L.J. muttered, but read on. " 'A blood carbon monoxide (COHb) of only forty percent was measured, using ventricular blood preserved in the heart. While the CO level is low, the lungs and blood pathways show evidence of emphysema and arterio'—something—'heart disease; such findings would indicate a lower-than-normal CO reading consis-tent with death due to smoke inhalation.

" 'Summary: A white, middle-aged man of less-than-average height and less-than-average weight, exhibiting symptoms of heart and lung disease which accelerated the effects of smoke inhalation. Attendant changes in skin and characteristic muscle contraction from exposure to high temperatures observed. Cause of death: smoke inhalation.' "

We both sat a moment. I didn't know what L.J. contemplated, but I considered how clinical our exit from life could be. Of course, I'd read enough labor and delivery records to know that physicians made our entry into life equally clinical.

"Do you get from that, that he would've died even if he hadn't had heart disease and—what else?—emphysema?" I asked.

L.J. shrugged. "Can't tell from this. Who'd understand half the words? But I can tell you what a doc won't say on a witness stand. No way a medical examiner's goin' to let an arsonist off by sayin', 'Gee, if the victim had taken better care of himself when he was alive, he might have been able to hold his breath long enough to escape the fire and he might not be dead now.' Good try, Counselor. But no go."

So much for trying defense strategies out on L.J.

"Interesting. And sad," I had to admit.

L.J. shrugged and tossed the autopsy report on top of the stack of papers. She didn't bother filing it somewhere she could find it more easily the next time she needed it.

"Thanks for your time, L.J. I'd better get to work."

"Try gettin' a better class of client, A'vry. You're goin' to ruin your reputation, the trash you keep time with."

I refrained from saying *oh, that reminds me,* but I

asked, "Have you had any word on Donlee Griggs?" With a pang, I realized I hadn't asked about him earlier.

L.J. pushed her protesting chair back from her desk, shaking her head. "No sign of him. The rescue squad got tired of dicking around and gave up about sundown yesterday. If he's there, he'll float up sooner or later. Big as he is, probably sooner. If he ain't there, he best not be showin' his big, dumpy ass anywhere in my line of sight or I'll shoot him right between his two stupid eyes."

L.J.'s a born peacekeeper.

"And A'vry, while you're lookin' for better clients, you might try attractin' a better class of boyfriend. Donlee Griggs, sheesh. In high school, who'd'a thought that's what little A'vry Andrews'd come to."

She smiled, her toothpick hanging precariously from her bottom lip as she showed me to the door.

Since my visit with L.J. had been so much fun, I decided to prolong my morning's frivolities with a quick visit to Sylvie Garnet's. Of course, I could've gone back to the office, past the Dragon Lady's gorgon eye, and waited on some other nutball like Geneva Gadsden or Nila Earling to call or come by. The more I considered my options, the better Jake Baker's offer to chase ambulances looked.

In violation of what I remembered as the Dacus code of conduct, whereby one should call before dropping by, I brazenly rang the Garnets' front doorbell.

The Garnets lived in a grand old house just down

the street from my aunts'. They'd bought it a few years back from an elderly lady and had turned it into a showplace. Even in November, monstrous ferns hung all along the wicker-furnished front porch—a porch large enough to host a full-dress ball.

I had just pressed the doorbell when a young woman climbed the steps at the far end of the porch to join me. Lindley Garnet, Harry's wife, wore a subdued ivory coatdress, matching pumps, and, when she noticed me, a determined expression.

"What a surprise to see you here," she said as she strode across the expanse of porch. No warm hello, no polite observations about the weather.

"I stopped by to see Mrs. Garnet for—"

"She has an appointment. I'm here to pick her up." She motioned with a flip of her wrist toward the driveway at the side of the house. Over her shoulder, I could see the roof of a car on the other side of the boxwood hedge.

Easy to see Lindley wasn't raised in a small town. Folks tend to get their messages across without such stridence.

Before I had time to look surprised, the front door swung open. Dressed in a goldenrod silk shirt-dress with a matching clutch, Sylvie Garnet looked as though she were on her way out to a luncheon appointment. And late.

From the expression on her face, I sat low on the list of people she'd expected to see on her doorstep.

She recovered quickly, though. "Avery, I'd intended to call you today. Come in." The sweetly ominous tone in her voice set off warning bells. She stepped back and held the door open for Lindley and me. Lindley gave her a peck on the cheek as she passed, their only acknowledgment of each other.

"Avery, I have an appointment," she said. The curtain on the heavy, glassed door shuddered slightly as she swung the door shut. "So I don't have much time. But we might as well attend to this now, rather than later."

The three of us stood in the dark, shadowy entry hall, Lindley throwing off the balance of our circle by edging a step closer to Sylvie. I glimpsed the parlor's patterned roll-armed sofas and wool rugs through the open French doors, but no one offered me a seat.

"Avery, I'm singularly disappointed," Sylvie said. "You must know."

I patiently waited for her to finish a reprise of her phone diatribe.

"I ask Harrison to throw a little work your way, help you get started. As a kindness to your family and all. And what do you do but betray us at every turn?"

I opened my mouth to answer, but she didn't stop for a breath. "You anger that inspector to the point he's called in reinforcements. They're threatening now to shut down the plant while they dig up the entire parking lot. And force us to pay for it!

Sylvie smacked her purse against the palm of her hand. "Avery, I surely don't have to tell you how that behavior's going to look to the people of this town. If you plan to do business here, you've got to keep in mind that you'll have both a personal and a professional reputation to maintain.

"Not that your family has ever paid much attention to what others think. Your parents certainly play by their own rules, your mother with her little projects." Her sneer really raised my hackles.

"And I suppose you heard, Mother Sylvie, that some absurd person tried to commit suicide to get her attention."

Sylvie nodded, her lips pursed in disapproval. "Avery, I don't have to tell you what that sort of publicity means if you want to attract the right kind of clients. You know, the kind who can pay. Of course, why any of this would surprise anyone in this town—anyone who knew your grandfather knew he was no better than he ought to be."

I couldn't believe I could just stand and listen while two cats batted me around like a catnip ball. Those childhood warnings about respecting elders short-circuited my responses. This must be how the snake charmer's victim feels: irritated at the noise but strangely unable to strike back.

"Of course, your grandfather didn't always exhibit much restraint in his love life, either." Sylvie's voice took on a goading edge. "After Emmalyn died, he really showed himself to be a lusty old goat. Jumping everything in sight, from Olivia Sterling right on. He even tried to keep time with me—and me thirty-five years his junior, if you can imagine such a thing!" She directed that last comment to Lindley, then preened and feigned a shudder almost at the same time.

I struggled not to slap her. I bit my tongue, not trusting myself to say anything. What could I say to a lunatic?

"Does incompetence run in the family, Avery? Or did you deliberately set out to harm Harrison and his business? Jealousy? Incompetence? What? I should have known, after those stories about you being asked to leave your law firm. Did you start screaming sexual harassment after the affair went bad?"

"Or after they found out you'd been evaluated on your bedroom skills rather than your courtroom skills?" Lindley added her own cheap shot in her honeyed low-country drawl.

I ignored Lindley. "Miz Garnet, I know you must be upset, so I'm not going to grace any of that with a reply." I struggled to keep a businesslike condescension in my voice. "Actually, I came by to tell you that Nebo Earling's sister is concerned about the mysterious circumstances of the fire that killed her brother."

Even to my ears, I sounded surprisingly calm. Judging from her rapid eye blinks, I'd landed a surprise punch. "She needs help with the burial expenses, which might be a cheap way to avoid answering difficult questions in a wrongful-death lawsuit. Maybe you could mention it to Mr. Garnet."

Nila Earling hadn't actually mentioned a lawsuit, but zinging that one at Sylvie felt good.

Sylvie's lips tightened, creasing the thick pancake of powder around her mouth. "I really can't see that we owe her anything. That derelict brother of hers mooched off Harrison for years. For all we know, he started the fire. For all we know, you suggested it, to divert attention from your incompetence in dealing with that environmental inspector."

"I'm sure Mr. Garnet's got his hands full right now, dealing with that illegal waste dump."

That one hit home, too. "We have to go now, Avery. I have an appointment with Sheriff Peters. Was that your idea, too? That the sheriff question Harry again, dredging up all that nonsense from all those years ago? Is that another sick attack you've launched on this family? I don't know what we could've done to merit this. All I can assume is that the damage you've done has been the result of incompetence rather than malice. But, then, I prefer to think the best of people."

She purposefully swung the front door wide, indicating that my audience was ended. "I'm sure I don't need to spell it out, but your services will no longer be required at Garnet Mills. Harrison feels quite strongly about that. Now, if you'll excuse me, I must go have a word with the sheriff."

In the doorway, I turned. "I take it that I should tell Miz Earling that you have no intention of offering a settle—"

I skipped a half step to keep from being hit by the door as it thudded shut.

Perhaps to avoid focusing too much on the personal gut punches she'd thrown, I found myself gloating over the L.J. aspect. So they'd invited little Harry Garnet in for questioning, had they? And his mother, the Lady Sylvie. And the sharp-faced Lindley Garnet, first lady in training—was L.J. questioning her, too?

Sylvie hadn't mentioned that my check was in the

mail. I'd get my bill to Rita Wilkes first thing tomorrow, including the trip to Columbia and the time in the library and both—no, all three trips to the mill.

Where did Sylvie Garnet get off firing me from a job her husband had hired me to do? As I strolled back toward Carlton Barner's office, I took a one-block side trip to the graveyard. Sunlight glinted off the polished marble and the occasional Mylar balloon. But no cars or people were about. I sat on Aunt Letha's bench.

I stared across the sun-bleached stones, bright flowers, and brown grass for some time before I realized that this bench overlooked the Howe plots. Somehow, the other day, I hadn't noticed. My grandfather's stone, with the names Avery Hampton Howe and Emmalyn Guest Howe and their dates, was the newest one in the family plot. Plenty of other Howes and relations rested there, most names I really didn't know.

I dissected the encounter with Sylvie and Lindley, trying to decide what about the conversation knotted my stomach, what left me with this sense of sick unease. Was it the calculated maliciousness of the outburst? Was it that Sylvie had claimed to remember my grandfather in ways I'd never heard anybody talk about him? Maybe he had tomcatted around. Certainly nobody would've discussed that with me. What really left the bad taste in my mouth was the way she'd said it, dripping with nasty innuendo.

I couldn't possibly have known my grandfather the way others had. What had he been like when he was younger? Had he consoled Olivia Sterling when

Sylvie stole her beau? In ways other than as the so-licitous big brother of Olivia's friends Hattie and Vinnia? Had it taken time for him to grow into somebody I adored?

I'd been around some masterful manipulators, but Sylvie Garnet took the prize for punching hot buttons. I wanted to physically shake myself to shed the nasty feeling that clung to me like stable muck.

My mama had taught me not to sass my elders; she hadn't said anything about letting lunatics rant unchecked. Sylvie's diatribe had been too ven-omous. She'd protested too much, and I wanted to know why. Was Lindley along for more than a ride? True, she and Harry met while finishing their MBAs, long after Lea Bertram had sunk from sight. But she had her eye set on the governor's mansion, and she wouldn't let even Harry get in the way of that.

Sylvie hadn't hired me, so she couldn't fire me. And I could think of nothing that prohibited me from following up on a few things.

I left the graveyard and headed toward Carlton Barner's office and my car. Even if Sylvie saw to it that I got fired, I might as well enjoy myself.

Fourteen

I'd been so busy talking to unpleasant people and weirdos that I'd let most of the day get by and hadn't eaten a bite. I stopped by the newspaper office first, for both food and information.

With an RC in a glass bottle and a pack of Nabs from the print room cracker machine, I climbed the creaky stairs to Dad's new office.

New is not a good word, though. From the threadbare carpet faded into a dusty brown to the dented file cabinets and the cantilevered worktable, everything wheezed with age and hard use—a place where people had long been too busy with the more important affairs of the world to worry about interior design.

My dad, a burly man, filled the space as if he'd been born to it. The top of his heavy thatch of reddish-brown hair faced me over the desk as I walked in and sprawled in the wooden armchair opposite him.

"So, Dad, who's getting married and who got arrested?"

He started a bit. He'd been concentrating on

some sort of drawings spread out on his desk.
"Um . . . yes," he said, then tapped the drawings.
"Think I've come up with a way to solve a product
flow problem on those little advertising weeklies we
print for that fella."

I nodded. I'd have to read the paper to catch up
on the news.

"Dad, what do you know about Nebo Earling?" I
popped a cheese cracker in my mouth and waited.

He pushed back from his desk and studied the
floor underneath for a minute. "Crippled when he
was born. Worked for old man Garnet. Lived with
his sister—when he wasn't holed up in somebody's
hunting shack drinking himself stuporous. Same as
his momma, sometimes."

"What did he do for Harrison Garnet?"

"Odd jobs. Mowed the lawn at his house. Gofer
work around the plant."

"You remember anything about him operating
some kind of heavy equipment for Garnet? Around
the mill?"

"Now you mention it, yeah, he did. I remember
thinking what a damned fool thing, letting Nebo operate a backhoe when he couldn't walk a straight
line most days and didn't have the sense God gave a
turnip."

He absentmindedly rolled up one of the sheets on
his desk. "'Course, they were working around in
that back parking lot then, clearing off. Reckon
there wasn't much there he could hurt."

"But he hurt himself somehow? Collected
worker's comp?"

He shrugged. "Don't know anything about that. Might have." His gaze wandered back to his drawings—some sort of flowchart.

I took a long last swig on my RC, then let out a quiet little burp. "You know Geneva Gadsden?"

His brow furrowed and he nodded. "Yeah. I know her husband better, though. Why you ask?"

"I can't place her. She called about something. We're to meet tomorrow."

"Ought to warn you, she's a bit of a kook."

I tried not to smile. "I gathered that in our phone conversation."

"Your mother knows her better." He stood when I did and walked with me across the musty carpet to the door. "She ought to be home later."

I nodded and gave him a quick hug. "Sorry to interrupt."

He looked at me—actually locked gazes—and said, "We're glad you're home, Avery. Hope you'll be staying."

I gave him a crooked smile and creaked down the protesting stairs. I didn't say good-bye. That way, he wouldn't hear a catch in my voice. I didn't have the heart to tell him that dealing with the likes of Sylvie and Lindley made leaving look sweet indeed.

My next stop was Nila Earling's house. Since I had no address for her, I detoured into the paste-up room to call Nila's neighbor.

After four rings, I heard the receiver on the other end lift. I waited for someone to say hello. Instead, a slurry voice speaking a bit too loudly said, "Shee-ut," adding more vowels than any word needs.

I paused, then offered a cautious, "Hello?"

"What?" Then more forcefully, "Shit."

"Is this a bad time?" I couldn't decide if the voice sounded old or drunk or weak from exertion.

"Spilled gahdam Cheerios and Hawaiian Punch all inside the sofa. Shit." Heavy mouth-breathing followed.

"I'm trying to reach Nila Earling. Or at least find out where she lives." I talked fast.

"Can't get her now. Takes too long for her to waddle her fat self over here. She's at Palmetto Trailer Park. Number 'leven. Shit." The receiver slammed down.

Perhaps I'd just wander over to Miz Earling's house without further attempt to forewarn her.

I checked the phone book, then asked the three folks working around the downstairs offices if they knew where I could find the Palmetto Trailer Park. I got three different answers, all prefaced with "hmm" or "let me see." The name Palmetto didn't help any, since the state tree only grows on the coast, not anywhere near the foothills. But I knew where three, maybe four trailer parks were. I'd try them all. It's not like driving around Dacus takes all that long.

The first one, near the city basketball and tennis courts, didn't have a name, just a string of mailboxes clinging desperately to a swaybacked board nailed to two posts.

The second one was the Heaven's View Motor Court. Why hadn't I noticed that glaring misnomer before? The red dirt from the rutted drive that wound through the house trailers had blown and spattered the trailers, the cars, the bushes, the discarded tricycles, and the red-stained children playing in their grassless yards.

Finally, on the opposite side of town—all of about six blocks from Garnet Mills—I found Palmetto Trailer Park. No palmettos, but there was a tidy stand of spindly pine trees and almost as much red dust as Heaven's View.

As with the other parks, the trailers here had been parked in their spaces too long. Spots of rust, stains from the overhanging pines, faded paint, lopsided add-on porches, and tired houseplants hanging limply in plastic pots all spoke of folks hunkered in.

Number eleven had once been a pale blue rectangular box. Now it sat, paler still, with one end crumpled in like a half-squashed beer can. No one had bothered to add a porch or anything more than the narrow metal steps that had come with the thing, back when it was much newer and much less faded.

I cautiously tested the bottom step and reached up to rap on the metal door. After three consecutively more insistent knocks, the door opened and Nila Earling filled the doorway. She hadn't first called out "Who's there?"

"Miz Ear—"

"Why, Miz Andrews." She blinked slightly in the afternoon sun like a mole peeking out its hole. "Come on in here."

She stepped back and made a little space for me to enter. The television blared the boxed intensity of a talk show.

The room's darkness wasn't all a trick of light.

Weak sunlight filtered into the narrow room through the flowered, scantily ruffled curtains. But the dirt-brown carpet, lumpy flowered sofa, and dark chipboard furniture gobbled all the light. While my eyes strained to see, my nose begged me not to breathe. The dusty air swam with stale cooking odors and stale body odors and ripe cat-box stink.

"Have a seat." She pushed a stack of newspapers off the sofa. A fruitcake-colored cat fell out of the papers and lay in the heap on the floor. I stepped over the jumble, eyeing the cat, hoping it wasn't dead. I hated the thought of that stench being added to the rest of the potpourri.

"How nice to see you, Miz Andrews. Can I get you something to drink? Some ice tea?" She stood over me, smiling down and ignoring the cat.

"No, no, thank you. And I apologize for stopping in without calling first, but—"

"Better you stop by than you make me walk next door so you can tell me you're comin'." She slapped her thigh. "Sure I can't get you somethin' to drink?" She spoke loudly over the television's noise.

I shook my head and she sank into the butt-sprung recliner that faced the TV. The chair sighed. From the folding TV tray next to her chair, she grabbed a sweaty glass of tea and gulped.

"Miz Earling—"

"Call me Nila, please. You come to my house, you call me Nila."

"Nila. Thank you."

Nila Earling did seem the queen of her castle, not the beseeching person who'd been in my office. A woman at home—with herself and her trailer.

"Nila, I have some bad news and I wanted to deliver it in person. I spoke with Mrs. Garnet about Nebo's funeral—"

"And she said they wouldn't pay." Nila Earling took another gulp, wiped the corners of her mouth with two pinched fingers, and nodded. "Figgered as much. You gonna talk to Mr. Garnet?"

I shook my head. "I doubt seriously that'll do any good. The Garnets—"

"Thought as much. So we gonna sue 'em?"

That one took me by surprise. "Um." I rested my elbows on my knees, trying not to settle too far back into the sofa. For some reason, I kept thinking of Nila Earling's neighbor and the Cheerios and Hawaiian Punch in her sofa.

"I really don't think that's an option, Miz, um, Nila. And, in any case, I would have a conflict of interest, carrying this any further. Perhaps I could recommend a lawyer you could talk to about your options."

"Figgered as much. It just don't seem right."

Fortunately she didn't seem inclined to beg me to reconsider. But I moved to change the subject.

"M—Nila, I was curious. You mentioned that your brother, that Nebo, had operated heavy equipment for Mr. Garnet."

"Sure did."

She didn't look surprised at my question. I felt a

twinge of guilt. She probably thought my exploration would lead to finding her some cash.

"Tell me some more about that. When was it?"

She settled her head against the back of her chair and studied the leak-stained ceiling. "Lemme see. Probably some time about 1970, I reckon. It 'uz about a year after Mama died. He 'uz button-popping proud of that job. 'Course, Nebo never did 'mount to much. Pains me to say that." She lay her puffy hand across her bosom. "But one's got to speak truth, even of the dead."

I murmured sympathetically.

"But he 'uz so proud of that job."

"What—could you tell me something about what he did for Mr. Garnet?"

She shook her head. "Don't know too much. They 'uz doin' some expansion over to the plant. They had Nebo diggin' holes and movin' tree trunks and stuff like that."

"Expansion?" I tried to keep my voice conversational.

She shrugged. "They cleared off that back part. Needed some more parking spaces. And they were building some kinda outbuildings. I'm not sure. Things 'uz goin' big over there then. Lotsa people around here worked at Garnet then." She shook her head, her jowls jiggling. "Things hadn't been so good for some time. Sad to see."

"Mm-hmm."

" 'Course, Nebo set up his own hard times," she acknowledged.

A surprisingly candid assessment, I thought.

"Nebo never did have right good sense. So gettin' that job humpin' that big digger around went to his head. Nebo always managed to mess in his own bed, if you'll pardon my language. Had to go flip that back loader over down the creek bank. Now how's that for fixin' your own little red wagon?"

"Is that when he hurt his back?"

"Yeah. 'Course, he tole ever'body he lost his job because he'd hurt his back and had the permanent rheumatiz. But truth be told, his supervisor fired him. Stood over him there, upside down in the creek, screamin' that he 'uz fired. Didn' faze Nebo. Rode outta there on a stretcher, and probably worked out for himself how to turn a buck somewhere between there and the hospital. Nebo wasn't smart but he could figger. Usually figger some way to get hisself into more trouble and more work than if he'd just done it the right way to begin with."

I nodded. I'd been to law school with guys like that—smarter, maybe. But always "figgerin'" a short cut.

"He received a worker's comp award?"

She nodded, her chins participating fully. Then she pursed her lips. "They keep payin' on any of that disability that he got? Like to a survivor or anything?"

I shook my head. "No. I doubt that." Figgerin' must run in the family.

She sighed and stared at the television screen. A local used-car commercial jerked across the screen. She'd muted the sound, but still couldn't keep her eyes off the bucktoothed guy on the screen.

"Nila, did Nebo ever talk about building that parking lot?"

She blinked, breaking the TV's hypnosis. "Lemme think. He did mention how they had to build up the back part of the lot, back toward the woods. It shelved off there. I 'member him tellin' about it 'cause he 'uz so proud about bein' the one to do the diggin' and the movin'. Like it 'uz some manly thing."

She rolled her eyes toward the ceiling. "Seems like they used some stuff from the plant that they had to get rid of anyway—you know, junk they 'uz going to have hauled off. Scraps and trash and such. And he got to be the one to bury it." She pronounced *bury* as an odd cross between *burro* and *berry*.

"Guess Nebo was one of the first recyclers," she said and giggled, her hand flapping to her mouth, then back to her lap.

I smiled at her joke, hoping the bells clanging in my head weren't sounds she could see reflected on my face.

"So Nebo stopped working for Garnet in the early seventies?"

"We-ell, not egg-zactly. He did get fired from his regular job and got the worker's comp. But Mr. Garnet musta felt some soft spot for him. Which, truth be told, always surprised me considerin' Nebo pulled that stunt about hurting his back and got the disability. But he kept giving him odds and ends to do. And sometimes givin' him a place to stay."

She sighed another bosom-raising sigh. "Guess things come around. That free place to stay got him kilt. And if Mr. Garnet hadn't been so free and easy with a ten here and a five there, Nebo wouldn't'a had to sleep it off up there. Some might think ill 'a me for this"—her hand went back to the wide expanse of her neck—"but I wouldn't never let him sleep it off here. He knew that better'n he knew his own name when he 'uz drunk. Some might say my hard heart killed him. But I ain't hearin' none of it. Nebo picked his own path."

"Yes, ma'am. I guess we all do."

"We surely do. You sure I can't get you somethin' to drink?" Her glass sat empty and she was back to staring at the TV.

"No, thank you. I really need to get going. Again, I'm sorry about your brother. And sorry I couldn't do more to help."

"Ah-h." She hoisted herself out of her chair. "I just didn't want to be missin' out on somethin' that shoulda been comin' to me. But . . ." She shrugged and picked up her tea glass.

I let myself out, since any other maneuver would have resulted in us both being wedged inextricably in the narrow door opening.

Leaving Nila Earling's, I steered the car around the track through the trailer park, trying to avoid kids and dogs and those little orange and yellow plastic toddler cars.

At the exit, I stopped, my feet holding both clutch and brake to the floor. Where to next? Nila Earling hadn't told me anything earth-shattering, but she'd told me enough.

I had a few more questions that needed answers. But the only place I could think to go ask them was a place nobody in her right mind would go. I sat, the engine throbbing, the sun soaking through the window glass into my bones, and tried to think of another option. Any option.

The horn blast behind me startled my foot off the clutch. I choked the engine and had to restart it, shift gears, and wave apologetically at the panel van that had come up behind me.

Fortunately, when I turned right, he squealed left onto the paved road. I drove slowly toward Main Street, trying to think through how I would approach them and what I would say. And whether I could fathom any other way to find the same information. After all, our last conversation had not been altogether satisfactory.

But at least it gave me a direction. I turned left and headed toward the old Heath house—the house that, much to the consternation of both the County Historical Society and the sheriff, had been purchased a decade ago by the Posse biker gang. For cash.

Fifteen

Few people in Dacus knew the Posse motorcycle gang personally. But everyone in town had known when they'd moved into the area. Admittedly, they were little more than a group of aging, husky guys with ponytails who frowned menacingly at grocery clerks and gas station attendants. They kept mostly to themselves.

That didn't keep the town's collective nose from sniffing around the edges of their affairs. If they engaged in anything illegal, they kept a pretty low profile because it never showed up on the arrest records printed in the newspaper. But as far as most people in Dacus were concerned, the gang's unforgivable sin had been buying the old Heath place.

The historic Heath house sat far back off a rough-paved county road, out of sight in a thick stand of trees. Nothing more than a large white farmhouse, it had once presided over a sizable pre–Revolutionary War farming operation and had boasted amenities such as glass windowpanes and more than two rooms long before such affluence became common in the upstate.

The rim of deep blue mountains overlooked fields now choked with slash pines and weeds. But, in the area's backwoods primitive days, the house had hosted visiting dignitaries, including a French naturalist who'd extolled the Heaths' hospitality in his 1780s travelogue. Thus the house had earned itself a spot in Camden County history back when few houses could boast of indoor toilets.

Having it fall into the hands of a motley assortment of questionable characters had drawn attention. The gang had ridden into town—reportedly from Charlotte or Miami, some city forcing out adult bookstores, prostitution rings, and mud wrestling. No one really knew what they did, how many of them lived here, or why they'd chosen Dacus. After all, they hadn't joined the Chamber of Commerce. But folks still speculated.

I'd heard a rumor that, shortly after they'd moved in, a delegation of local ladies had paid a visit. A sort of stern, impassioned No-Welcome Wagon. The reports of what transpired had grown bigger and better as time went on. Best I remembered, Sylvie Garnet herself had been on that visit—probably led it.

I turned the long nose of my Mustang onto the rutted washboard dirt road—overgrown on both sides by an impenetrable tangle of brambles, cedar, broom sage, and saplings—and bumped the half mile to the house. I wondered how the ladies had been received. Not that it mattered. Max and I were on a first-name basis.

Now that I was here, ten miles from town and too far from any hope of help, I strained to remember why I thought this trip so necessary.

I pulled into the weedy yard and around the circular drive. The house needed paint and the landscaping made a strong back-to-nature statement. It looked like a house where an elderly couple on a fixed income lived. After I turned off the ignition, I noticed the Harley chopper displayed on the second-floor porch.

No one stirred. No vicious guard dogs rushed out. No armed sentries pointed automatic weapons at my head. No questioning eyes peered around the Confederate flag that served as a downstairs curtain. Nothing.

Did one get out and ring the doorbell? Honk the horn? Start the car and drive furiously back to the road? The eerie calm of this place held their thunderous visit to my cabin in stark contrast.

I focused so intently on the front door that, when knuckles rapped on the car window beside my ear, I jumped. An embarrassing reaction, since it was my old friend Do-Rag.

He'd appeared out of nowhere, artfully sauntering up in my blind spot, which was amazing, considering his sheer size. I smiled up at him and cranked down the window, an awkward act in the little car. The air outside carried the faint smell of wood smoke and the customary late-November nip, although the sun had warmed the inside of the car nicely.

Nothing in Do-Rag's tone or manner radiated any particular warmth. He just stood there, his beefy arms slack at his sides, his head slightly cocked to see me under the car's convertible top. No "Hi, how are you? Care to come in?" Just the stare.

"Wondered if Max was around." I tried to keep my tone casual, as if this sort of house call was not at all out of the ordinary for Avery Andrews, attorney-at-law.

He shifted his weight slightly from one foot to the other, but didn't respond.

"I spoke with Sheriff Peters. About Max's request. I need to follow up with Max about something."

That might not create an exactly accurate picture of the reason for my call. But L.J. had spurred their visit to my cabin. And this time, the mention of her name got Do-Rag to bend over and pull the latch on the car door.

Of course, the door didn't open. I always lock it. So we entertained ourselves for a few seconds with a silly routine of fumbled locks and latches before he swung the long door open and I crawled out. No graceful way to extricate one's self from a low-slung Mustang. Good thing I'd worn slacks with my navy blazer.

Do-Rag, without uttering a word, walked around the front of the car, clomped up the steps, and opened the front door. It hadn't been locked. Guess there was no need for that out here in the country. I pushed the car door shut and followed Do-Rag into the house. In the front hallway, he said over his shoulder, "Wait there." Then he disappeared down a dim hallway beside a narrow set of steps that led to the second story.

The floor, made of heart-of-pine boards that are impossible to find now, lay scuffed and gouged. No antique oak hall tree or credenza overflowing with flowers graced the dingy foyer. Autumn sunlight streaked through windows that might not have been washed since the Battle of the Cane Break. A card table and a scattering of cardboard boxes, topped with everything from a motorcycle headlamp to the week's mail, completed the foyer's decor.

Eyeing the mail, I tried to picture one of the outlaw bikers perched at the kitchen table with checkbook and calculator, paying the light bill and the department store charge cards. I bit the inside of my lip to keep from grinning. If I allowed myself even a chuckle, I'd collapse in a giggle fit. This felt too much like being in church—quiet, serious, and alien to other experience.

The creaking floorboards and scuffing boot treads warned me of Do-Rag's return. He brought Max with him.

Max thudded to a stop, his fingers hooked loosely through his jeans pockets, with Do-Rag a step behind him. Max wore a faded flannel shirt unbuttoned enough to reveal part of the words printed on his T-shirt. On his thin chest, the only word fully visible was *bullshit*.

His bucked front teeth remained hidden inside his bushy beard, but he gave me a half nod. When I didn't speak right away, he did the polite thing by asking, "Yeah?"

"I appreciate your agreeing to see me on the spur of the moment." Maybe an extremely formal tone would provide some balance to his insolent stare. "I hoped you could answer a couple of questions for me."

He didn't invite me into the parlor for tea and scones, but he also didn't spin on his boot heel and leave me alone, so I continued.

"I delivered your message to the sheriff. She says she's following up on it."

He nodded. His expression said he'd already known that. He still hadn't blinked.

"When we talked at my house, you indicated that Noodle had gone out on his own. Can you tell me if Noodle—if he had anything to do with Garnet Mills, other than burning it down?"

Max gave a small blink of surprise. But he quickly returned to his accustomed unblinking stare.

I rushed on with my explanation. "I realize your group has certain—rules of conduct. But there's more at stake here than an arson. Did Noodle ever do any work for Harrison Garnet?"

Max just stared. Do-Rag shifted from one foot to the other. I'd struck some kind of chord. I just didn't know what tune.

"It's important. I know you're concerned—sensitive to—" I took a deep breath. "I'm not handling this very well. What I really want to know is, do you have any idea why Noodle set the fire? Did he do it on his own? Or did Harrison Garnet hire him to do it?"

Max stared that bald-eyed stare of his. Finally, the set of his mouth said he'd made up his mind about something.

"I don't know how Noodle came to get mixed up in it. Like I said, he went off on his own." He propped himself against the stairs that led to the second floor, looking thoughtful. I hadn't noticed that the banister was completely missing, the railings broken off in splintered nubs.

"Clyde." He turned to Do-Rag. "When was it Noodle did that hauling?"

Clyde?

Do-Rag screwed up his mouth. "Don't recall. Back before he did that stint on that distribution charge."

"That'd be what? Twenty-five years ago? Thirty?" He stared at the floor near Do-Rag's— Clyde's—scuffed boots. Then he stared at me.

"Noodle used to do some contract hauling. Had his own rig, till he lost it. Hard to make payments from inside CCI."

His inside joke stopped me a minute until I realized that the Central Correctional Institute—the crumbling nineteenth-century prison on the riverfront in Columbia—would've still been operating when Noodle got sent "up the river."

"Yep," Clyde said. "Hauling watermelons to New York. Thought he'd pack some of 'em with snow."

He almost smiled at the thought, then frowned. "Musta made somebody mad. Cops pulled him before he made it to the state line."

"Made somebody mad?"

They both shook their heads solemnly, knowingly.

"Cops don't just happen to have a drug dog along when they pull a watermelon truck heading outta Hampton."

I nodded. So Noodle had gotten himself ratted out before. Interesting fellow, with some nice friends.

To get back to the subject, I asked, "So he did some hauling for Harrison Garnet, before he got arrested?"

Max nodded, staring now out the front door behind me. "Yeah. That was about his only local customer."

"What got him into the trucking business?"

Max shrugged. "His brother or brother-in-law. I dunno. Somebody had a rig. Noodle's always thinking of an angle. Angled himself right into fifteen years."

"What'd he haul for Garnet? Any idea?"

Another shrug. "Garnet's in the furniture business. I remember a load of school desks going somewhere in the Midwest. Big trip for Noodle. One of his first long-distance jobs."

"He always carry—um, contraband on his trips?"

Max shook his head. "Naw. Not at first. But Noodle's greedy. Always looking for an angle."

"That all he did for Garnet?"

"Did some short-haul stuff—equipment, supplies, something. Once he worked several days, helping move stuff outta the plant. Remember 'cause he needed some guys to help. These guys here told him to stick it. But he hired a coupla derelicts to help him."

"Help him?"

"Load and unload. Noodle's not one to do too much actual work if it can be avoided. Delivering to a business, he could usually contract so he didn't do the grunt work. But not on this project. Ol' man Garnet wanted the barrels moved out, loaded, and unloaded."

At the mention of barrels, my shin twinged from its remembered meeting with the rusted barrel ring in the woods behind Garnet Mills. Now the warning bells clanged in my head. I'd been looking for a connection. This proved to be more than my half-hatched plan had expected.

"Do you remember when he hauled those barrels? About what year?"

Max blinked, finally. My eyes burned just from watching him stare. "Sure do. That was his last big job before he left to work out his Hampton watermelon scheme. Again, that'd've been twenty-five years ago, at the least."

Do-Rag nodded.

"Come to think of it, about that time he got that contract to back-haul some stuff down here. From some place in upstate New York. Figured he had himself quite a business—snow-filled melons up and storage drums back. Then he got himself ratted out and busted."

"Storage drums? What'd he do with those?"

Max shrugged, looking bored. "Dumped 'em somewhere. I don't know. Wouldn't have amounted to much. Noodle only made two, maybe three trips."

Sunlight streamed through the windows around the front door, warming the broad, dusty hallway. But I felt an excited chill. Not only had Noodle worked for Harrison Garnet, he'd helped fill the field of drums that now had Garnet over a barrel with the environmental boys. Dawson Smith's soil bores might yield him more than he imagined—two, maybe three extra tractor-trailer rigs more, brought from somewhere else to add to Garnet's barrels.

Noodle had known Harrison Garnet for years. He'd been his partner in crime before. Why not again? When Harrison had needed his pesky records destroyed, who better to call than his old pal Noodle? After all, Noodle had his own reasons for a coverup. In addition to destroying records, had they arranged the fire to get rid of one of the other witnesses to the barrel burial? That thought chilled me.

I'd had trouble picturing Harrison Garnet torching his own place. And I'd wondered where he'd find someone to do it for him. In truth, he hadn't had to look very far. Noodle had been right there, fiddling with his bike in the back parking lot at Garnet Mills, waiting for the shift change. How convenient.

I glanced at Max. He stared back.

"Thanks," I said. "That—may help." I fumbled around for a gracious way of saying *Thanks for helping me put a noose around somebody's neck. Your friend Noodle won't dangle alone.* "Thanks. I appreciate your time." I turned to go, then stopped.

"One other thing. I'm just curious. How'd Noodle get that name? I mean, it's—kind of unusual."

Some of my earlier questions had made Do-Rag—I couldn't call him Clyde—shift uncomfortably. This one made him scuff, almost dance on the dusty floor. Max stared. That fanatic-looking quirk of his made my eyes burn in sympathy.

"Noodle earned that name when he first joined a club." Something that might have been a little smile spasmed at the corner of his mouth. "He'd ridden as a Maniac for awhile. That club was a tough one to pledge in those days. Noodle locked his place the day he took another pledge and his woman out on a wildlife excursion in one of those Florida swamps."

The more his mouth shadowed closer to a smile, his prominent front teeth peeking through his beard, the more my stomach clenched.

"A group of 'em stayed out there several hours one night with the pledge who'd crossed the line on a deal. Unfortunately, the pledge didn't come back with the rest of 'em. He couldn't manage to get his intestines gathered up and stuffed back inside and get himself to a hospital before he died. The club pledged Noodle soon after that. His nickname stuck, just to remind anybody who might cross him how he left the guy in the swamp. Effective don't you think?"

I hoped my face wouldn't betray the knot of disgust in my stomach. It must have, though, because his thin-lipped mouth almost blossomed into a smile.

"Don't worry, though. The rat's girlfriend came back okay. After they pulled the nails out of her hands. Noodle had pinned her to a tree, so she could watch the guys conduct their business. She must have learned a lot that day. She rode with Noodle until he came up here. Made a lot of money for him, I'd guess. Once the infection in her hands healed up and she could get back to work."

Max's face settled back into its bland stare, the hint at animation around his mouth disappearing as he finished his horror story.

Do-Rag had the decency to look a bit sick to his stomach. Had he been there, that night in the swamp? Or was he remembering his own initiation, somewhere else?

Looking at these two guys, I knew no easy door opened to their group. They were frighteningly serious.

"Sorry I asked," I said, surprised at my own candor. Might as well be candid. He'd wanted to see if he could shock me. And he could.

No one escorted me to my car, though I'm sure someone watched to make sure I left. I might have been crazy enough to come calling, but I wasn't dumb enough to wear out my welcome. Chills shivered the back of my neck as I drove the Mustang a tad too fast down the washboard drive. I tried to slow myself down, so as not to appear frightened. But it didn't work.

When the back tires burped onto the rough asphalt of the county road, I turned toward town. Despite the prickling from too much adrenaline, I was glad I'd come. Max had told me more than I'd bargained for.

Not only had Noodle—I shivered at the name—worked for Harrison Garnet, but he'd worked on the back lot, with the barrels that now interested the environmental guys. By indicating what had been purchased for use at the plant and what had been properly disposed, the records Noodle had amateurishly tried to burn would probably give the inspectors a road map to the contents of most of those barrels.

But, of course, Noodle wasn't a professional arsonist. He'd branched out to handle this little matter. And the answer to why he'd handled it for Harrison Garnet now seemed clear—he had his own additions to Garnet's dump to hide. I mused over the news that Noodle had done other short hauls for Garnet—school desks? Or visits to other illegal dump sites? That would've raised the stakes for both him and Garnet.

The other question—the one that didn't yet have an answer—was how did Lea Bertram fit into all of this? Too much had happened, all of it circling around Garnet Mills. I just couldn't quite buy the coincidences. How badly had Harrison Garnet wanted a son in politics? How much could his money buy?

The only person who could jiggle all the pieces until they fit neatly together was Harrison Garnet, though I doubted he'd want to sit around with me this evening putting together jigsaw puzzles.

I headed toward Mom's house, the sun a blinding ball on the crisp blue November horizon.

The surface calm at my parents' rambling house belied strong undercurrents. Mom, the phone caught between her shoulder and her ear, paced the kitchen to the length of the phone's cord and then back in the other direction.

"Cha-rles," she drawled with exasperation. She nodded absentmindedly at me as I came in the door, then continued with her lecture into the phone. "You know good and well I've talked to Petty about her so-called complaint. After thinking about it, she decided that he really hadn't harassed her. More that he made her uncomfortable. She hadn't expected him to ask where someone could buy large-size lingerie around here. He—"

Charles must have interrupted her. I ducked under the stretched phone cord to get a Coke from the refrigerator. Then I perched on a stool at the counter. This one sounded too good to miss.

"Charles, it's perfectly understandable that a man might want to buy lingerie, for a wife or—" Charles interrupted again, but then Mom talked on. "—or a girlfriend. Just because Petty was a bit taken aback by the question doesn't mean it was harassment.

"Yes. I know perfectly well that the board could be sued for allowing a hostile work environment to exist. But Petty's not suing. And even if she did, she really wouldn't have a case. Even she doesn't think the environment is all that hostile, now that she knows the whole story."

That brought another tinny tirade through the receiver from Charles. Charles Press, maybe? At the Economic Development Board?

"Well, Avery's sitting right here. If anyone knows about harassment, it's Avery."

I hoped my mom was selling my lawyering skills and not revealing that she knew more about my former supervising partner than I would want her to know.

"Charles, the bottom line is that Petty's fine about all this now and isn't considering any harassment charges—"

She nodded at an interruption, then said, "Charles, I simply don't see how we can help but support Sy. Buying women's lingerie really isn't the issue here—I know we have to consider the public relations aspects of this, I know this is a small town. But you might be surprised how accepting folks can be—"

At the next interruption, my mom rolled her eyes. "Charles, honey." Uh-oh, the tone she uses when she's not placating any more had crept into her voice. "The bottom line is Sy Bonifay may have a claim against us if we try to dismiss him."

The buzz on the other end of the phone turned into a squawk.

"Charles, honey, there's such a thing as the Americans with Disabilities Act. Now, I'm sure Avery could answer any questions you have, but my guess is that some psychological thing, whatever it is that's led Sy to do this, would constitute some sort of disability. We can't fire somebody because he has a disability, Charles. Not as long as he can do his job."

The squawking sounds quietened. Maybe Charles needed to catch his breath.

"That's fine, Charles. We can talk about this some more tomorrow." Her voice lost its purr, like a cat who'd played its prey, toyed, pounced, then ended things. "Okay."

She hung up the phone, the extra-long cord twisted from her pacing. I took another swig from my Coke can and fixed her with an expectant stare. "Well?"

"Well what?" Then she shrugged, resigning the innocent act. "That situation I mentioned to you, at the Economic Development Office? Can a female harass another female?"

"Sure. Same-sex propositions are treated just like—"

"No, no. Not that quid-pro-quo stuff you told me about. I mean creating what you called a hostile work environment. Saying things that make somebody uncomfortable to the point she can't do her job. But what if it's just girl talk? Can a woman do that to another woman?"

She stood with her hands on her hips, her head

cocked, her Reeboked feet in a fighting stance; she had no idea how anachronistic her conversation sounded, standing there surrounded by her white kitchen appliances.

"Well," I mused, "that's a tougher question. I can imagine situations where it would create a hostile work environment—"

"But just a simple question like, Where around here do you buy really nice big-size lingerie?"

"A woman got offended because another woman asked her that?"

"No, not exactly." She pulled open the refrigerator and poured herself an orange juice. "No, she thought a man was asking her that."

"Where to buy lingerie? Like for a girlfriend?"

"No, no. But would that be harassing, if a man asked it?"

"Probably not to most people. He'd have to know she found it offensive. She'd have to tell him. But if two women are talking, like you said—"

"No." Mom pulled out the bar stool opposite me, settling in for an explanation. "You don't understand. She *thought* he was a man. But he isn't."

I just stared. When I think I've learned not to be surprised by anything she throws at me, Mom comes up with a new one.

"A woman got offended because a man asked her where to buy lingerie, but—"

"But now she's not offended because now she knows that he's not really a man. He's undergoing a sex change."

My mouth hung open. "The guy you all hired to head the Economic Development Board is in the process of becoming a woman?"

She nodded. "So now Petty's not offended at all. But Charles Press is about to throw a blood clot."

"Sy Bonifay's the new guy, the one you found strange? You thought his eyes looked funny."

"Sure. But he doesn't look funny now." She gulped some juice. "I mean, before, something just didn't seem quite right. Before, he was in the wrong context. He didn't ring true. Now," she shrugged, "he makes sense."

Unlike the low-country flatlanders I'd left a few weeks ago, the citizens of Dacus, with their mountain leanings, seemed more inclined to accept people in all their weirdness. But this would be a bit of a stretch, even for Dacus. It obviously didn't stretch my mom, who hopped up and started pulling leftovers out of the refrigerator.

"Meat loaf for supper?" she asked.

"Great." Leftover meat loaf is always better than fresh meat loaf—and an infinite improvement over the culinary wasteland in the cabin's cupboard.

For I while, I played couch potato in front of the TV, mulling over what I knew about Harry, Lindley, and Sylvie, and particularly about Noodle and Harrison Garnet. Then I puttered around setting the table for the three of us while Mom made mashed potatoes. Dad arrived in time to catch the weather on the Greenville station's evening news.

"Oh, Avery," Mom said, startling me as I dumped a blob of ketchup on my meat loaf. "In the midst of everything, I forgot all about your phone message. I'm so sorry, honey. It might be important."

She scooted out of her seat at the kitchen table and reached across the counter to push the button on the answering machine.

His voice came through slow and clear. "Avery? Jake Baker here. I been waitin' and waitin' to hear back from you. You comin' to Charleston to help me whup these insurance bastards' asses or you gonna hole up there in that godforsaken backwater writing wills and dyin' of boredom?"

The look that passed across my dad's face read as a confused mix of hurt and embarrassment. Then, perhaps sensing my glance, he focused on working more butter into his mashed potatoes. Both he and Mom kept their eyes on their plates while Jake's booming voice rambled on.

"You know I can beat the socks off any deal you had at that prissy-pants Calhoun Firm. If we're as good together as I think we're going to be, you can make more in one good case than you can in ten years up in those hills. You ready to roll the dice and get in the game? You hurry up and give me a call before I come up there and load you in the Lamborghini myself."

The machine announced the end of the messages and recited the time and date.

My dad, his eyebrows furrowed together, finally broke the silence. "You thinking about leaving?"

The hurt on his face and the stiff control in his voice made it hard for me to look him in the eye.

"Jake Baker's offered me a job in Charleston."

How to explain Jake Baker and the confusion of
pros and cons: a real job, the chance—though
maybe remote—of big money, fighting for the
Davids rather than the Goliaths, the slimy lure of
success and the chance to shove it back in the Calhoun Firm's face.

"But," I said, "we really haven't talked any details. I'll have to find something sooner or later."

Dad nodded. Mom—who'd certainly heard the
message earlier and hadn't mentioned it—changed
the subject, filling Dad in on the Economic Development office excitement. And Dad, getting into the
spirit of being a parent who wants a kid with a mind
of her own, chatted about how he'd isolated the
short in the delivery van's electrical system.

Against the background of that comforting chat-
ter—and trying to forget the look on my dad's
face—I made a decision. After helping Dad clear
the table, I went to the den to call Harrison Garnet.

His voice sounded surprisingly cordial. "I'll be
home all evening, Avery. Feel free to come on by."

Sixteen

I still hadn't gotten used to it getting dark before six. By the time I rang the bell beside the Garnets' front door, the walkway and porch were visible only because the entry-hall light shone through the lacy door curtains.

Inside, Harrison Garnet rolled into view before the chimes stopped sounding.

"Avery," he said, leaning forward to pull the door open. "You got here sooner than I expected. I meant to turn on the porch light for you. Come on in."

His casual hospitality took me by surprise. He wheeled ahead of me into the parlor and offered me a seat. I had to perch on the edge of the wingback chair so my feet would touch the ground.

"I heard on the news," he said, settling back in his chair, "that the sheriff has just arrested the fellow they suspect burned down the office."

He sounded relieved, almost excited about the news.

I'm sure I looked puzzled. "Where'd they find

him?" I asked, buying more time to study his reaction.

He shrugged. "Some trailer north of town. His name is Dorrance—or Noodle Waitley, I think. Something like that."

"Mr. Garnet, that's what I wanted to talk to you about."

I watched his face. He sat, his elbows on the chair arms, his hands in his lap, his face open and polite, like a round-faced balding child on his best company manners.

"Mr. Garnet, I won't beat around the bush. I'm rather surprised you're so relieved they caught that guy."

He crooked his head slightly to one side, puzzled.

"Aren't you afraid of what he'll say?"

He raised his hands slightly, palms upward. "I expect him to admit he burned my office, put my company in danger, and left my people without jobs."

"But aren't you afraid he'll tell them who put him up to it?"

"If he had an accomplice, I certainly hope he'll name him. I'd like to know who thought it was such a good idea. And I want to know why they took such pains to throw suspicion on me."

His mouth twitched in an exasperated grimace. "Even if he confesses on the courthouse steps at high noon, I doubt that'll convince Dawson Smith that I didn't try to burn my own records."

"You didn't hire Noodle—um—Dorrance to set the fire?"

"Good God, Avery. Certainly not. How could you

think such a thing? And you the one that made them so suspicious in the first place. Avery, I—"

"I'm sorry, Mr. Garnet. I had to ask. We have an attorney-client relationship. I need to know what's protected under that and what's not."

The quizzical tilt of his head returned.

"You see," I glanced down at my hands. "I found out today that Dorrance—who goes by the name Noodle—used to work for you."

He pursed his lips and shook his head absently. "I—don't remember anybody in the plant by that name. A lot of those folks have been with us for decades, but some of them—"

"No, Noodle drove a truck for you. Back in the early seventies. Back when you were paving the parking lot and clearing the plant of all those barrels. Those barrels that Dawson Smith and his merry band are interested in."

I paused, but he said nothing. His eyebrows knit together and he clenched his fingers into a knot.

"Dawson Smith is poring over what's left of your records—and the arson investigator indicated they had plenty to work with. I imagine he expects to find proof—probably in purchase invoices—of what materials you bought for the plant. Then he'll compare those with the records of what got hauled off legally. Then he'll compare that with what they find leeching into the soil and groundwater behind your plant."

Harrison Garnet shook his head, looking not like a belligerent businessman but a bewildered child. "I could tell them what's in those barrels. Just some old rags. That's ancient history. Why would that concern anybody today?"

I have learned, from years of talking to people who want to keep things from me, that I can't always tell when somebody's lying. But if Harrison Garnet wasn't telling the truth as he knew it, then he won the prize as the best liar I've ever seen.

"What's in those barrels?"

"I told you. Rags. They're the trash barrels we used to catch the rags they used to wipe glue. You know, when they fitted furniture pieces and such."

"But that glue is a hazardous material, Mr. Garnet."

"Hazardous? It's glue. I guess if you ate it or took a bath in it or used it for eye wash, it'd be bad. But it's just glue."

I could actually believe he was as naive as he sounded. He really didn't have a clue.

"The EPA and the state guys won't see it that way, Mr. Garnet. They suspect it contains phthalate, an EPA priority pollutant. And maybe some other materials." I didn't mention my suspicions about Noodle's little back-haul scheme. Maybe, just maybe it had nothing to do with Garnet's property.

"So what's this phthalate stuff supposed to do to people?"

"They don't really know, though it causes tumors in lab rats."

He pursed his lips into an expression of mild disgust. "Why are they wasting time on this? Why not spend time with the really dangerous stuff? They cry wolf—everything's dangerous, nothing's safe. Avery, people worked with that glue day in and day out their whole lives with no problem. How can somebody come along now and say, Oh, that's dangerous?"

"Maybe they were harmed."

He snorted. "Life's tough, Avery." He patted his knees. The wheelchair wobbled a bit with the force of his movement. "Then you get to die. But before that, you get to listen to a lot of government research that tells you don't drink coffee, don't eat shellfish, don't eat peanut butter. For God's sake, you can't even drink water anymore because it might have something in it."

The irony of his last example missed him completely. When he got really worked up, his voice developed a televangelist's passion and lilt. He could offer to host one of those conservative antigovernment radio talk shows.

But I believed him. He genuinely saw nothing wrong with burying a parking lot full of phthalate-loaded barrels.

"You may be right, Mr. Garnet. But the government won't see things that way."

"Well, tell me, Avery. Just how in the hell can they come on my place so many years later and tell me I can't use my own property as I see fit? How can they come marching in like gahdam storm troopers and force me to pay through the nose to have barrels dug up? They use big words like *remediation*. But what they're talking about is screwing me out of a business I've worked decades to build. It's just glue, for God's sake. Nobody saw anything

wrong with what we did back then. What's the big
stink now? Damn barrels been there so long, there
won't be enough of 'em left to fool with."

I didn't mention that phthalates degrade slowly,
so there would be something left to dig up. Not to
mention whatever else Noodle might have dumped
there.

"Mr. Garnet, you have no idea why Noodle would
try to destroy your records—particularly the older
records from the late sixties and early seventies, the
ones in the bound journals?"

"I told you. I have no idea. But I do know that I
had nothing to do with it. And that Noodle fellow—
if he tells the truth—will clear me. That's all I
know." His face had flushed during his tirade and he
held his hands in clenched fists.

I didn't volunteer that I knew why Noodle might
want to destroy the records. As a waste hauler, he
could be held liable and could do some more jail
time.

"Harrison." Sylvie's voice behind me caused
both her husband and me to start. "Harrison, you're
getting yourself all worked up. You know that's bad
for you."

She sauntered into the room, crisp-looking in a
navy pantsuit with gold soutache braid scrolling the
cuffs and lapels. Her honeyed voice sounded like
she was greeting the pastor on Sunday morning.
"Why don't you go on back to the den? Avery and I
have some unfinished business to discuss."

I had watched Harrison transform from an innocent, kindly older gentleman to a rabid antigovernment reactionary in a matter of moments. When Sylvie entered the room, he transformed yet again. His eyes narrowed and his lips tightened.

But Sylvie didn't notice the change. She crossed the room to where he sat and bent to release the brake lever on his wheelchair.

"You run along now. Avery doesn't need to be upsetting you."

He made no move to leave. And he didn't look at her. Rather, he frowned at a patch of carpeting somewhere between his feet and mine.

"Harrison—"

"I'm not going anywhere, Sylvie." His tone carried the subtle hardness of metal filings.

"Harrison, you know how upset you've been—"

"Sylvie, dammit. Avery and I are talking."

"And I couldn't help but hear how overwrought you were getting. I could hear every word you said when I came in the back door. Avery, how you can come around here yet again stirring up trouble—"

"Avery, I don't know anything about this Dorrance fellow—or Noodle or whoever. But Sylvie might be able to tell you about him." He stared at her with a fierce intensity. "Can't you, Sylvie?"

She jerked her hand from where it had rested on the handle of his wheelchair, almost as if it had burned her.

"Harrison, whatever are you—"

"Tell Avery, Sylvie. Tell her about the fellow who owned his own truck. The one you knew could give us such a good deal when we cleared out the warehouse storage. Tell her about those other barrels, too. Tell her, Sylvie."

The passion with which he'd attacked interfering government wastrels had vanished. His voice had calmed to a dangerous quiet.

Sylvie didn't move. She stared down at him in icy, mute anger.

"I never did quite understand how you met him. Certainly not on one of your church social committees. Wasn't he a cousin or something? I really didn't pay much attention at the time."

Something furious flared in Sylvie's eyes, then she seemed to collect herself. She turned and walked to a small Governor Winthrop secretary that sat under the far window.

Harrison didn't turn to watch her go. The tension firing between them was so intense, it made me feel shaken. Then I realized what Harrison now knew—that Sylvie, through Noodle, had burned down his plant, threatening the people he'd taken care of for years.

Sylvie twisted the key in the top drawer of the secretary. Her back to us, she stood stiffly.

"Are you looking for this?" Harrison asked, without facing her.

Sylvie's quick whirl as she spun to face Harrison drew my attention. At first, I didn't see the gun resting in Harrison's lap.

"Harrison, give me the gun." Sylvie's honeyed tone returned, one that sounded like she was used to it getting her what she wanted.

"You did it, didn't you?"

Sylvie just stood there, her arms stiffly at her sides. With her glittering gold braid and her tense stance, she looked like a slender toy soldier.

"You did it, didn't you," he repeated, this time less a question than a statement.

At first I couldn't keep my eyes off the revolver Harrison held so calmly in his lap, so out of place in this elegant parlor. Then I couldn't take my eyes off Sylvie. Emotions I couldn't read passed across her face like cloud shadows across a mountainside.

Then her thin lips parted, words hissing past the darkly lipsticked gash. "Yes. I killed the bitch."

With his left hand, Harrison twisted his chair a quarter turn toward her. His right hand held the gun, level and steady, pointing straight at her. His profile appeared calm, an old hunter comfortable with guns.

I thought they'd forgotten about me until he spoke. Then I knew he'd needed an audience.

"She did it, you know. She killed her. I've known ever since they found her car. I knew it was Lea. And I knew she'd done it." He looked directly at Sylvie's face for the first time.

"All those years, I wondered. I knew you'd had something to do with her leaving. But I thought she'd just left town. I never dreamed—"

The dam that had held Sylvie back broke. She shook with rage. "All you've ever done is dream. You pathetic, shriveled worm of a man. You've floated along, falling into that furniture business, falling into a land deal or two. You never could see more than two steps in front of your stupid face."

"Did you get him to help you?" Harrison's voice stayed as steady as his gun hand. "Did you get Cousin Dorrance to help you? Or did you take care of Lea all by yourself?"

Sylvie's hands clenched so tightly her nails had to be cutting into her palms. She stood rigid, leaning forward slightly, her eyes blazing. "That little slut? I certainly didn't need any help handling her." She spit the words at her husband.

"Sit down, Sylvie." He calmly waved the gun, indicating a chair to her left, the companion to mine.

Sylvie didn't move. She shook with rage, her eyes darted. I hoped he knew he might have to use that gun.

"Sylvie, I said *sit*." He enunciated the last word as if to a wrongheaded puppy in training class.

His voice stayed calm. But Sylvie saw something in his face. The man she'd treated like a worm had turned. Recognition flashed in her eyes and she moved woodenly to the chair. She sat stiffly on the edge, her hands clenched in her lap.

"So you didn't need your cousin Dorrance's help with Lea. Why did he burn the office? Was that your idea?"

"You idiot. Those government inspectors are going to hang you by your toenails. And you don't even have sense enough to see it coming. Those records needed to be destroyed. And Dorrance said he could take care of it, that he knew all about it. Half-wit."

"He's your cousin, dear." Harrison said. And he quickly got the effect I suspect he wanted.

"He's not my cousin," she spit. "He's daddy's cousin's nephew. Hardly—"

"I know. I know. Not really quite on the family tree. But some acorns just don't get scattered as far as one might like, do they?"

The quiet taunt in his voice acted like a gasoline mist on her fury. But she stayed in her chair.

"You're a fine one to talk." She leaned forward, her hands on the arms of the chair. "Do you have any idea what a fool that little slut played you for? What were you thinking? That she loved you?" The shrillness in her voice gave *love* a particularly loathsome sound. "What a fool. And no bigger one than an old one."

Harrison's face, in profile, remained calm. "Oh, I had no illusions about what kept Lea Hopkins around. But I didn't have to worry about looking like a fool to anybody in this town. That'd already happened. When I married you."

A vein pulsed in Sylvie's neck. But she sat still, her head held regally on her stiff neck.

He pursed his lips, then quietly said, "But I certainly didn't know that she and Harry . . ." His voice trailed off.

"Do you want to know what happened?" Sylvie cocked her head slightly, a teasing tone in her voice. "To little Lea? I'll tell you. She wasn't the brightest bulb on the Christmas tree. I sure hope she was good at something besides thinking. She didn't realize it wasn't you in the car until she'd climbed in and closed the door. She had the good grace to be startled, maybe even a little embarrassed. But I put her quickly at ease. Offered her a warm toddy from my thermos to calm her. Told her we needed to have a friendly chat. Between two women with something in common."

My fingers went ice-cold as I watched her. Her drawl deepened and a tiny smile played at the corner of her mouth. It scared me to think how easy it would be to fall for the gracious, charming act she could put on.

"As soon as she started wheezing, she knew what had happened. She tried to explain to me about her fruit allergies. I helped her back to her car so we could look for her antihistamine injection, and assured her she could save her breath. No need to explain." Sylvie's teeth glistened frighteningly against her burgundy lipstick. "I told her I already knew all about her dreadful allergy."

I bit the inside of my lip to keep my teeth from chattering. Something about the derisive calm in her voice made her replay one of the scariest things I'd ever witnessed.

"She leaned into the backseat, fumbling in her handbag. A simple shove and she collapsed onto the floorboard. She'd parked her car in the absolute best possible place. All I had to do was turn the key, push the door lock, and pull the gearshift before I shut the front door."

She watched Harrison's face. From where she sat, she could see him better than I could. Her story must have been having the desired effect, because she continued.

"I couldn't see her. I thought she might climb up

into the seat so I could wave good-bye to her through the back window, but," she shrugged dramatically, "she didn't. The car did take an inordinately long time to sink. It floated like a boat a good ways out, then just sat there."

She smiled, her hands folded calmly in her lap, her feet crossed at the ankles.

"I must admit, I had a few dreadful moments of doubt about what I'd done. What if the wretched thing floated and refused to sink? But," she sighed, "finally. The front end began to tip under the water. And it slipped completely out of sight."

Her hands fluttered, then settled. "I must say I was surprised that nobody ever found her. I thought surely, that first summer or two, somebody would find her car. Imagine missing a car that big in that little bitty ol' mud hole."

I felt as though I must be shaking all over. But Harrison Garnet sat rock solid, his profile toward me, the revolver aimed directly at his wife.

"I never would touch fish that came out of that lake. Did you ever notice that?" She smiled. With a jolt, I was struck that she and I had had the same thought. I remembered scaring myself half to death as I lay in the johnboat, staring at the moon.

"Avery," Harrison said without turning toward me. "There's a phone in the hallway. Would you call the sheriff? Sylvie, stay put."

His no-nonsense tone stilled her reflexive movement. But it didn't still the fire in her eyes. She clutched the arms of the chair, calculating her next play.

"Harrison, have you lost your mind? What would you gain by that? Avery here's not going to talk to anybody, are you, darling? Why, Avery'll be so glad to have a full-time job again, so people will stop talking about what happened to her in Columbia—"

"Avery, get the phone."

"Harrison, you know I made all that up. I just said it to see if I could hurt you. Like you hurt me so much all those years ago with that dreadful little affair. I've tried to forgive you, Harrison. But it hurt so much. I'm sorry. It all just bubbled up in that frightful, awful lie I just told. Nobody in their right mind would believe I would do any such thing. Why, what kind of monster would I have to be?"

"Avery?"

I stood slowly, keeping my hand on the chair as I backed around it. I kept my eyes focused on her, whether because I didn't believe what I saw or because I was afraid to turn my back on her, I couldn't quite say.

As I moved, the venom returned to Sylvie's voice. "You idiot. Think how this is going to look. You'll be ruined. And for what? Think, Harrison. For God's sake."

From the hallway, I could hear Harrison begin to speak. "Sylvie, I truly wish I could roll you off into the lake." He sounded weary. "I wish you had the chance to claw at the door handle as you watch your watery casket settle into the mud. How long do you think it took?"

After my earlier bad experiences with the sheriff's dispatchers, I was pleasantly surprised when my call transferred directly to L.J. As I talked to L.J., I could see Harrison Garnet's back, his bald head shiny, his shoulders steady. But I couldn't see Sylvie until I crossed the hallway back into the parlor.

Apparently Sylvie had opted to play the teary-eyed wronged one.

"Harrison, you wouldn't actually shoot me, would you? After all you put me through. Can you imagine how fearful I was—of what that girl might do to you? Of what she might do to us—and little Harry just getting started out on his own, his political career so young and fragile. I just snapped, Harrison. It was as if I'd just been struck crazy. I—" She sniffed daintily, her hand to her mouth, her eyes glistening.

"Of course I would shoot you, Sylvie. And much worse. You know I would. So you won't give me an excuse." He actually sounded as though he regretted that she wouldn't.

He continued. "I have something much worse in mind for you. A nice, nasty, prolonged trial. Right here in Dacus. Imagine, the Dacus DAR regent, Garden Club president, and mother of a state gubernatorial candidate on trial for a sordid and bizarre murder. Tabloid TV will love that. You'll probably make all the talk shows and the grocery checkout lines. Like that Texas cheerleader's mom who tried to kill her daughter's rival. Avery, you reckon those Court TV folks'll come to Dacus for the trial?"

He didn't turn to face me, but Sylvie shot me a venomous glare. Neither of them expected an answer.

L.J. got to the house faster than I'd expected. Of course, the Law Enforcement Center's only a few blocks away. By the time I opened the front door for L.J. and two deputies, Sylvie was screaming, looking like a candidate for the psycho ward.

"You little worm," she shrieked. "You torture me and abuse me all these years. Your sordid little affairs, your evil accusations. I can't take it anymore."

Foolishly, she tried to jerk away as L.J. leaned over to cuff her. Jerking away from L.J. wasn't her best move. One of the deputies closed in and they quickly cuffed her hands behind her.

L.J. had relieved Harrison of his gun as soon as she'd entered the room. She'd emptied it of bullets and spun the cylinder into place with a practiced quickness while the deputies had stood, like left and right tackles, in front of a seemingly deranged Sylvie Garnet. The deputies and L.J. appeared completely unmoved by the scene.

As the two deputies led her past me toward the parlor's lace-curtained French door, I noticed spit flecking her lipstick. Some strands of her Queen Elizabeth lacquered hair had shaken loose. Shards of hatred stung her eyes.

I could see Sylvie's planned defense already. She must watch enough TV to know that, in the South, a wronged woman has a better-than-average shot at getting away with murder.

I shuddered as I thought of her smiling and waving good-bye to Lea Hopkins Bertram. Sylvie Garnet was sane. Frighteningly sane.

Seventeen

The next morning, I forgot my ten o'clock appointment with Geneva Gadsden. I belatedly remembered Geneva and her crusade to silence the defiler of Katie Hope's memory as I pulled my lunch out of the cracker machine at the Law Enforcement Center.

Great. Two clients down in two days—no, three, if I counted both Nila Earling and Harrison Garnet.

L.J. had obviously enjoyed herself. She had questioned me, Harrison Garnet, Noodle, and who knows who else late into the night, then invited me back early this morning. I earned a cracker break only because somebody had to type my statement so I could read and sign it. Typing it with two fingers, if I had to guess, judging from how long I'd been waiting.

At least I hadn't had to face Geneva Gadsden. One crazed woman in a twenty-four-hour period filled my limit. I toyed with the idea of calling Lou Wray at Carlton's office to see if she could get a message to Geneva. But I didn't toy with that idea long. I strolled across the waiting room to the phone, my footsteps loud on the tile floor.

The phone book fell open easily to the Yellow Page listing for bail bonds. The White Pages listed only one Gadsden. Then I discovered I'd spent all my change in the snack machines.

Maybe I could use a phone back in the cop cubby-holes. What were the odds Geneva would have an answering machine so I wouldn't have to talk to her in person?

I'd balanced my crackers on top of my Coke can and reached for the door when a loud voice behind me boomed in the hollow room. I almost dropped my lunch.

"A'vry. Why the hell didn't you stay the hell in Columbia?" Rudy Mellin strode toward me and pulled open the door. "Since you been back, what? Two, three weeks now? We've been puttin' in over-time like nobody's ever seen. And incidentally, the county doesn't pay overtime. She-ut, A'vry. Give us a break, why don'cha? Just get the hell outta town."

During his speech, Rudy ushered me down the hall and out the back door.

"Rudy, I'm waiting to sign—"

"No, you're not. You're comin' with me. We just got a nine-one-one dispatch. There's a crisis inter-vention needed. Up at the water tower near the ten-nis courts. And I b'lieve you're just the one to help."

He didn't walk around the patrol car to open the door for me, so I swung open the door and plopped inside, tearing open my crackers as he cranked the car.

Then he just sat, staring at me.

"You want one?" I mumbled through orange crumbs.

"Your seat belt, A'vry. Cops have to set an example."

"Pfft." I blew crumbs all over my lap, snorting. "Guess that's why you never see a cop driving the speed limit," I mumbled.

He heard me. He spun out so fast, my head snapped back and I almost spilled my Coke all over the weaponry on the seat between us.

"Where are we going?" I asked.

"I told you. The fucking water tower. A'vry, I want this over with, once and for all. If you don't get something worked out with that fat idiot, I personally am going to pull my pistol and shoot him."

"What are you talking about?"

"Shit, A'vry. What else? Donlee damn-his-ass Griggs."

My stomach lurched as he took the turn onto Main Street at a screech. I decided I wouldn't ask Rudy any more questions—at least not while he was swerving around slow drivers and bumping into the recreation center parking lot. I could only guess that Donlee had not been found at the foot of the waterfall.

A small crowd had gathered. And they were all staring up. I had a momentary vision of what the Second Coming would be like, although I hoped I wouldn't be one of the ones left standing around staring up.

But this was no Second Coming. This was Donlee Griggs, up on the water tower catwalk.

Rudy slammed his door and stood with his hands on his hips. "A'vry, dammit. This itn't funny anymore. You gotta get him reined in before he hurts hisself."

"Rudy—"

"A'vry, he ain't bright. Hey!" Rudy called to a group of cops and firemen who clustered around one of the picnic tables. "Who's got a bullhorn around here?"

From somewhere, a guy in a jumpsuit produced a battery-boosted megaphone. Rudy thrust it at me.

"What?"

"Talk to him, A'vry."

"About what?"

"How the hell should I know? He's the one wanted to see you. Haven't you noticed what he's been working on up there?"

I squinted up at the water tower. An amateurish scrawl arced behind Donlee—at least he looked big enough to be Donlee, but he was really too far away to make out his features. The letters, painted in brilliant purple across the belly of the pale blue tank, were easy to make out after I studied them a minute.

Donlee Luvs Avry.

"The dumbshit even misspelled your name," Rudy said, shaking his head.

"Rudy, I need a little help here. What the heck am I supposed to say?"

"Nice work, Donlee? I want to have your children? How the hell should I know? You're the one's got him whipped into such a frenzy. You tell me."

"Rudy, I represented him in a court hearing a

couple of weeks ago, on a disorderly conduct charge. That's it. End of story."

"Not for Donlee. Apparently he survived his fatally false leap off the waterfall. Now he's threatening to jump off the tower unless he gets to speak to you."

"Why the hell doesn't he just call me on the phone?" I muttered.

Rudy shot me a sharp look. "Just tell him you're here."

I fumbled with the button that activated the speaker. The thing was hard to hold.

"Donlee?" My voice echoing out the other end startled me—and the rest of the crowd. And Donlee. He swayed woodenly, his tall, awkward frame leaning dangerously over the catwalk railing.

The crowd gasped.

"Donlee, it's Avery Andrews."

Donlee waved, both arms gyrating wildly over his head. He gave a little rabbit hop of excitement.

"Donlee? Donlee, don't—"

My warning didn't make it out the other end of the speaker.

Donlee looked for a moment like an energized rap dancer as his arms windmilled and his body torqued, trying to regain his balance. Then he toppled headfirst over the railing.

The gasps from the crowd turned into disbelieving shouts. And moans. Several people shrieked. I might have been one of them. Those crowded closest to the tower ducked as a shower of purple paint splattered over them and a paint can clattered to the ground.

After a split second of distraction, I looked back up. Donlee swung in space. Back and forth, a few feet beneath the catwalk. With his arms crossed tightly over his chest, he looked like a Christmas ornament suspended from the belly of an alien space craft.

"Good Gawd a'mighty." Rudy whistled in disbelief.

The crowd chattered, nervously relieved. And pleased that the show had taken an interesting turn.

"Harv!" Rudy called to a group of firemen clustered near one of Dacus's two red fire engines. "What you got that can get him down?"

The man named Harv just stared up at Donlee, then said, "Short of shootin' him down, damned if I know."

"No ladder? Anything that'll—"

Harv gave Rudy an idiot look. "Rudy, why would we need a crane that'd reach a water tower? We ain't got a building in this town over three stories high. They prob'ly ain't got shit that'd go that high in New York City."

A conclave gathered around Rudy to hatch a rescue plan. Someone came and took the megaphone away from me. He called up to Donlee and told him not to worry, to just hang tight.

Donlee gave a feeble wave, then crossed his arms again.

"What's he hanging from, anyway?" somebody asked.

Somebody else—a man with a pair of binoculars trained on Donlee—said, "Looks like he's got himself a safety harness. It's hooked to the railing up there. Must be around his chest."

"Big as he is, that must hurt like hell, hanging like that."

Somebody snickered. "Yep, ever'body figgered a guy Donlee's size must really be hung." Nobody else laughed.

I kept my eyes on Donlee. I'd been going to tell him that if he didn't come down off that tower, I would come up and kick him off. In that way my mama always said she'd skin me alive. In that loving way. Thank goodness I hadn't had an opportunity to broadcast my message before he fell.

I went back and sat in Rudy's car, watching the rescue efforts from that haven. Out of respect for the near-tragedy, I refrained from eating the rest of my crackers.

A couple of guys climbed the tower ladder, which must be like the StairMaster from hell. But apparently they couldn't pull him up. So two more guys climbed the stairs.

I couldn't bear to watch as they struggled to hoist Donlee, the giant Christmas ornament, to safety. For one thing, I feared something other than a can of purple paint might hit the ground. For another, craning to look up through the windshield was giving me a headache.

When everybody returned safely to earth, Donlee got hustled off to another patrol car, still clutching his chest and looking around over the crowd.

Rudy eventually came back to join me. Most of the crowd had broken up by that time. I had finally broken my voluntary fast and eaten the rest of my crackers. Now I really needed something to drink.

Rudy drove me to the station without saying much, except that Donlee would be held at the Law Enforcement Center at least overnight. "And you better get in there and have a word of prayer with that boy before he does something really stupid. Shit, what am I saying? What could be more stupid than faking a drowning, pretending to jump off a waterfall, and hanging yourself from a water tower?"

I couldn't answer that. "I'll talk to him, Rudy. But he needs some professional help."

"I'll say." He jammed the gearshift into "park" and stomped into the building.

Which left me with several choices. Should I go in and sign my statement about Sylvie Garnet's confession? Did I try to see Donlee now, before they finished processing him? Should I call Geneva Gadsden and apologize for missing her appointment? Or did I just sit and wait for all this to filter through the gossip network back to Aunt Letha?

I opted to sign my statement, but postponed everything else. I somehow hoped time would work it all out.

When I drove to my parents' house, I found I had the house to myself. I got a glass of milk and some graham crackers and stretched out on the sofa.

I hadn't even finished my grahams when the phone rang.

"Avery? Melvin Bertram." He didn't need to introduce himself. "I heard about Sylvie Garnet." He didn't need to say anything else.

"Yeah," I said. After a pause, I added, "I guess that settles things with L.J.—the arson and—everything."

"I hope so."

Another long silence lay between us.

"Avery, I wanted to apologize. About the other night."

Before I could say *Oh, what for?* he continued. "I'm afraid I got a bit—maudlin."

"I'd say you were entitled. After what you'd been through."

"I don't know about that. But thanks anyway."

I didn't try to fill the silence. I sensed he had something more to say. Finally, he said, "Avery, I've been thinking. About a lot of things. This—well, this may sound crazy."

Probably not, I thought, not after what I've seen the last couple of days.

"But I'd—well, I'm not at all sure it would work out. For me personally, that is. And I certainly don't know what kind of plans you've made for your future. But, if they should include staying in Dacus, I wondered—well, how you'd feel about sharing office space?"

"Office space?"

"Sure. You know the old Baldwin and Bates Funeral Parlor? That huge Victorian on Main, not too far from the courthouse? My brother and I own that. He wants to sell it, and I've been thinking about buying him out. It's actually our grandparents' old house—my dad grew up there.

"The family rented it to Baldwin and Bates, I guess for so long that nobody remembers it as the

Bertram house. Which," he gave a wry chuckle, "considering how that name's been bandied about lately, is probably for the best."

"You're really thinking about settling in Dacus? Opening an office?"

"Um-hm. Guess I'm hoping for some—I don't know, remediation, perhaps." He paused, then asked, "What about you?"

I didn't answer right away. Even when I did, it wasn't much of an answer. "I don't know. I really just planned to light here awhile. You know, rethink some things, get my bearings."

"I didn't mean to jump to any conclusions. I guess I'd just gotten some impression that—well, think about it. No rush. My brother won't be sending his kids to college for some time yet, so he's in no hurry for the money. And that monstrosity of a house isn't going anywhere. If you'd like to have a look at it, though, just give me a call. There's living quarters upstairs, too, you know."

Over a funeral parlor? I didn't ask that out loud.

"Thanks, Melvin. That does give me something to think about. I—I'll let you know."

"Fine. No rush. To tell you the truth, I've got some thinking of my own to do."

After I hung up, I lay back and studied the ceiling, the wooden cornices over the tall double-hung windows, the plaster medallion around the ceiling fan.

Avery Andrews, attorney-at-law. Black letters on a discreet white sign. Maybe hung on a wrought-iron signpost, in front of that rambling Victorian. Close to the courthouse. With its wide wraparound porch and a witch-hatted circular section on one side. I bet it had central heating. The lack of that luxury in my cabin had begun to evidence itself as nighttime temperatures stayed in the thirties.

I lost myself in a daydream of decorating my gracious office with resplendent antiques and of drawing clients who knew the meaning of the word *retainer.* Then the phone rang again.

"Miss Andrews. There you are. Mr. Barner asked me to call."

At the mention of Carlton Barner's name, I recognized Lou Wray's clipped voice.

"He wanted me to let you know that this is a place of business and that we really cannot be bothered with taking personal messages for you."

"I—"

"I'll be happy to read these over the phone to you. But you really should make plans to relocate yourself to more permanent office quarters as soon as possible. Mr. Barner's quite insistent on that."

"Yes, ma'am, but—"

"The first message came in about an hour ago, from one Donlee Griggs. He wished to inform you that this constituted his one phone call." She said those last words as if they had a bad taste.

"His message said, and I quote: 'It's my car, isn't it? That's why you won't go out with me?'" Lou read in an unamused monotone.

"I didn't know he had a car."

Lou Wray continued. She clearly had no time to find humor in any of this. "This second message came in only moments ago. A reporter called from the Greenville paper, wanting information that I clearly could not give. Apparently Mrs. Geneva Gadsden has chained herself to the Confederate war monument in front of the courthouse, engaging herself in some sort of civil disobedience. She insisted that you were her spokesperson and that the newspaper should contact you."

"How did the *Greenville News*—"

"I'm sure you can see why Mr. Barner has insisted that the time has come for you to sever any relationship with this firm. Our clientele—"

"Yes, ma'am," I said. "I'll be by later to pick up my legal pad and my pencils. Thanks for calling with my messages. It's been such a pleasure working with you."

After I hung up, I thought momentarily about calling Jake Baker, to politely but firmly turn him down. I couldn't think of any reason not to stick around Dacus awhile longer. And I couldn't think of a good reason to leave. Even Jake's wildest promises couldn't pay me enough to watch the disappointment on my dad's face again. And he certainly couldn't compete with the entertainment value around here.

Maybe in a few weeks I'd call Andie, the law school classmate who worked at the state bar association and knew everybody in South Carolina. But I was in no rush. I grabbed my jacket and headed for the courthouse and the Confederate war monument.